The
Reason Why

Also by Vickie M. Stringer

STILL DIRTY

DIRTY RED

IMAGINE THIS

LET THAT BE THE REASON

The Reason Why

A NOVEL

Vickie M. Stringer

ATRIA PAPERBACK

New York London Toronto Sydney

ATRIA PAPERBACK

A Division of Simon & Schuster, Inc.
1230 Avenue of the Americas
New York, NY 10020

First Atria Paperback edition August 2009

ATRIA PAPERBACK and colophon are trademarks of Simon & Schuster, Inc.

For information about special discounts for bulk purchases,
please contact Simon & Schuster Special Sales at 1-866-506-1949
or business@simonandschuster.com.

The Simon & Schuster Speakers Bureau can bring authors to your live event. For
more information or to book an event, contact the Simon & Schuster Speakers
Bureau at 1-866-248-3049 or visit our website at www.simonspeakers.com.

Designed by Nancy Singer

Manufactured in the United States of America

10   9   8   7   6   5   4   3   2   1

Library of Congress Cataloging-in-Publication Data

Stringer, Vickie M.

  The reason why: a novel/Vickie M. Stringer.—1st Atria Paperback ed.
    p.   cm.

  Prequel to: Let that be the reason.
  1. African American women—Fiction.   2. African Americans—Fiction.
  3. Drug dealers—Fiction.   I. Title.
  PS3569.T69586R43 2009
  813'.54—dc22   2009018265

ISBN 978-1-4391-6609-3
ISBN 978-1-4391-6610-9 (ebook)

CHICAGO LAWN BRANCH
6120-24 S. KEDZIE AVE.
CHICAGO, ILLINOIS 60629

Chino, my first love,
this one's for you!!!

It is better to be feared than loved.

—Machiavelli

The
Reason Why

Intro

"What a bitch gone do?"

Pammy loved Chino, because he could make toe-curling love. He could make her laugh or smile when all the chips were down and the shit was hitting the fan. He had taken an innocent little cookie from Detroit and turned her out with the street life. More than the money, the hairdos, the clothes, the cars, the status. The love was intoxicating, healing: like chicken noodle soup when Pammy was sick, Chino protecting her body with his when the bullets were flying, the dreams that they shared together. Knight in shining armor my ass, he was her everything.

Imagine This. The Reason Why.

Chapter 1

A Dream

It was the summer of 1988. Jazzy Jay's was the premiere hot spot in the city on Saturday night. The converted storefront with a massive bar and a thumping surround-sound stereo system was the club of choice for all Columbus, Ohio ballers and cluck-cluck heads who were after the ballers' money. Dope boys and gold diggers alike dressed their best when stepping up in Jazzy's and made sure that their whips were fresh to impress. But for all Jazzy's promises, its shortcomings were the 2 a.m. closing time and that it didn't serve food. For this reason, the Waffle House was the place to head after the club.

The Waffle House was often packed to capacity, and this breezy night it was no different. The washed, waxed, and chromed-out rides filling the parking lot looked like a car show. Jimmy Blazers rolled through bumping EPMD; IROCs burnt rubber up and down the street, racing and showing off their acceleration. BMW 325s were here and there, along with several 5.0 Mustangs and chromed-out Cutlass Supremes and Regals, while Pete Rock & C.L. Smooth, Run DMC, and

LL Cool J provided the soundtrack for the night—that was, until the police showed up and mobbed the place.

Some folks fled, others stayed. This was typical. The police knew that the Waffle House was where everyone hung out after Jazzy's closed. They also knew that people raced . . . and they weren't going to stop. We were just young people having fun and we were going to continue. Depending on the po-po's mood, they'd run up on us like Rambo just to see folks scatter like roaches.

"Look at those fucking idiots in the street drag racing!" Chino said, protesting to Fabian when he saw the swarm of officers. Leaning up against his Jeep Cherokee, Chino shook his head in disgust.

The officers climbed out of their police cars and started herding the crowd back against the Waffle House's side wall. Some of the officers began searching the gathered crowd. "Damn, I'm strapped, yo!" Chino whispered into Fabian's ear.

"Shit, get rid of it, kid!"

"They searching!"

"Peep game!" Fabian nodded to his right. "They ain't searching the boppers!"

"Well shit, I need to slip my jammy to a chicken head," Chino said.

"Do that and kiss it good-bye, man," Fabian told him. "Damn, that was my favorite pistol of yours, too. You should have sold it to me when I asked you to. You'd let some chick hold it, risk not getting it back, but you couldn't sell it to me. Dude, that's fucked up. "

"You trippin' rap," Chino told him. "I got my Ruger P-89,

not the Beretta but I'll sell this bitch to you right here, right now." Chino looked at Fabian seriously. He didn't care about his piece. He just wanted it off him.

Fabian laughed. "Nigga, you crazy. That's yo' case. Enjoy it."

"Bullshit!" Chino told him defiantly. He maneuvered away from Fabian and into the crowd. He squeezed his way through until he found what he was looking for—a female with a large purse. He slipped his weapon inside the slit on the side.

"What are you doing?" Pam asked, turning in his direction.

Pam Xavier was fresh to the city. She had grown up in Detroit's famed LeDroit Park area, the daughter of upper-middle-class parents who gave her the best. Private school, lessons in piano, French and Spanish, the best of everything. She was sixteen and already a graduate from Catholic school. Pam was an all-American girl who was away from the watchful eyes of her parents, living it up in a place she knew little about. She was totally brand-new.

"Yo, check it, lil mama," Chino told her. "They checking the hard heads, not the chicken heads, so you can just close up your purse and hold on to that for daddy."

"First of all," Pam said, craning her neck, "I'm not your little mama, you're not my daddy, I'm not a chicken head, and I'm not holding shit for you." Pam looked inside her purse and her eyes became large when she saw what he had placed in there. "Hell naw!" she screeched in an angry tone. "Definitely not this!"

Chino held up his hands. "Okay, say it a little louder. I don't think the po-po heard you. Damn, give a brother a case, why don't you."

"This is your case," Pam told him. "You shouldn't be carrying a gun anyway. It's guys like you that mess things up for everyone else."

"Hey, we can debate the merits of being judged by twelve or carried by six another time," Chino said with a smile, trying to defuse Pam's anger, "but for right now, a brother really ain't trying to go to jail. Can you be a soldier and help out a general?"

Pam turned away and smiled. He had a way with words that made her laugh. She turned back toward him. "A general? You mean a private, don't you?"

"No, lil mama, I'm a straight up commander in chief. If stars and bars indicate rank, you can just call me General Milky Way, 'cause I got enough stars to be my own galaxy, and enough bars to open my own candy factory."

Pam smiled.

"Guys over there. Ladies to the side!" An officer yelled, pulling Chino away, separating him from Pam. He winked and blew a kiss her way.

"Hey, how will I find you?" Pam shouted.

"Don't worry, I'll find you!" Chino shouted back.

He was cute, Pam thought. Cuter than cute. Pearly whites that looked like he just stepped out of a dental factory. Low-cut, curly hair, smooth peanut butter skin, hazel eyes that look like crushed brown and green crystals. And he had the gift of gab. He probably had a saying for everything. If he didn't find her, she certainly would have to find him.

"Did you get rid of it?" Fabian asked, gathered with the group of young men the police had snatched up.

Chino nodded. "Nice little red bone. See the one over there with the red Coca-Cola shirt?"

"Where?" Fabian asked, stretching his neck and using his six-foot-three height to look over the crowd.

"The one with the mushroom hairstyle," Chino told him.

"Cute," Fabian nodded his approval. "One question, though."

"What's that?"

"What if she turns you in?"

"Then that's her shit," Chino declared.

"And if she tries to press the issue?" Fabian asked.

Chino shrugged. "Then you know how we do it. She does some shady shit like that, then she'll be dealt with."

Chapter 2

We Belong Together

Pam sat on her bed inside her dorm room at the Ohio State University, staring at the black handgun lying just in front of her. She couldn't believe what had happened at the Waffle House. It was surreal. Her brazen attempt at trying to be cute now crumbled. She had never seen a real handgun, let alone touched one, until last night. It took her two hours of pacing and debating just to get up the nerve to pull it out of her purse. She slept little during the night, thinking of it in her room. Should she call the police? Should she go to the dean of students? Should she call the campus police? How about just toss the thing inside the nearest trash can? But what if she ran into him again, and he wanted it back? What would she do? What would he do if she didn't have it to give back?

"So, what are you going to do?" Tomiko asked, looking at Pam, then at the gun.

Tomiko Harrison was Pam's roommate. She was nineteen, a sophomore from Houston, Texas. She had run to Ohio State because it was the first place she could think of that was far enough away from her parents, particularly her mother.

Tomiko wasn't going to be the long-haired, green-eyed, yellow-skinned AKA with the Fisk degree and fiancé from Meharry Medical School. Those were her mother's dreams, not her own. She was determined never to set foot on that campus in Nashville, if she could help it.

Her mother was crestfallen at Tomiko's graduation when she had broken the news, but her father had given her a secret thumbs-up. To gain her own identity, Tomiko had stripped the perm out of her hair and did everything she could to lock it. She wore it in twists, and braids, and even had coarser hair braided into her fine locks so that she could have the appearance of dreads. It was her personal declaration of independence from her mother.

Thanks to Tomiko, Pam was quickly learning where to get a decent hot meal on High Street, away from the dorm cafeteria, how to balance school and her blooming social life, and where the hottest nightspots were nestled in the bustling streets of downtown Columbus.

"I don't know!" Pam answered Tomiko's question.

Tomiko sat on Pam's bed, with the handgun sitting between them. "Well, you better decide something quick."

"I know, girl!" Pam sighed, frustrated. "What do you think I should do?"

"Get rid of the thing! I would have given it to the police last night!"

"No," Pam said, shaking her head, "he would have gone to jail."

"So?" Tomiko said, turning up her palms. "You don't even know him!"

"I know he's black . . . and there are enough black men in jail already!"

"He was carrying a gun, Pammy! You wonder why there are so many in jail. Maybe it's because they do stupid shit like carry guns to places where people are just having a good time. This is how so many of our guys also end up in the cemetery."

Pam nodded. Tomiko had a point.

"I say we take it to him, and throw it at him," Tomiko suggested.

"What?"

"He didn't give a shit about you when he stuck it in your purse last night!"

"He did. He just knew that the police weren't searching the women."

"Make excuses for him," Tomiko said with a teasing smile. "He must have been cute."

"That has nothing to do with anything," Pam protested.

"Was he cute, Pammy?"

Pam hesitated and then nodded reluctantly. "He was kinda cute. Girl, he had some pretty-ass eyes."

Tomiko nodded. "Um-hum, that's what I thought. Girl, you willing to go to jail for a cute face. I really need to school you."

"I ain't stupid, girl," Pam confirmed, rolling her eyes. "You don't need to school me."

"This isn't you." Tomiko pointed toward the gun. "In the streets, you're like a babe in the woods. I knew I shouldn't have took you to the spot last night."

"Girl please, that has nothing to do with anything."

Tomiko grabbed her purse. "Look, let's hop in the Beemer and go and find this mystery man."

"How are we going to do that? It's Sunday afternoon, and shit, I don't even know his name!"

"You know what he looks like, don't you?" Tomiko quizzed. "Besides, we know he carries a gun, so he's probably one of those fools that hang out at the gambling shack, or over by the projects selling that stuff."

"You want to go over there?" Pam said, with her eyes bucked out of her head.

"Girl, we can leave the top up on the ride and just roll through real quick to see if you spot him."

"Two females in your car, rolling through the hood, and you think nobody is going to pay any attention to us?" Pam asked sarcastically. "And even if we do find him, then what? I'm gonna just walk up to him and say, 'Hey, stranger, here is your murder weapon back'? Girl, what if he shoots us?"

"And you didn't think about that when you accepted the damn thing?"

"I didn't accept anything!" Pam protested. "He stuck it in my purse!"

"And you could have stuck it back in his face and told him you didn't want it. Or you could have given it to the police."

Pam folded her arms and crossed her legs.

"Okay, okay, you ain't down for turning brother-man in," Tomiko told her. "I'm cool with that. But damn, girl."

"Let's just find him, and you can give it back to him."

"Me?"

"Yeah, Tomiko, you ain't scared of nobody. Hell, you carry guns in the back of your pickup truck down in Houston."

"Ha, ha, real funny. Does it look like I drive a pickup truck?"

"Girl, you know y'all be hunting down in Texas."

"Pam, don't make me front on Detroit, 'cause you know better. Even the babies carry guns in their diapers in that dangerous mother."

Pam laughed heavily. "Get off my city. I'm from Motown, baby!"

"Girl, get your illegal-ass gun and let's go find this nigga."

Pam took a sock, lifted the gun, and put it inside a paper bag. She was determined not to get any of her fingerprints on it.

"You think it done killed somebody?" Pam asked.

"Girl, let's just hope it don't kill nobody today!" Tomiko told her. "And by nobody, I mean us!"

"Amen!"

Chapter 3

Be Careful

Sunday afternoon in the hood, Chino and Fabian sat in their regular spot, in Fabian's car, checking out the honeys. In the reflection of the passenger's mirror, he saw two chicks walking up the street. They were both sucking on lollipops and switching their asses to get attention.

"Watch this, man," Chino told Fabian with a mischievous grin on his face. Once they got close enough, Chino leaned out the window and grabbed a handful of firm, thick booty that passed by him.

"Fuck you!" the girl in the Daisy Dukes shouted.

"You offering?" Chino quipped.

"Hell naw, I ain't offering you, asshole!"

"Well, damn, I thought since you was showing off all that ass, you know . . ." Chino laughed with a smile.

"Just 'cause I'm wearing these shorts don't mean I'm a ho!" she retorted.

"My bad!" Chino looked up and down at her body. "It's

just that you're wearing a ho's costume, so you can see how I made a mistake."

"Fuck you, nigga!"

"Chicken head!" Chino shouted.

Fabian laughed as he pulled away in his black Porsche 928 GT. "Man, you're crazy!"

"Man, these bitches are crazy," Chino declared. "They putting it all out there on display, and get mad when you react to it."

"You can look, but not touch," Fabian told him.

"I'll bet you if I tossed her ass a C-note she'd let me touch."

"Bet!"

"Bet!" Chino told him.

Fabian stopped the car and busted a U in the middle of the street. They pulled up on the two young ladies strolling down South High Street. One was wearing extremely high-cut Daisy Dukes that exposed nearly half her ass. She had on a half-shirt that tied at the midriff, which exposed her taut stomach and her perky breasts. Her hair was done up in a pixie cut, and she sucked seductively on a lollipop as she strolled the street. Her companion wore tight, form-fitting spandex shorts and a matching spandex top. The spandex bodysuit showed off her voluptuous figure and bodacious buttocks. She wore her hair in a mushroom, and she too sucked seductively on a red Blow Pop. The temperature outside was moderate for the fall, and people were out in droves taking in the warm weather. The hood was buzzing with activity today.

"Yo, yo, yo!" Chino called out from the Porsche.

"Fuck off!" Daisy Duke told him.

"Naw, baby, that was my bad!" Chino said, in his most sincere voice. "I thought you were someone else."

"You sure in the hell did!" she snapped.

"Aw, girl, don't be like that," Chino told her with a grin. "Let me make it up to you."

She continued to stroll away, but this time with a little more swing in her walk.

Chino smiled at the show, leaned back inside the car, and looked at his boy.

"The usual?"

Fabian nodded. "Bet!"

Chino pulled a wad of cash out of his pocket and peeled off a hundred-dollar bill. He held it out the window. "Aye," he yelled. "This for you, lil mama!"

Daisy Duke turned and looked at Chino. Her face twisted up with confusion and disgust when she saw what he held in his hand. "What's that for?"

"It's my apology to you."

She waved her hand dismissing him. "That's okay, you keep it. I ain't no ho."

"This is the way we apologize," Chino told her. "When we mess up, we make it right. We come out of pocket as a penalty."

Daisy Duke thought about what he said and made her way to the Porsche.

"I guess so." She extended her hand and accepted the money. Before she could take her hand out of Chino's he grabbed it slightly.

"Let me make it up to you with a little dinner." He smiled and eyeballed her body.

"Dinner?"

"Yeah, a nice romantic dinner somewhere. You pick the place."

She hesitated for a moment, then a smile spread across her face. "I guess."

"Well check it," Chino said. "I'm gonna need to get your number so I can call you."

Daisy Duke took her hand back, dug into her purse and pulled out her phone number, which was already written down. "You better call me," she told him, handing him the small piece of paper.

"Bet!" Chino said. "I'm gonna call your sexy self tonight." He definitely wanted to get into her high-cut shorts.

"Okay, I'll be waiting."

"I bet you will," Chino said, biting down on his bottom lip. "Damn, girl, you really wearing those shorts. I couldn't help but want a piece of that cake earlier."

Daisy Duke laughed. "You crazy!"

Chino held out his hand. "You mind?"

Daisy Duke smacked her lips. Normally she would have for free, but when she saw the wad in his hands, and that he was rolling in a Porsche, she complied. Daisy Duke had found herself a true baller.

She turned to the side and Chino rubbed on her ass again, but this time he had her permission. He caressed her butt gently, and then grabbed a handful of butt cheek. "Damn, you fine!"

Daisy Duke laughed.

"Tonight, little mama," Chino told her. He turned to Fabian. "Let's roll."

"Damn!" Fabian exclaimed, pulling away. He pulled out a wad of bills from his pocket and handed Chino a hundred-dollar bill.

"Thank you very much," Chino said with confidence. "You just bought that pussy for me."

"Damn, at least you could have plugged me in with her homegirl."

"Damn, my bad," Chino said. "Don't worry, I'll find you something."

"Yeah, something ugly or fat!"

"Yo, check out the honeys in this red BMW," Chino said. "They rolled up and down the street like three times already."

"Think they're one-time?"

Chino shook his head. "Naw, they too pretty to be police. Those are bona fide good pussies from the college."

"Woooweee!" Fabian held out his hand and Chino gave him a handshake. "You know I love square pussy. You get to fuck 'em, use up their daddy's credit card, and then leave 'em in time for Valentine's Day!"

Chino laughed. "And I thought I was a dog. You're a real Fido, you know that?"

Fabian pulled up alongside the BMW.

Chino leaned forward so that he could talk to them. "Hey, baby girl!"

Pam turned to see who was talking to her. "Oh, shit!"

"Oh, shit!" Chino said.

"What?" Tomiko shouted nervously.

"What's up?" Fabian asked.

"That's old girl from last night!"

"Girl, that's him!" Pam shouted.

"Pull over!" Chino told them and pointed to where they should meet.

Fabian pulled over into a nearby store parking lot and Chino climbed out of the car. Tomiko pulled in behind them while Chino walked up to the passenger side of the car and leaned inside.

"What's up, baby girl?"

"My blood pressure," Pam said.

Chino laughed. "You sure helped a brother out of a jam last night. I owe you big time."

Chino pulled out his wad of money and tossed five one-hundred-dollar bills into Pam's lap.

"What's this for?"

"What a five-thousand-dollar bond would have cost me."

"Girl, shut up and take the money," Tomiko said under her breath.

"You don't have to give me anything."

"Thank you!" Tomiko blurted out over Pam.

Again, Chino laughed.

Pam folded up the money and handed it back. Chino was stunned. No female had ever given back his money and been serious about it.

Pam reached down on the floor, under her seat, lifted the paper bag, and handed it to Chino. "I believe this belongs to you."

Chino opened the bag and looked inside. "You sure you didn't use this?"

"No!" Pam said, indignant at first, and then realizing it was a joke, broke into a wide smile.

"You look like a killer," Chino told her. "What's your name, killer?"

"Pam."

Chino nodded. "You look like a Pam. My name is Chino."

Pam smiled. "You look like a Rico."

"Ahhh, that's my alias," Chino confirmed with a smile.

"You have an alias?"

"Um-huh, that's my out-of-town alias, when I go to get them thangs!" Chino rubbed his hands together and howled.

"Boy, you're crazy!" Pam shouted.

"Pam, where you from?"

"D-Town."

"D-Town?"

"Detroit."

"The Motor City, huh?" Chino asked. "First female I ever met from Detroit. Congratulations."

"Congratulations or beware?"

Chino laughed. "Oh, yeah, you're definitely from Detroit. You got one of them fly mouths."

"I thought I was the first female you met from Detroit," Pam challenged.

"I done came across plenty of fly mouths in my day and you're not an exception." Chino glanced around, peeped his surroundings, then brought back up the subject at hand. "Look, I ain't trying to get caught up in the hood with this jammy, so I got to get out of here."

"Bye." Tomiko spoke harshly with an attitude.

Chino looked at Tomiko, then at Pam. "But why don't you give me your number so that I can properly thank you."

"Just say thank you, that's fine."

"Not good enough," Chino told her. "A general has to properly reward his troops so that they stay loyal."

"What makes you think that I want to be one of your little soldiers?" Pam asked, looking at Chino like he had lost his mind.

"You do."

"How do you figure that?"

"Because you ain't never met a nigga like me before."

"A dime a dozen in Detroit."

Chino shook his head and chuckled. "I doubt that. So, you gonna let me take you to dinner or what?"

"Dinner?"

"A picnic on the Scioto. I'll make the sandwiches myself."

Pam laughed. "Okay, a picnic on the river? This I gotta see."

"Okay, so what's your number?"

Pam shook her head. "Give me yours."

Chino gave her his pager number.

"My code is all ones." Pam replied.

"All ones?" Chino quizzed.

Pam nodded. "Yep, I'm number one."

"We'll see," said Chino, rising up from the window. "We will definitely see."

Chapter 4

Keeping Promises

The following Tuesday evening, when Pam strolled out of the Friendship Village nursing home where she worked, her mouth fell open in surprise. Chino was outside waiting for her on a black and purple Kawasaki Ninja motorcycle. She could hear her mother screaming in her ear at that very moment about how unsafe motorcycles were.

"When you said that you were going to pick me up from work, I thought that you meant in a car," Pam told him.

"What difference does it make?"

"It makes a big difference!" Pam said, pacing. "I was expecting to be driven inside of a nice comfortable, safe vehicle. I wanted to hear the radio."

"I'll sing to you," Chino said.

"You sing?"

"No."

"Then what are you talking about?"

Chino shrugged. "Wait till you hear this engine sing."

"I'm not going with you anywhere on this thing!" Pam crossed her arms defiantly.

"Why not?"

"Because these things are dangerous!"

"This," he pointed, "is a bike. Bikes are not dangerous, the rider is," Chino explained. "If the rider does dumb and dangerous shit, then the bike is dangerous. I'm not going to do dumb shit with you on here."

Pam exhaled and rolled her eyes upward.

"I promise you, no crazy shit."

Pam looked at Chino and lifted an eyebrow. "Nothing crazy?"

Chino pressed his hand against his chest. "Would I lie to you?"

"Yes!" Pam said, and then smiled. "Maybe."

"Never."

"I don't even know you," Pam said. "You could be the biggest liar in the universe."

"Hey, Chino does not lie. Not never."

"You're referring to yourself in the third person?" Pam smiled again. "I see that you have your ego in check."

Chino laughed, and nodded toward the bike's rear seat. "C'mon, big head. You're burning daylight."

"Big head?"

"Yeah. You know you got a melon on top of that poor neck of yours."

Pam's mouth fell open and she hit Chino playfully. "Forget you! Is this how you treat your dates? You talk about them?"

"Only the ones that I really like."

"Oh, really? So you really like me?"

Chino nodded. "Yeah, you got a lot of appeal with you, youngster."

With that, Pam climbed on the back of the Ninja and wrapped her arms around Chino's waist. Chino revved the engine and pulled out of the parking lot of Pam's job.

"So what's with the old folks' home?" Chino asked.

"It's a retirement home," Pam corrected, emphasizing the word *retirement*.

"It's got old people in there, right?"

Pam nodded. "It's home to seniors who want a more relaxed lifestyle in their golden years."

"Damn, girl. Why you got to be politically correct all the time?"

"Why you got to be so rude and boorish?"

"Boring?"

"No, not boring. Boorish."

"You calling me an ogre?"

"No, you're more the caveman type."

Chino had to laugh. She wasn't impressed with his street status, or his dope money. She was real. And in his life, he didn't meet that many real people, people who weren't out for his money. "So what do you do there?" Chino asked. "You like wash they shitty asses, and change they beds and shit?"

"No!" Pam said, hitting Chino on his shoulder. "That's nasty."

"So what do you do?"

"I work at the cash register."

"The cash register? They got bread up in there?"

"Yes, they have a store for the community," Pam explained. "It's not just one retirement home, it's an entire residential community."

"Damn, so you a cashier and shit?"

"Yeah. You sound like you got a problem with that."

"That's a gig for niggas who just got out of the joint."

"What?"

"You heard me!" Chino switched lanes and accelerated.

Pam clutched his waist tighter and buried her head in his back. "Chino!"

"It's cool! Girl, I ain't going but forty!"

"Still, you gotta let me know when you're going to speed up!"

"You need to ride with me more often. As a matter of fact, I need to teach you how to ride."

"No, thank you!"

"We going to start your lesson this weekend."

"I work on the weekends," Pam told him. "And I definitely ain't riding with you on this thing at night!"

"That's cool. I can teach you during the day."

"Didn't you hear me? I have to work. Some of us have legitimate jobs."

"And some of us got bullshit house-nigga jobs, like we fresh out the joint."

"There's nothing wrong with an honest day's work!" Pam shot back. "Maybe you should try it sometimes."

"Maybe you should quit."

"Quit? Yeah, right! And who's going to pay my bills, you? Are you going to take care of all my expenses?"

"Yeah, I can do that."

"Yeah, right!"

Chino pulled the clutch and downshifted. He broke the bike down to first gear and pulled over into a shopping center parking lot.

"Why are we stopping here?" Pam asked.

"Because I can show you better than I can tell you," Chino said. He pulled out a wad of money and placed it in her hand.

"What's this?" Pam asked. "I told you, you don't owe me anything."

"That's not because I owe you, that's what I'm giving you so you can quit that bullshit job."

"Chino, I don't want to quit my job!"

"Yeah you do, ma. Nobody wants to be on their feet all day, working for minimum wage. Why work for them, when you can work for Chino?"

"Doing what? I'm not selling anybody's drugs."

"Not hustling, girl. You can do other things for me."

"I'm not a hooker either."

"Not that either, big head!"

"What?"

"You gonna be Chino's soldier."

"What?"

"You're going to be General Chino's national security advisor."

Pam burst into laughter. "Boy, you're crazy!"

"Quit that bullshit job, Pam. Your new man is gonna take care of you."

"My new man?"

"Yeah." Chino leaned forward and kissed her softly on her lips. "Hang out with the Chino, baby girl. I promise you, it'll never be boring."

"Yeah, not boring, but something tells me that it'll be plenty dangerous."

"Not dangerous. Adventurous." Chino gave a big Kool-Aid smile.

Pam didn't know why she didn't push away his first kiss, let alone why she had allowed him to kiss her again. Ignoring her gut, Pam wrapped her arms around Chino's neck and kissed him slowly . . . passionately. Maybe it was because she was feeling Chino. Not because of his looks, his fast talk, or his fast money. It was something more than that. Something she couldn't put her finger on. She was definitely down for a little adventure, although her sixth sense warned her that messing with Chino was going to be dangerous. Perhaps even deadly.

Chapter 5

You Bring Me Joy

Chino pulled up to Pam's dorm in his black IROC-Z with the T-Tops off and the car's custom stereo system booming. Whodini was singing about friends, and how many of us have them. Pam was waiting on a bench, absorbing the bursts of cool air, sunlight, and breathtaking autumn scents. She heard Chino before she saw him, and stood up to watch his ride roll in.

"Now this is more like it!" Pam shouted.

Chino turned down the volume on the stereo. "What?"

"I said, this is more like it."

"Girl, you know you like my bike," Chino said with a smile.

Pam shrugged. "It wasn't as bad as I thought."

"C'mon," Chino said, nodding toward the passenger seat.

Pam climbed inside the IROC. "So, what's in store for today?"

"You'll see." Chino smiled.

Chino ejected the Whodini cassette and popped in Soulsonic Force. He always played "Planet Rock" when he wanted to show off his stereo system and impress people.

Pam and Chino pulled up to City Center Mall in downtown Columbus, parked, and headed inside. Chino led her into Dillard's, into the junior misses section. He began pulling Troop warm-up sets from the rack and holding them against Pam's frame.

"What are you doing?"

"Springing for you some fresh gear."

"I can buy my own clothes."

Chino walked his eyes up and down Pam's blue jeans, pink polo shirt, and pink Adidas. She quickly became uncomfortable, as she checked out his snow white Le Coq Sportif warm-up set. He was dressed to impress. He wore a matching white Kangol, clear Gazelle glasses, and a pair of all-white Pumas with fat white laces. On his fingers he wore a massive gold four-finger ring, and on his neck hung a fat gold dookie rope.

"I'm gonna make you look like you work for Chino."

"Oh, really?" Pam asked, lifting an eyebrow. "And what's wrong with what I'm wearing?"

"Nothing, if you want to look like you work in an old folks' home."

"I do."

"You did."

Chino picked out a couple of outfits and then headed to the even more expensive Gucci rack. He pulled off a black and gold and a brown and gold Gucci warm-up set.

"Chino, these things are like three hundred dollars!" Pam said, looking at the price tags.

Chino ignored her. "We need to get you matching Gucci hats and shoes."

"Chino, I can't accept these!"

"It's a done deal, lil mama. You're my girl now. Ain't no more protesting. It's my right as your man to spoil you and to buy you things."

"Chino!"

"C'mon." Chino nodded, leading her to the checkout counter where the handbags were kept.

"May I help you?" an older white woman asked. She looked to be in her mid-fifties. The woman looked at Chino and Pam suspiciously. She knew that all the clothes they were carrying came to well over one thousand dollars.

"Yes, I'd like to see that brown Gucci purse with the gold Gs"—Chino pointed—"and the black Gucci purse with the gold Gs."

"I'm sorry, I can only let you see them one at a time," the saleslady told him. "They're three hundred and up."

"I know the cost. I want to buy them both," Chino told her.

"Both?" The woman gave a fake smile. She looked at Chino, then back at Pam and continued, "Somebody must be having a birthday."

Pam shook her head. "No, it's not my birthday."

"Why it got to be somebody's birthday?" Chino asked.

"I . . . I was just commenting on what a special gift," the woman stuttered. She turned to Pam. "Are you graduating?"

"Why it got to be a special occasion?" Chino asked.

"Chino, stop."

"I'm just saying. Black people buy something nice, it's got to be a birthday, a graduation, a Christmas present, a wedding, a funeral, something. Why can't I buy it because I can. Damn!"

"Chino, let's go," Pam said, pushing him away from the counter.

"No, we ain't going nowhere. I want service. I want her to shut her damn mouth, stop with the racist comments, and just ring up my shit!"

"Chino, no," Pam said, trying to push him away from the counter.

"She's a worker and can't afford a damn thing in here," Chino said. "So she just needs to be courteous to the people who can afford this shit."

Chino pulled out a massive wad of cash and peeled off six one-hundred-dollar bills. He tossed them onto the counter. "I'll take both the purses, like I said before." He peeled off ten more hundred-dollar bills and threw them on top of the clothes he laid on the counter. "And then you can ring this shit up, too. After you're done with that, you can point me toward a jewelry store in the mall. My girl needs some fat gold earrings, and a fat gold dookie rope to go around her neck."

Chino leaned over and pulled Pam close. He kissed her on her lips. "And when you get through, you can put all this shit in gift boxes and wrap it up. This is a special occasion. We gonna celebrate being black and rich."

The cashier's face turned red with anger, mixed with frustration, mixed with envy.

Pam burst into laughter.

Chino peeled off ten more one-hundred-dollar bills and gave them to Pam.

"Chino, what's this for?"

"Because I made you a promise, that if you quit your job, you wouldn't miss it."

Pam grabbed one of her new Gucci bags from the saleswoman's hands and stuffed her money inside it.

Miss her old job at the nursing home? She didn't think so! Fuck that job!

Chapter 6

Everything That Glitters
Ain't Gold

"*I* can't believe that you agreed to do this," Pam said, smiling.

Chino shrugged. "It's officially our second date, so that calls for a special sacrifice on my part."

"Are you sure you want to do this?"

"I'm the C-H-I-N-O, don't you know? I can do this. I can do anything. Don't you realize that? You ain't fucking with no ordinary nigga. Girl, I'm like Superman, except I don't even bar no kryptonite."

"Yeah, well, what do you bar, Superman?"

"What all niggas bar. The courtroom, and them Klansmen in them black robes."

Pam threw her head back in laughter. "Boy, you silly."

Chino finished lacing up his ice skate.

"You don't have to do this," Pam told him.

"Hey, a promise is a promise. I said that you could pick the second date, and this is what you picked."

"I just wanted to see if you would agree to it. I don't want you to fall down and kill yourself. What would your mother have to say to me? She'd come after me!"

"Don't worry about that. My moms was killed by some people who wanted their secrets kept when I was twelve. Besides, ice-skating is just like roller-skating. And back in the day, your boy Chino couldn't be faded on them roller skates."

Pam's eyes softened. "No, Chino, it's not like roller-skating." She paused. "I'm so sorry about your mother. It has to be rough without a parent."

"Yeah, I know all about that. My pops is in lockup and won't be out any time soon. Charge it to the game."

"I'm so sorry. I don't know what to say."

"It's nothing you can say. You know what I mean, see what I'm sayin' is some walk it, some talk it. "

"Chino, you making a joke about something that's not funny."

"Sometimes you laugh to keep from crying. My father is doing life for drugs and my mother is dead for drugs. And I sell drugs."

Pam and Chino sat quietly on the bench outside the rink. Pam glanced up at Chino, who was staring down at his skates. She placed her hand on top of his. Chino folded her hand into his and smiled to himself. He shook his head and stuck his leg straight out into the air.

"See these blades on the bottom? They just like razor blades. And I can work a razor blade blindfolded. When it come to blades and white shit, I'm the master. Don't start panicking if the fiends see me out here cutting up and want to start bagging up this ice and shit."

"Boy, be quiet!" Pam stood up, held out her hand, and Chino clasped it. She gently pulled him up, and he began rocking back and forth and swinging his arms, trying to gain his balance. Pam wrapped her arms around him to keep him from falling. "Be careful!"

Chino leaned in and kissed her. "Wheew! Works every time!"

"Boy!" Pam pulled away. "I should push you down!"

"For stealing a kiss?" Chino shook his head, smiling. "Damn, you're a hard one."

"Come on, hold my hand," Pam said, leading him onto the ice in the rink.

The Chiller was a popular indoor all-year-round ice-skating rink, and the perfect excuse for new couples to hold hands or wrap themselves around each other to prevent spills. The hot chocolate bar was always crowded with pairs of all ages warming up after a flirty four dozen trips around the rink.

"Whoa!" Chino shouted, again thrashing his hands about, trying to gain his balance.

"I'm not falling for that again," Pam warned him.

Chino fell on his behind, pulling her down to the ice with him.

"Chino!"

"You could have kept me from falling!"

"I thought it was another one of your tricks to steal a kiss."

"Like this?" Chino said. He leaned in.

"Chino!" Pam softly called out his name and moaned. His kiss had her feeling moist in places. She didn't want that, at least, not yet. She wasn't ready to take that big step in her life. She had held on to her virtue for sixteen years, and she wasn't sure about giving it away. Since age fourteen, Pam had been pleasuring herself more and more with each passing year. She wanted to experience a man, but the fear was overwhelming. Especially with a boy she had just met . . . a boy like Chino. He was nice, and sweet, and cute, and funny, but still . . .

She had heard moaning in bed one night and woke to find Tomiko's ex-boyfriend on top of her roommate, handling his business. Tomiko sounded like the angels were beneath those covers blowing her like she was a trumpet. It was the first time she had ever had an orgasm listening to someone else make love. Tomiko told her that her ex, Daryl, had a dick like a brontosaurus bone. Who wanted something like that up inside them? Tomiko promised that it didn't hurt, and that it felt good in places that she didn't know existed until she had a stiff one up in her.

Despite Tomiko's guarantees, Pam still felt that she wasn't ready. But still, Chino had her nipples swollen, as well as her labia. She had never had feelings like this for a boy. High school was all about the academics, and social activities with her girlfriends. Her mother and stepfather were protective, making sure that teenage boys weren't on the agenda.

Pam wondered if she was just caught up in being on her own in a new and thrilling city, with a boy who was two years older than her. He was more than just older too; he was completely independent and making it without a college education.

She wanted to try having sex, but then again, she didn't.

Her mother had always told her that she would know when the time was right, and when she was ready to take that step. "Just make sure you protect yourself," was the advice her mother had given. Damn, why couldn't there be a manual that said, when this happens, do this. When you reach this age, you're ready for this.

"You okay?" Chino asked.

Pam snapped out of her thoughts. "Yeah, I'm all right."

Chino stood, and helped Pam up.

"Hey, you stood up by yourself!"

"Duh, no shit, Sherlock!"

"Chino, you better not!"

"Better not what?"

"You better not have been acting all this time."

"What? Acting like I couldn't skate?"

"Chino!"

"Tag, you're it!" Chino tapped Pam on her shoulder and took off. He sped around the rink like he was Scott Hamilton on steroids.

"Chino, you asshole!" Pam took off after him. "I can't believe you've been making a fool of me this whole time!"

"You're the one who assumed that because I was a dude I couldn't ice-skate!" Chino told her. "I'm from Cleveland, girl. There's only one thing to do in the winters when you can't drink, and that's ice-skate."

"Chino!"

Chino spun around facing her, while skating backward at high speed.

"When I catch you, I'm going to kill you!" Pam shouted.

"You can't catch me, slowpoke!" Chino said with a smile. "Your head's too big, and it weighs you down."

Pam sped up. Chino spun and accidentally bumped into some young ladies. He tumbled to the ground, and Pam slid to a stop next to him.

"That what your sorry ass gets!" Pam huffed.

"Sorry!" Chino shouted to the girls.

Pam extended her hand, and Chino clasped it. She began to pull him up, and then let go, allowing him to fall back down to the ground. "Now you're it!"

Pam sidestepped Chino and quickly raced off. Chino got up and went after her. He caught up with her halfway around the rink, and pulled her to the center of the rink, where he used his weight to pull her down.

"Chino!"

He pulled her close and kissed her again.

"Don't."

"Don't what?" Chino asked softly.

"It's too soon."

"What are you trying to say?"

"It's too soon for this."

"I don't understand, but whatever it is, I'm cool with it. Don't worry about anything, Pam. I'll wait for you, for as long as it takes. We're in this thing together, understand?"

Pam nodded. Her mouth wouldn't say what her heart wanted it to say. Her brain had interceded. What she wanted to say was that it was too soon for her to be feeling the way she felt about him. What she wanted to say was that it was too soon for her to have fallen in love.

Chapter 7

Slow It Down

Pam strolled down Neil Avenue, on her way to her Sociology 100 class. She had on a pair of jeans, a jacket, and a scarf to keep her face warm. Pam's eyes teared as the brisk November wind snapped across her face. Drawing her scarf closely to her chin, she continued to walk, shielding her face with her textbook. Turning right to walk past Mirror Lake, one of her favorite outdoor spots on campus, she saw that the water was now sprinkled with orange, yellow, and red leaves from the various trees. She smiled at its spendor and its beauty. It made her feel special.

Although it was cold outside, she was anything but anxious to reach Mendenhall Lab in the South Oval. Pam was slacking off in school because she was either with Chino or thinking about him when she should have been listening to a lecture or studying. Her mom and stepdad crossed her mind. They wouldn't be happy with her upcoming quarterly report card.

"Hey! Pam!"

Pam quickly turned around. She hadn't heard the deliberate footsteps behind her. A tall, well-dressed boy stood before her, grinning widely. Pam searched his face but couldn't place him.

"Yes?" she asked as she stared at his beautiful smile with pearly white teeth. The brisk wind blew the scent of his cologne into her nostrils and she inhaled the smell. His skin was a smooth semisweet chocolate, pulled delicately against his high cheekbones and masculine jawline. He was dressed in a Karl Kani jean outfit. Her heart fluttered briefly.

"Hey, I'm Erik." He extended his hand. Pam gave him a blank look. "I'm in this class." She searched her memory again but still didn't recognize his face or name, and her face told it all. "You're in sociology, right?"

"Oh, yeah . . . Hi. I'm in this class." She looked at him quizzically again. "What did you say your name was again?"

Erik thought he was tripping. He thought he had seen Pam in his class, but the way she reacted to him, he was now uncertain.

"Well, damn, I can see that I really made a good first impression on you," Erik said playfully. "And again, my name is Erik."

"I'm sorry, Erik, my mind is somewhere else." Pam smiled, but only to be polite.

"C'mon," Erik said as he began to talk toward the class. Pam followed; she didn't want to be late. When they reached the classroom, Erik opened the door and kindly extended his hand. "After you, my lady."

Pam rolled her eyes and stepped inside. Erik laughed and followed her in.

"So, when we consider what is 'normal' or what is 'abnormal,' we have to evaluate the standards in regards to accepted and rejected, or 'taboo,' behavior. Understand that African tribes operate at a completely different level of behavioral standards than—" The professor was cut off abruptly by a series of rapid beeps, signaling that class was over.

"Eesh, already? All right folks, remember that our exam review is next Wednesday, and don't forget that your research papers are due Monday. Oh, and I won't be in my office tomorrow. I have a seminar to attend. See you next week!"

Pam collected her things and walked out of the lecture hall. "Hey, what did you think about that lecture?" Erik asked, trailing behind her. "I think he was on point about what's considered normal versus abnormal. The rituals in other countries that are considered customs are barbaric and—"

"What are you saying?" Pam asked, continuing to walk.

"You weren't listening? Girl, you trippin'. Hey wait up! How could you not pay attention to that mind-blowing shit?" he asked sarcastically.

Pam laughed and slowed down a bit so Erik could match her pace. The stream of students that burst through the building's front doors were met with a fierce wind.

"Where you goin' next?"

"My dorm room." Pam kept walking.

"I'll walk with you," Erik offered, hunching his shoulders against the cold.

Pam stopped and turned toward him, shielding half her face from the wind with her scarf. "Look, Erik, I know what you're doing, but I have a man."

Erik looked at Pam, threw his hands up, and smiled. "Hey, I'm just tryin' to make new friends. No harm intended."

Pam tilted her head to the side to evaluate his personality. Erik looked away and back at Pam.

"Hey, why don't we get together and study for this damn test?" he asked her. "You know you'll be needing some help because you didn't hear a thing dude said the entire hour."

Pam laughed and thought for a second. He was right. She knew her grades were about to go down the shitter, and agreeing to a study session would at least make her feel obligated to hit the books.

"You know what?"

"What's that?"

"I need all the help I can get at this point," Pam answered. "Let's go."

Chapter 8

Straight Ballin'

"Face, nigga!" Chino shouted, as he swooshed the ball into the basketball net.

"Fouling-ass nigga!" Rock shouted.

"That wasn't no foul!" Chino shouted back. "Quit crying. You doing all the crying, what the baby gonna do?"

"C'mon, let's school these niggas!" Rock shouted.

Chino, Fabian, Infa, and Chris J were on one team, while Rock, Ant, Corey, and Joe Bub Baby were on the other. They were playing their weekly Saturday afternoon basketball game on the neighborhood court. All of the hood gathered at the court on the weekend and balled, or lounged at the park. Everyone had their whips shined to perfection, while the young ladies wore their latest outfits and had their hairdos in the latest style. Pam and Tomiko sat in the stands watching.

"Pass the rock!" Joe Bub shouted, clapping his hands. Rock passed him the basketball, and Joe Bub pulled up and made a three-pointer. "Face, niggas!"

Joe Bub Baby was six feet tall, heavyset, and the spitting

image of Gerald Levert. In fact, Joe Bub swore that he could sing like the megastar. He walked around constantly singing "Casanova" and other Levert hits. He was a dope boy who swore he was an R&B singer, and even went so far as to spend his drug proceeds on studio time, professional production, and R&B tracks.

"That ain't shit!" Infa told him, while dribbling the basketball back down the court. Infa was one of Chino's main men. Half black and half Panamanian, he was fluent in Spanish and English. He got his looks from his Panamanian mother. He had her curly jet black hair, light brown skin, brown freckles, and brown eyes. He also had her hot Latin temper. Infa carried his father's full lips, full nose, and athletic build. He was the Latin lover in the crew. He could charm the socks off a nun.

Chris J pointed toward the net, and Infa tossed the ball up toward the basket. Chris J snatched the ball in midair and slam-dunked it over Ant and Corey. The crowd went wild.

"Face that, niggas!" Chris J said, laughing and jogging back down the court. Chris J was the b-boy in the crew. He was six-four and could ball but was known as a b-boy because he could b-bop, and breakdance like no other back in the day. Spin on his head, windmill, eggroll, fourplex, 360, handstand, poplock, you name it, he could do it. He idolized the New York City Breakers and the Rock Steady Crew. When he was a kid, he had a life-sized poster of Crazy Legs thumbtacked to his wall. Chris J could also name every rapper, rap group, and rap song that ever existed. He was do or die true to hip hop.

Ant ran down the court and clapped his hands. Rock passed him the basketball. Ant turned to pass it to an open

Corey, but Chino jumped into the passing lane and stole the ball. He tossed the ball to Fabian, who was racing down the court. Fabian passed it to Infa, who passed it to Chris J, who threw it to a trailing Chino for another slam dunk.

"Wheeew!" Chino shouted. He pounded his chest and turned toward Pam. "That was for you, baby!"

"I see you, baby!" Pam shouted back. She blew Chino a kiss.

"This is for you, baby!" Ant shouted to Tomiko. Ant was the pretty boy in the clique. He was six-one, with emerald green eyes, high yellow skin, and low-cut, wavy hair. He could have been a model under other circumstances, but he had been born in the hood.

Tomiko held up her hand, giving him her palm. "I don't even think so!"

"Girl, he's cute!" Pam whispered.

"He's too cute," Tomiko told her. "He probably has about twenty bitches that he fucks with on a regular basis."

"That don't mean that you can't make him yours," Pam said.

"That statement right there gives up your age, girl," Tomiko said. "Guys like that can't be changed or tamed, they are just gonna be whores their whole life, until they grow old. Then they want to settle down."

Rock pulled up, and the ball clanked off the front of the rim. Chris J got the rebound and passed the ball to Fabian, who dribbled downcourt.

"Game point!" Infa shouted.

"We make this, it's over!" Chino told them.

"Man up!" Rock shouted to his team. Rock was known for

his ludicrous basketball skills and he could handle the ball like no other. He was the Michael Jordan of Columbus. He had been one of those kids that everyone just knew was heading to the NBA. But somehow, like most of those hood superstars, Rock had fallen victim to the glamour of street life instead of paying his dues on a college basketball team. Rock got his name from being able to cook dope like he was Chef Boyardee. He could take a mayonnaise jar, an ounce of cocaine, an ounce of baking soda, and some water, and get back two ounces of crack. His cooking skills were legendary in the streets of Columbus, and throughout much of Ohio for that matter.

"Defense, y'all!" Joe Bub shouted. "Don't let 'em score!"

Fabian passed the ball to Chino, who threw it to Chris J, who immediately swung it round to Infa. Infa drove toward the net, and everyone collapsed on him. He tossed the ball to Chris J, who drew a triple team. Chris J then found Chino and he immediately swung the ball out to Fabian, who had set up in the corner for a three-pointer. Fabian shot the ball and hit nothing but net.

"It's over!" Chino shouted, throwing his hands up. "It's over!"

"Champions, baby!" Infa shouted.

"You niggas can't fade us!" Chris J shouted. "I'm a beast boy!"

Chino raced into the stands, up the bleachers to where Pam was seated. He leaned in trying to get a kiss, but Pam pushed him away.

"Boy, you're all sweaty!" Pam shouted.

"A little bit of your man's sweat ain't gonna kill you."

"Yes, it will!" Pam said, continuing to push Chino away.

"Peep game, y'all!" Infa shouted.

Chino turned to see what Infa was talking about. His crew on the court was staring at the adjacent street. There he noticed a black GMC Jimmy was slowly creeping past the park. Suddenly several weapons came out of the window.

"Get down!" Ant shouted.

Gunfire erupted and sparks flew off the asphalt court and the metal bleachers. Chino shoved Pam down and dove on top of her, shielding her body with his own. With his other arm, he pulled Tomiko down as well.

"Stay down, baby!" he whispered to Pam.

The loud pop of gunfire rang out for several moments before the screeching of the Jimmy's tires. They were gone.

Total silence.

Then tears.

Screams and people running.

"Are you all right?" Chino asked, removing his body from hers, all the while protecting her from the chaos.

Pam was able to produce a nod through hysterical tears.

Helping Pam up, he looked at Tomiko. "Are you okay?" Chino extended a hand toward her too.

Grabbing Chino's hand, nervously she answered, "Yeah, I'm all right."

Infa ran over. "Anybody hit?"

"Them hoes can't even shoot straight!" Rock said, dusting himself off.

"Who was that?" Corey asked, looking spooked. Corey was the nerdy one in the crew. He was a good kid who desperately wanted to live the street life. He hung around Chino and the rest of the fellas for excitement and acceptance. They knew he was perpetrating; however, Corey was cool. Although he wanted their life, if they could have traded theirs with his, the crew would have given their right arm to do it. "That was them Cleveland niggas!" Chris J exclaimed. "I seen them at the club the other night."

Pam stared at Chino with a tear-streaked face and spoke angrily. "I want to go home!"

"All right, baby girl. Just checkin' out my boys here, then we can burn out."

"Now!" Pam screamed.

"Okay, baby," Chino said, holding up his hands to calm her down, "c'mon."

"Chino, did you know those people? Why were they shooting at us?" Pam questioned.

"They were just tripping."

Chino pulled Pam close, to calm her shaking body.

"Baby, I won't let anything happen to you," he whispered into her ear. Kissing the top of Pam's head, he held her.

Pam hugged him tightly. "Promise me, Chino."

"I promise you, Pammy. I'll give my life to keep you safe."

Looking into his eyes, Pam believed him. "I know you will," she told him, thinking about how he had thrown his body on top of hers to keep her safe. His safety wasn't an issue, hers was. *If I stay with him, how many more times will I get shot at?* she thought to herself. *What else will happen next time? Next time . . .* Pam pondered.

She looked at Chino and a pang of hurt crossed her heart

at the thought of not seeing him again. Quickly, she brought herself back to reality and erased the thought of him not being around out of her mind.

Pam knew that Chino was a baller and with the lifestyle came risks; risks she was willing to take because she knew that he would protect her or die trying.

Chapter 9

Forever True

"Aaaaaaaaaaah!" Pam screamed at the top of her lungs as the Ferris wheel spun through the air.

Pam had not been the same since the shooting. She stayed close to home, in the safety of her dorm room. Regardless of how much Chino urged, she had refused to go out. After a few days of chilling in Pam's dorm room, Chino knew that he had to do something to get her mind off what happened and back into the swing of things.

Chino watched Pam smile and laugh. He wanted to make sure that she was enjoying herself and having a great time. He was truly catching feelings for Pam. He had never fallen for a girl so quick. He felt close to her. He felt like he could trust her. She was young, and naive, and new, and she was completely different from the hood rats that he was used to dating. Pam showed him that the world could be different. She was proof that there was a better world out there.

"You having fun?" Chino asked.

Pam nodded. "A lot."

The ride came to a stop, and Chino helped Pam out of her seat. The two of them began to stroll through the amusement park. Chino clasped her hand and felt her shiver.

"What's the matter?"

Pam rubbed her arms. "It's a little cold out here."

Chino pulled off his jacket and wrapped it around her.

"No," Pam protested, "you'll be cold."

Chino shrugged. "I'll be all right."

"Thank you," Pam said. They walked for a few moments and Pam stopped to look at Chino. "Is it going to always be like this?"

"Like what?"

"Are you always going to be my knight in shining armor? Are you always going to come to my rescue?"

Chino laughed and nodded. "Always. Just call me Sir Chino, Duke of Columbus."

Pam laughed. "And what would that make me?"

"Lady Pam, the Duchess of Detroit."

"Oh, a royal marriage, huh?"

Chino pulled her close. "I didn't want to tell you at first, but this whole thing was arranged. I paid your father a bride price."

"Oh, really? And how much did I cost you?"

"Three chickens, two cows, two goats, and my favorite bull."

"Damn, that's a high price for a bride."

"You're African? Damn, I thought I was getting an Asian chick."

Pam nudged Chino in his side and the two of them laughed. They walked for a bit without talking.

Chino finally spoke. "Pam, what is it you want to do? You know, like really *do*. What are you in college for, anyway?"

Pam thought for a moment. "Well, I'm a business major. I've always pictured myself running something. My mom always said I was an entrepreneur. I had lemonade stands every summer, all summer long growin' up." Pam paused and laughed to herself. "I didn't even care about going to the pool or playing in the sprinklers. I was out there stackin' quarters!"

"Nickelin' and dimin' at an early age. I knew you were the one for me!" Chino bent over laughing, and Pam joined in.

"You know it!" she exclaimed.

Chino sucked in his breath. "If you had to run something starting now, a business, what would it be?"

"Hmm . . ." Pam considered her options. Two children burst suddenly between them, yelling excitedly about their next ride. A frustrated mother trailed behind them, carrying coats and cotton candy.

"Excuse me," she said as she passed through the couple.

Pam smiled at the woman and watched as she caught up with her children, calling after them, telling them not to go too far.

"A salon," Pam said finally.

"You wanna do hair for a living?" His eyebrows were raised. "My woman gets her hair and nails done. She ain't gone be standin' behind no one's back, pampering them!"

"Chino!" Pam swatted his shoulder. "I want to *run* the place. That's a whole lot different than shampooing!"

They came upon a booth with a shooting gallery. Chino guided her toward it.

"It's time for the general to do his thing!"

"What?"

"It's time for me to show off my shooting skills," Chino told her. "You don't get to be a general without being able to bust some ass."

Pam laughed. "You have too many titles for me."

"I was a general, then I conquered Ohio and became the Duke of Columbus," Chino explained.

"And a very active imagination," Pam continued.

Chino lifted the rifle. "How much?"

"Five tickets," the booth operator told him.

Chino pulled a wad of tickets out of his pocket, tore off five of them, and handed them to the operator.

"You shoot ten ducks, you get to pick from these stuffed animals," the operator explained. "You shoot twenty, you get to pick from these." He pointed to another group of stuffed animals. "You shoot thirty, you get to pick from these. Forty will get you anything on the top rack, and fifty you get to pick from over there behind that case."

"What's the catch?" Pam asked.

"You only have five misses," the operator told them. "Miss five times, and it's over, the gun cuts off."

Chino peered through the sights of the electronic rifle and took aim. He waited for the first of the tiny automated ducks to roll by and then began to squeeze the trigger. Duck after duck quacked and fell to its side.

"Go, baby, go!" Pam clapped enthusiastically.

Chino continued to shoot, nearly earning a perfect score. He shot forty-eight ducks before the gun cut off on his fifth miss. Pam jumped up and down.

"How many did I get?" Chino asked.

"A whole helluva lot," the operator told him. "I'll count the tickets up for you."

"Which one you want?" Chino asked.

Pam shrugged. "I don't know."

"How about that big-ass Winnie the Pooh bear over there?" Chino said to Pam, pointing.

"Yeah, that's a nice one."

"Yo, give me that Winnie the Pooh," Chino told the operator.

"Sorry, you needed fifty for that one."

"Damn, how many did I get?"

"You got forty-eight."

Chino reached into his pocket and pulled out some more tickets. Pam stopped him.

"That's okay, you don't have to do it again."

"You sure?"

Pam nodded. "Yeah. Let's go ride some more rides."

"Well, what does forty-eight hits get me?" Chino asked, determined to win Pam an animal.

"You can have pretty much anything, except the stuffed Winnie."

"Fuck it, give me that big-ass Tigger then."

"This one's my favorite," the operator told Chino as he pulled down the gigantic stuffed animal.

"Yeah, Tigger is cool," Chino confirmed.

"He's not as big as Winnie to snuggle up with, but he'll do," the booth operator told them.

"I don't need that Winnie," Chino said, grabbing Tigger

away from the operator. "I got my own Pooh to snuggle up with."

Pam smiled.

"Ain't that right, Pooh Bear?" Chino asked.

Pam nodded. She liked the name. He was her Chino, and she was his Pooh. It was the first time anyone had given her a pet name. It made her feel really special.

Chapter 10

Me Against the World

"What's up, kinfolk?" Chino said, greeting Fabian as he strolled into the house. Fabian had two trap houses that he used for business, where big-timers went to score. He was meeting up with his boy to conduct business.

"What up, my dude?" The two exchanged handshakes and a quick embrace.

"Your world, baby," Chino told him. "I'm just a squirrel trying to get a nut."

"Right . . . right," Fabian confirmed. "Come on." He led Chino to the kitchen where two of his business partners from LA awaited him.

"Sup y'all." Chino spoke to the dudes sitting around the kitchen table where twenty kilos were stacked.

Chino lifted one and examined the red scorpion on the packaging. "What happened to the tarantula?"

"New supplier, baby boy!" Fabian said excitedly. "This shit is coming up from Texas. Thirteen-five a key."

"Get the fuck outta here!" Chino told him.

"I'ma hook you up with a eighteen-five ticket."

"Shit, bet!" Chino said.

"Hey, you remember Lupe and Pepe, don't you?" Fabian asked.

"Yeah," Chino nodded, and shook each one's hand in turn. "What's happening, fellas?"

"Shit, long-ass drive," Lupe told him. "I'm about to get outta this muthafucka and go get some sleep."

"Hell, yeah!" Pepe agreed, rubbing his tired eyes.

"Damn, you short today." Chino examined the pile on the table.

"Man, you crazy," Fabian told him. "You just late, kinfolk. I done already moved thirty of these things."

"Damn, what was it, a fifty stack?"

"You know it!" Fabian said, holding up his hand.

"All right, you the man!" Chino said, shaking his hand once again.

"You muthafuckin' right, I'm the man." Fabian grinned. "With this new connect, I can come up strong within a few months. A few months I'll be out of this shit for good!"

"Damn, you thinking about getting out?" Chino asked.

"That's the object of the game, holmes," Fabian told him. "Get what you need and get the fuck out. Don't make a career of this shit. I'm trying to sit on a coupla mil so I can bust out in a "fat ass" crib, some "tight ass" whips, open my own business, and never have to worry about shit for the rest of my life."

"Sounds like a winner," Chino said, nodding.

"Take my advice, bro. Get your money, and get the hell out the game."

"When I get to where you are, then I can talk about getting out," Chino said with a smile.

Suddenly a loud noise resonated from the living room. It sounded like glass and wood shattering, then came a barrage of voices.

"Police!" several voices shouted from the living room. "This is a narcotics search warrant!"

Pepe raked the keys off the table into a metal bucket of acid that they had sitting next to it. A couple of the kilos burst open, scattering powder as they struck the corner of the bucket. The vast majority of the kilos landed inside the large vat of acid and dissolved instantly.

"Let me see your hands!" "Hands!" a second officer shouted. "Get down on the ground!" yelled the first officer to enter the kitchen.

Chino held his hands up. "Damn!"

"Slowly, with your hands above your heads, turn around!" the first officer shouted.

Chino, Fabian, Pepe, and Lupe all turned around, leaving their backs to the officers.

"Get down on the ground!" another officer commanded.

Chino dropped down to his knees, with his hands held high above his head. Suddenly he felt his wrists being cuffed.

"You gentlemen are under arrest," one of the masked officers told them. "You have the right to remain silent. Anything you say can and will be used against you in a court of law. You have the right to an attorney. If you cannot afford an attorney, one will be appointed to you. Do you understand these rights as I have read them to you?"

One of the officers turned Chino around. "Do you understand your rights?"

"Yeah, man."

The officer turned Pepe around. "Do you understand your rights as they have been read to you?"

"*Sí!*" Pepe confirmed.

An officer turned Lupe and Fabian around. "Do you understand your rights?"

Lupe nodded but Fabian spoke. *"No habla Inglese."*

The officer's masked face looked at Fabian. He could tell by the squint of his eyes that he made the officer mad.

"We need a Spanish-speaking officer in here!"

"Right here!" one of the masked officers said, walking over to Fabian. *Tu hablas español?"*

"Portuguese," Fabian confirmed, smiling.

"He speaks Portuguese," the Spanish-speaking officer told his counterparts.

"This muthafucka speaks English," one of the masked undercover officers declared. "He's just trying to bullshit us. Fabian, you know yo ass speaks English!"

"Who do we got here, gentlemen?" another masked plainclothes officer asked.

"We got our target. Quintanilla is here, so are the two drivers, and we got Christonos here as well."

Another officer scooped some of the wasted powder into a test tube and shook it. The blue liquid inside the tube turned red. "We got a positive for cocaine here!"

The officers cheered.

"Quintanilla, Fabianico, is going away for a long time!" one of the officers declared.

"We got trace residue in the van as well," the other officer chimed in. "We can connect the two drivers to the conspiracy. Bring me Christonos."

Two officers grabbed Chino and led him into the next room. A chair was brought in behind him, and he was shoved into it.

The officer bent down and stuck his face in Chino's. Chino could see the officer's day-old stubble sprouting from his face. "Your partners are going away for a long time," one of the undercovers told him. "You're in a shitload of trouble too. The only question is how much trouble. I'm going to give it to you straight with no chaser. You have two choices. One, you can get a little bit of time by helping us out, or you can get a lot of time by not helping us out. But let me tell you this, it's time to help yourself. Those guys in the other room, they're going away regardless. We just need you to fill in the blanks for us on some things. We want to know how much they had, how often those guys brought the drugs, where they came from, and who has been sending the drugs up here to Columbus. Help us out with that and we'll tell the judge that you cooperated, and we may even work you a supersweet deal where you walk with just probation."

Chino laughed in their faces.

"What's funny?" The officer asked. "I didn't say anything funny." He turned to the other officers. "Did you say something funny?"

"Nope," the older officer replied, "but what's funny is this nigga right here going away for a long time. You son of a bitch!" the officer shouted at Chino. "Let's get that straight right now! You can do a lot of time, or no time at all. It's your choice!"

"I want a lawyer," Chino said calmly.

"You ain't getting no fucking lawyer, you black muthafucka!" the officer shouted.

"Fuck you!" Chino shouted.

"Fuck me? No, fuck you!" The officer swung and struck Chino in his jaw. "Talk, you black muthafucka!"

"Fuck you!" Chino shouted.

"Where are the drugs coming from?" the officer said, striking Chino again.

"Fuck you!" Chino shouted.

"How much did they have?" the officer said, striking Chino again. This time, blood flew from Chino's lip.

"Suck my dick, bitch!" Chino shouted.

The officer struck Chino again, this time leaving a gash across his right eye.

"Fuck you!" Chino shouted. "I ain't talking! I ain't telling you shit!"

The officer knocked Chino from the chair and kicked him in his stomach. Chino curled into a ball.

"You talk, you son of a bitch!" the officer shouted.

"Fuck you," Chino said weakly.

"Get this asshole out of here," another officer ordered.

Two officers lifted Chino up and dragged him back into the room with Fabian, Lupe, and Pepe, who had heard the whole thing. They saw Chino's bloody face and beat-up body. Pepe and Lupe exchanged glances. Chino had taken an ass whipping and hadn't broken. He had held strong. They would report this back to their people.

"You all right?" Fabian asked.

"Fuck them hoes!" Chino said.

Fabian nodded. Chino had held his water under pressure. He hadn't just been interrogated, he had been beaten. That kind of loyalty meant the keys to the city. Fabian knew for certain he was going away, but he would make sure that Chino was taken care of. He had a cousin in New York that he would hook Chino up with to make sure that he was all right.

"It's going to be okay, bro," Fabian told Chino. "You'll see. Stay strong, and the world is yours."

Chapter 11

Giving My All to You

"Dang, Pooh, you feel warm as hell." Chino placed his hand over Pam's forehead.

"I know. I don't feel so good."

Chino wrapped his arms around her, pulling her close to him. He kissed the back of her neck and then climbed out of the bed. "As a matter of fact, you're burning up."

She started shivering. "I didn't feel well yesterday. I woke up last night with a headache, and now I have a fever."

"Just get some rest, baby. I'll take care of everything."

"I can't just lay in bed all day," Pam protested. "I have clothes to wash, an exam to study for, I have—" Pam sneezed.

"Bless you!" Chino told her.

"I can't—"

"You won't," Chino interrupted her. "I'll take care of your clothes and help you study for your test."

"Yeah, right!" Pam said, trying to sit up. She sniffled and coughed.

Chino gently pushed her back down. "Baby, lay down. I'll

get your books and throw your clothes in the washing machine. Your books are in your backpack, right?"

"Yeah."

"Okay, then," Chino said, turning to head out of the room.

"Separate my whites!" Pam told him.

He turned to look at her with a grin on his face. "Duh! I know how to wash clothes, girl! I even manage to dress myself some mornings, isn't that amazing?"

"Okay, you got me," Pam said mustering a laugh, lifting her hands, signaling no contest.

Chino turned and headed out of the bedroom into the living room. He grabbed her basket of clothes and carried it into the kitchen, where his washer and dryer were tucked away inside a closet. He pulled out her white clothes, placed them inside the washer, added a cup of bleach, a scoop of laundry detergent, and turned the washer on. When he was finished, he closed the top on the washer and walked to his pantry, where he found a can of chicken noodle soup.

Chino carried the soup to his counter, looked inside a drawer, found his can opener, and opened the soup. He looked inside his cupboard, found a microwave-safe bowl, and poured in the chicken noodle soup. He placed the bowl in his microwave.

The microwave beeped to let him know that his soup was done. He found a spoon from his dish drawer, placed the bowl on a plate, and then found some fresh saltine crackers inside his pantry. He placed a sleeve of crackers on the plate next to the bowl, and then carried it all into the room to place the bowl of soup on the nightstand next to the bed. He left and returned from the kitchen with an ice-cold glass of lemonade. He wished that he had some Sprite or 7UP to give her, but he was out. He would have to run to the store and pick some up for her later. He searched his medicine cabinet for a couple of Tylenol to help break Pam's fever. He found a couple of extra-strength tablets and carried them back into the room with him.

"What's all this?" Pam asked.

"It's your breakfast," Chino told her.

Pam waved him off. "I really don't feel like eating anything."

"You're going to eat and get better, young lady," Chino said, playfully. He handed her the Tylenol. "Take these."

Pam sat up, plopped the Tylenol into her mouth, and sipped on the lemonade. Chino took the glass, set it back down on the nightstand, as she lay back on the pillow.

"Sit up," Chino told her, sitting down on the side of the bed, with the bowl of soup.

"Chino, I don't feel like eating anything."

"Sit up," he gently insisted.

Pam sat up in bed, and Chino lifted a spoonful of soup to his lips and gently blew on it.

"I can't believe you're making me eat."

Chino fed Pam a spoonful of warm soup. "I have to get you better."

"Do you do this to all of your women?" Pam asked.

"Only the sick ones." Chino winked.

He fed her another spoonful of soup and then handed her a cracker.

"I haven't eaten soup and crackers since I was a kid," Pam told him. "I think the last time I did, I had a cold and my mother fixed it for me."

Chino smiled and continued to feed her.

Swallowing a spoonful, Pam looked at Chino, smiled, and continued. "I like how you take care of me, Chino. Are you always going to be like this?"

"I'm going to try."

Pam ate another spoonful and nodded. "I know you are."

"Is that a bad thing?" Chino looked at Pam and dabbed the napkin at her mouth.

"No, not at all. It's just scary, that's all."

"What's scary?"

Pam sighed. "I've never heard of a man fixing his woman chicken noodle soup, let alone feeding it to her."

"So, what are you saying?"

"I'm saying, you've earned some major points here."

"Sounds like you're feeling a little better already."

"A good man makes his woman feel good."

"Now I'm a good man, huh?" Chino asked.

"Maybe."

"Here," Chino said, handing her the bowl of soup. "Feed your damn self."

"Chino!" Pam's eyes grew big as saucers and her mouth fell open in surprise. "I was just kidding!"

Chino laughed at her expression, then suddenly his face became serious. "Hey, baby girl, I have to head to New York for a day or two."

Pam's heart thumped hard as she sat quietly and listened.

"My man, Fabian, set me up with his cuz to take over while he's on lockdown."

Chino's recent run-in with the cops had shaken Pam up. This hustla had her tripping, and she was strapped in for the ride. "Chino . . ."

Chino walked into the living room and pulled out the only textbook she had inside her pack.

"*World Civilizations!*" he exclaimed. "My best subject!"

Pam laughed. "Yeah, I'll bet."

"Girl, I used to teach world civilizations," Chino said smiling, sitting in the bed next to her. "What do you want to know about?"

"We're talking about ancient Egyptians."

"My people!" Chino said. "Invented all the important shit."

"Like what?" Pam asked, lifting an eyebrow.

"Oh, you trying to test me, huh?"

"What did they invent?" Pam asked. "Name one thing."

"The motorcycle!"

"Boy, get the hell outta here!" Pam laughed, trying to shove Chino off the bed.

"What?"

"See, that's what I'm talking about. How in the hell are you going to help me study?"

"Because I'm the man. Let's see." Chino reached for the history book.

Pam pulled it back.

"That's okay, I don't need no book to tell me about my people. We're an oral people anyway. I don't need no white folks to tell me that we were the first to navigate by the stars, or to invent the science of astronomy, or to domesticate animals, or to irrigate based on the seasons along the banks of the Nile."

"Chino!" Pam said. Her mouth fell open.

Chino laughed.

"How do you know those things?"

"Girl, don't underestimate me."

. "Chino!"

"You think that I'm just some dumb-ass street nigga, don't you?"

"No, I never thought that. I know you're smart, but . . ."

"But I shouldn't have any book-smarts, huh? I shouldn't know as much as my big-headed girlfriend? I shouldn't know that Akhenaton was the first to proclaim one true god and thus invent monotheism. I shouldn't know that the Egyptian pyramids were astronomically aligned, or that the pharaoh Sesostris had conquered the entire known world. I shouldn't know that Hatshepsut ruled as a man, or that Thebes was the center of Egyptian religious life, or that the Greek deities were copies of Egyptian ones?"

Pam's mouth remained wide open.

Chino pulled the book out of her hand. "Now c'mon, Pooh, let's study and get you an A on this exam."

Chapter 12

Right Place, Right Time

"*I love* New York!" Chino shouted out the window. "New York, New York, big city of dreams!"

Chino ducked back in the car; the biting December air was too much to bear hanging out of a moving vehicle. Chino and Joe Bub Baby rolled down the busy streets of Manhattan. One thing he loved about the city was its energy. It could be two or three o'clock in the morning, and Manhattan would be lit up like it was broad daylight. He particularly loved rolling through Times Square and the massive Port Authority Terminal to check out the wide variety of characters who hung out in those places. New York was like a zoo for humans. One could find a variety of different species wandering about.

"Yo, check that out, dog!" Joe Bub said, pointing to the white cats that had multicolored Mohawks.

Chino shook his head. "Only in New York."

"Yo, let's roll through Harlem."

"Mos def, but we can do that later. First we gotta meet Fabian's cousin."

"A'ight," Joe Bub agreed. "Aye, what's that cat's name again? Dragons, Dragoon, Dragoose?"

"Dragos, fool!" Chino spat. "This is my plug, remember that. You just along for the ride, so you be quiet and let me do all the talking."

"Bet," Joe Bub told him. "Hey, C, let's hit that club The Roxy while we up here."

"I'm cool with that."

"So old boy is Fabian's kinfolk?"

"Yeah, they moms are sisters or cousins or some shit."

"That's fucked up how them cops did you."

"Fuck 'em." Chino shrugged. "They just mad 'cause they knew I was gonna walk. My name wasn't on the warrant, or the house, or any of the bills. I was just a visitor and had nothing to do with anything. At least that's what the jury would have been led to believe."

Joe Bub held up his hand and Chino shook it. "That's how you beat that shit, baby!"

"They didn't really have shit on Fabian but about two ounces worth of powder that didn't fall into the bucket. That shit ain't nothing but about twenty-four months. As long as nobody talks, that's all he'll get."

"He'll end up in a camp doing sweet-ass fed time," Joe Bub added. "Golfing and playing tennis and shit."

"The good thing is, he got the paper to just kick back and do his time real sweet," Chino said. "He'll be good."

"Man . . . if I gotta do a bid, I at least hope it's a fed bid,"

Joe Bub commented. He glanced down at his Swatch. "Hey, where we gotta meet them fools at?"

"Right here," Chino said, pulling up to his destination, watching a car leave, "and there goes a parking spot right there."

Chino whipped his rented Corvette around into the newly vacated parking spot. He and Joe Bub climbed out of the Vette and made their way across the street, heads tucked down and hands in their pockets, protecting themselves from the frosty air. A group of Puerto Ricans were standing outside a deli.

"Yo, you know where I can get a good cheese steak sandwich?" Chino spoke, giving them the code that Fabian had told him. "A nigga hungry."

"Cheese steaks are in Philly," one of them replied, hunched over from the cold.

"Well, what do you have here in New York?"

"Coneys," another one answered correctly.

A slim Puerto Rican dude with a long mustache and slicked-back hair stepped forward. He wore a black leather jacket, some black jeans, and some black boots. He looked like a cross between the Terminator and Fonzie from *Happy Days*, but something about him was intimidating. Maybe even dangerous. Perhaps it was his unassuming manner, or the way he held his cigarette in his mouth, or the way he talked so slow and steady and sure but everyone could see that he wasn't one to be fucked with.

"I am Dragos." The slim man extended his hand.

"Chino." He took and shook Dragos's hand.

Dragos nodded toward the interior of the deli. "Let's step inside and talk."

Dragos led the way and Chino followed. The men stepped in front of the entry, letting Joe Bub know that he wasn't going inside with them.

"Shit, it's colder than a muthafucker out here!" Joe Bub said to himself as he turned around and bounced up and down slightly, trying to keep warm.

Dragos seated himself at a table in the corner, and Chino took the opposite seat.

"I've heard a lot about you, Chino." Dragos looked closely at him.

"I hope it's all good."

"It has been," Dragos told him, nodding his head in approval. "The family speaks highly of you and my uncle received some reports . . . impressive. Our family values loyalty, and a man who can take a beating and keep his mouth closed is thought of in highest regard."

"Man," Chino said, rubbing his hand across his chin, "there's no way I'll ever be a snitch."

Rubbing his hands together, Dragos stared long and hard at Chino. "You have proven yourself."

"Have you heard anything from Fabian?"

"Nothing since the last time we talked. The lawyers say that he is going to be fine."

"That's good."

"I thought it was important that we meet, so I could get a good gauge of your character since we are going to be dealing with each another from here on out. Fabian thinks of you like a brother."

"As far as I'm concerned, he is my brother." Chino and Fabian were as thick as thieves and their friendship was true.

"I don't know what kind of deal you and Fabian had, but I'm looking for someone who can move some serious merchandise for me in Columbus."

"How much?" Chino asked, never losing eye contact with Dragos.

"A lot. Basically, I'm looking for someone who can take Fabian's place. All of the people he was working with are going to need a new supplier."

"And you think I'm ready to move that much product?"

"Only you can answer that question, Chino. Are you ready?"

Chino looked out of the window and thought about what Dragos was asking. Was he ready to move that much weight in Columbus? Could he move that much weight? At least twenty birds a week. And depending on the ticket, he might be getting two or three thousand off each bird. Did he know enough niggas that moved at least a key? Could he depend on twenty niggas to each get a key each week, or ten niggas to get two keys a week? His crew would definitely have to step up their game. Money would be flowing like water, if they could find the customers. Could he do it? If Fabian could, then he could too. Fabian was from out of state, whereas Columbus was his. He was from Ohio, and nobody knew those streets or the players like he did. Yeah, he was ready.

"What kind of ticket are we talking?" Chino asked.

"We'll start off small," Dragos explained. "How about twenty keys a week?"

Chino nodded in agreement.

"The first month, I'm only going to send ten a week. I

want you to build up your clientele and get used to moving that kind of weight."

"You can go ahead and send the whole twenty," Chino told him confidently.

He was ready to ball and rake in all of life's rewards. The streets had not been kind to him as of yet. In fact, the streets had been a real bitch. But now, the bitch had just opened her legs up to him, and he was definitely going to fuck.

Chapter 13

Wait Till I Get My Money Right

Chino walked to his closet, pulled open the door, and kneeled down. He turned the knob on his metal safe, entering the combination. After correctly entering the four-digit number, he turned the lever and pulled open the heavy metal door. Inside the safe were his life savings. He had amassed roughly one hundred and eighty-five thousand dollars. Not enough for him to quit hustling for the rest of his life. Not enough for him to pack up and leave Columbus and go somewhere else and start over. Definitely not enough for him to buy a nice house out in the suburbs, furnish it, buy two cars, settle down, and raise a family; it was just enough for him to keep going. But with this new connect, things were definitely going to change.

Dragos was shipping him twenty kilos a week. If he made two thousand dollars a key, just by playing the middleman, he could definitely live with that. Forty thousand dollars a week meant that his dreams were within reach. In a year, he would be a millionaire. In a year, he could afford to quit. In a year, he could pack up, leave Columbus, leave the heartless and cold streets, leave behind all the death, destruction, and hard memories that seemed to plague him. In one year, he would be able to afford that life in the suburbs. In one year, he would be able to marry Pooh, start a family, have two nice whips in the driveway and a nice family dog in the backyard. He wanted it all. He wanted the American Dream.

The thought of waking up in the morning, taking the trash can to the street, and waving at his neighbors made him laugh. Hard-core Chino, gangsta from the hood, wanting to live the *Leave It to Beaver* lifestyle; but then again, wasn't that what it was all about? Getting out of the ghetto? White kids wanted to sag, listen to hip hop, talk black, dress black, and become a part of the hood. Real niggas from the hood wanted out of the hood. They would trade anytime. Give me Beverly Hills, you muthafuckas can have Compton. Deal. No backs, no jacks, no penny tax.

Chino counted out fifty thousand dollars and put the rest of his money back inside his safe. He gave the combination lock a few twists and pulled on the lever to make sure that his safe was secure. The worst thing in the world would be to get peeled by a fucking burglar. *Man, that would be so fucked up*, he thought.

Chino placed his fifty grand inside a large manila envelope and headed out the door. He was about to ball like crazy, but only if he could move that much yayo. How did one move that much product on a regular? By building up a customer base. How did a business build up its customer base? By advertisement. And in this game, how did one advertise, or let others know that you had product to move? By looking like you did. Nobody in the game would say two words to a scrub. The big-timers that he had just overshot wouldn't give him the time of day. Chino had always been known as one of Fabian's boys; now he wanted to be their supplier. He wanted to sell keys to niggas who had once been his peers, his competition, and even his suppliers when Fabian's supply had gone dry. But he had to let them know that he was open for business, and if it was any flack, he had to let them know that this was a new day and that he was the man now. First things first; he needed a whip that said he was the man. What better way than to go foreign?

Chino pulled into the Porsche dealership in his bucket and headed inside to the showroom. He was met with some strange glances, snares, smirks, but mostly the salesmen simply ignored him. They thought him just another kid from the hood with Porsche dreams with a lot of questions and a big waste of their time. One salesman didn't see him that way, though. He figured that the dreamers that walked into the dealership today were his customers of tomorrow.

"Hello," the salesman said, extending his hand toward Chino. "My name is Tom, what can I do for you today?" At least this guy was giving him some respect.

Chino pointed toward a Porsche 944 Turbo convertible on the showroom floor. The 944 Turbo had an almost butter smooth gray leather interior, a Blaupunkt stereo system, and a gorgeous candy red paint job. "Man, I like this one."

"Ahh, this is nice. The convertible nine forty-four Turbo," Tom confirmed. "We just got her in two days ago. She's a real beauty. Actually, the nine forty-four is our biggest seller, then the nine eleven, and our top of the line is the nine twenty-eight GT."

"Yeah, I know." Chino nodded. "My homeboy had a nine twenty-eight GT, a black one. It was nice."

"The nine twenty-eight is a helluva vehicle," Tom told him. "Expensive though."

"How much is this one?"

"This particular vehicle is fully loaded. It stickers out at forty-eight thousand. You can buy a 944 in the thirties; same thing with a turbo model. You can get a nicely equipped turbo for about forty to forty-two."

"How does it drive?" Chino asked.

"Like a beauty." Tom smiled. "Have you ever driven a turbo before?"

"Naw, man." Chino shook his head.

"Man, there is nothing like driving a turbo, especially one of these. This thing takes off like a fighter jet." Tom looked around the dealership. "If you brought your driver's license, I can take you for a test drive."

Chino nodded. "I got my license."

"I just need to make a copy of it for insurance purposes, and find us some keys to one of the demos, and we're outta here," Tom told him.

Tom returned and tossed Chino the keys to a demo. Eagerly Chino waved his hand to the other salesmen, opened the door, and climbed inside. He inhaled deeply. The new car smell, the smell of leather, and its soft, glovelike feel was a combination that Chino loved. Taking the car on the freeway and getting the feel of it, he was even more sure this was the car he wanted. Chino turned up the stereo system and found a hip hop station bumpin' MC Breed's "Ain't No Future in Yo Frontin."

"What kind of stereo in this?"

"Blaupunkt," Tom told him, trying to look cool but praying for a sale. "Blaupunkt, Alpine, and Nakamichi are the stereos they put in high-dollar foreign cars now."

"I see." Chino's mind was made up. He got off the highway and made his way back to the dealership.

This was the car that would tell the ballers that he was a serious player. That they could come and score from him, and that he would always be the man.

"I'll take it," Chino said, once he came to a complete stop on the parking lot.

Tom laughed. "Wow, I like a man who knows what he wants. I don't mean to pry, but you must have a heck of a job."

"Yup."

"You look a little young, though. Are you a lawyer or something?"

"I'll give you forty-eight for it, but that's with tax, title, and license."

Tom shook his head slowly. "I don't know if my general manager is going to go for that."

"It's the end of the month, you want to close out your sales month strong," Chino told him knowingly with a smile. "He'll take it."

Tom grinned at the slick-tongued youngster. "So, you're a car salesman, huh?"

"I'm a salesman."

"I knew it!" Tom beamed. "No wonder you knew exactly

what you wanted. Most customers have to be shown a couple of different models before settling on one."

"Forty-eight, cash."

"Cash?"

"Cash," Chino repeated.

Tom rubbed his face. "Let me talk to my boss and see what he says."

"Look, Tom, you and I both know that you're going to go around that corner, go into that office, and tell your boss that you just sold this car, but you want to see if you can squeeze a little more out of the deal." Chino looked at Tom. "It ain't gonna happen. I'm not paying a penny over forty-eight, so you better squeeze tax, title, license, and the extended warranty all into that forty-eight."

Tom looked at Chino and gave a fake smile.

Chino stole a glance at his watch. "I'm trying to pick my girl up from school in my new ride, so I don't have a lot of time, so we got a deal?"

"Yes, sir," Tom confirmed.

"Cool. I don't have a lot of time. Make this quick."

Chino opened his manila envelope and took two grand out of it. "Tell your finance manager and your sales manager to come and see me. I'll take care of the money and the paperwork while the service guys get the car ready."

"Yes, sir," Tom said again.

Chino handed the salesman Pam's information. "The car is going to be in my wife's name. I'll bring her in to sign whatever she needs to sign once I pick her up from school, but in the meantime, make sure that you register the car in her name. It's going to be a gift for her."

"I'll take care of everything right away, sir." Tom exited the car and disappeared inside the building.

Chino leaned back in the seat of his brand-new Porsche. He was somebody. Somebody who was finally on his way. He could definitely get used to giving orders, and he could definitely get used to having fine German leather beneath his ass.

Chapter 14

The Family

Chino gathered the crew together to let them know of their good fortune. He pulled up to Corey's house in his new Porsche and revved the engine. The loud, high-pitched whine of the turbo motor caused the guys to look outside.

"Chino, what the hell?" Rock asked, looking at the car, then back at Chino.

"No you didn't!" Corey shouted. "My nigga, tell me you didn't knock off this drop-top Porsche!"

"Cabriolet is what Porsche calls their convertibles, you uncultured fool," Infa told him.

"Whatever it is, this bitch is nasty!" Joe Bub Baby declared. "Stank nasty!"

"Kinfolk, what this set you back?" Ant asked.

"We gon' pull some hoes in this muthafucka!" Chris J declared.

Chino smiled and took in all the adulation.

"I know this muthafucka was a cool fifty Gs," Corey said.

"When did you knock this bitch off?" Infa asked.

"Yesterday," Chino told them.

"Yesterday? And you just now coming around your peeps to show it off? Fuck you, nigga," Rock joked. They all went to look inside the ride.

"Man, this bitch got a Blaupunkt in it and everything!" Corey exclaimed.

"How this bitch move on the freeway?" Ant asked.

"Shit, like that wind, my nigga," Chino confirmed.

"Damn, I want one of these hoes!" Chris J declared.

"We all gonna be rolling foreign . . . if y'all ready, that is," Chino told them.

"Hell yeah!" Ant said.

"I been ready!" Chris J chimed in.

"Nigga, what is you talking about?" Rock asked.

"We can all ball till we fall, if y'all ready to get ya grind on," Chino replied. "C'mon in, let me break it down to you."

The crew followed Chino inside and took seats around Corey's parents' dining room table while Chino sat at the head of the table.

"How was New York?" Rock asked.

"Lovely," Joe Bub replied.

"New York is what I want to talk to you about," Chino told them. "I met with my homeboy's cousin, and dude is promising a major ticket, if we can handle it."

Chris J rubbed his hands together. "If we can handle it? Man, bring that shit on!"

"No more quarter keys and halves," Chino told them. "Do each of you think that you can move at least a key a week?"

"A key a week?" Corey shouted.

"Hell yeah!" Infa stated.

Joe Bub chimed in, "A key a week? Bring that shit on."

"A least," Chino told them. If they could move a key a week, then that would mean that he had just gotten rid of six keys a week. He could probably move four on his own. That meant that he would have to find a home for the other ten. He could definitely find ten niggas in Columbus to get a key from him.

"Man, I'll be moving two keys a week in about a month," Joe Bub Baby declared.

"Me too," Infa said.

"Me three, nigga," Rock added.

"But no bullshit," Chino told them. "I know that I'm asking you to push more dope than you're used to, but be careful with that shit. Don't take no chances, don't make no stupid decisions and end up busted or short. I know you niggas like to go shopping as soon as you get some money in your pockets, but we can't roll like that no more. Pay me first, and put your profits up. I don't want to be getting fronted, I want us to be straight up buying weight from these dudes. They don't take no shorts; besides, we can get better prices if we buy straight up. I want all of y'all to come up. I want all of y'all to be buying two keys a week for yourself."

Nods went around the table.

"Bet," Infa said. "Boys, he's looking out for everyone."

"So, you gonna front us at first?" Joe Bub questioned.

"Yeah, at first, but like I said, save your money because I want us to start buying from dude instead of getting fronted. We can get a better price and that means more money for you." Chino looked at all his soldiers. "With shit like this, we can sew up Columbus, Cincinnati, Dayton, and Cleveland. We can be the kings of Ohio."

"That's what I'm talking about, nigga!" Chris J said. "Being the kings of this shit!"

"Winning it all!" Ant said. He looked at Rock. "What you think, man?"

"Like Seabiscuit or something, nigga! I want to win it all." Rock looked at Infa.

"The muthafucking Triple Crown!"

"That's what it's all about," Chino told them, looking over his crew. "Winning it all."

"The motherfucking clique that wins it all!" Corey suggested. "The Triple Crown Clique."

"Bitches run in cliques, nigga!" Ant replied. "We outlaws, fool. Outlaws run in posses."

"The muthafucking Triple Crown Posse, fools!" Chris J shouted and looked around the table. Smiles crossed all of their faces.

"Triple Crown Posse!" Ant confirmed.

Chino nodded. "I like the sound of that. From now on, this is the muthafucking Triple Crown Posse. A group of straight up outlaws dedicated to getting that paper and winning it all! Anybody who don't think they can cut it, feel free to walk now."

Chino peered around the table and all eyes remained on him.

Nobody moved. "Okay, then, this means it's for life, niggas. We in it together, we ball together, we fall together. Nobody snitches and tries to save they own ass, is that clear?"

Nods went around the table.

"You snitch, you die," Rock declared.

"Naw, nigga, you snitch, and your family dies!" Infa declared.

"Word!" Chris J said, nodding.

"If any one of us gets cracked, or we all get cracked, we keep our fucking mouths shut, is that clear?" Chino asked.

Again, nods went around the table.

"We're going to have a cook house. If we all chip in a hundred dollars a week, we can rent us a place. Everybody cool with that?"

"Uh-huh." Nods went around the table.

"Don't keep your dope where you lay your head," Chris J added. "Keep that shit at a bitch's house, at a kinfolk's house, anywhere but where you lay your head. Is that clear?"

Everyone nodded in agreement.

"And don't keep no guns with that shit," Chino told them. "We'll pull some bitches and use their house to keep our straps in. That way if a house gets hit, we won't lose all our shit. Is that clear?"

"So, you gonna give us a ticket of a key a week?" Ant asked.

"For right now," Chino said. "I want you buying your own keys as soon as possible. If I got you buying your shit, plus I'm buying my shit, we can all put our money together and score big. When a muthafucka fronts you, then you owe that nigga. Old boy in New York seemed okay, but I don't want to owe them cats shit."

"When we gonna get the first ticket?" Infa asked.

"This weekend. For right now, we gonna have to cook it here like we've been doing. Is that cool, Corey?"

"Hell yeah," Corey said.

"Then that's it," Chino declared. "The Triple Crown Posse is officially in business. We down for each other and we down for whatever. We're in it to win it all."

"Triple Crown Posse . . . TCP!" everyone yelled in unison.

Chino extended his hand to his boys. "Let's do this shit!"

Chapter 15

The Sky Is the Limit

"We rollin', baby!" Infa said, shaking hands with Corey outside the club.

The crew had decided to step out and hook up at Jazzy Jay's to celebrate their good fortune. It had been three weeks since that fateful meeting at Corey's house, and they had received three tickets since. That was sixty kilos total for Chino and he had been able to move them all. Soon each member of the crew would be pumping two keys apiece a week. With the exception of Joe Bub Baby, Infa, and Chris J, who had moved ahead and would be pumping three apiece. Times were good.

Corey pointed toward his new champagne-colored BMW 325i. "Just got her today."

"How are you going to explain that to your parents?" Chris J asked.

"My pops financed it," Corey explained. "As long as I keep my grades up, they're paying for it."

"Ah, ole schoolboy-ass nigga!" Rock said laughing.

"I thought you got her by balling, nigga!" Ant said.

"Me too!" Infa laughed.

"Why you acting like you balling out of control when Mommy and Daddy got this shit for you?" Chris J asked. "Faking the funk ass nigga!"

Chino and Pam walked up holding a large shopping bag.

"Damn nigga, you could have left your bags in the car," Rock told him.

Chino held up the bag. "These are gifts for you ugly-ass niggas."

Chris J rubbed his hands together. "Hell yeah. I like gifts, especially when they for me!"

"Gifts?" Rock asked, lifting an eyebrow. "Who you think you are, Santa Claus or something, nigga?"

"Shut up, black-ass nigga!" Chris J told Rock. "I want my gift. Kinfolk, what you get a player?"

Pam laughed. Chris J always made her laugh. He and Infa were the two in the crew that kept her rolling.

"C'mon," Chino said, nodding toward the parking lot. The crew followed him to a nearby car. It was cool, because Chino knew the owner of the black BMW 750i. He sat his large bag on top of the hood. "We a crew, we need to show these hook-ass niggas that we roll together. We need to let it be known that Triple Crown Posse is where the ballers are."

Chino reached inside the bag and pulled out a large gold rope chain with a large gold crown medallion attached to it. He placed it around his neck and then reached back into the bag and pulled out another one. He placed this one around Pam's neck.

"That bitch is clean!" Corey said excitedly.

"That ho is cleaner than a muthafucka!" Ant agreed.

"Where you get them hoes from?" Rock asked.

"I had them made," Chino told them. He pulled another chain out of the bag and placed it around Infa's neck.

Infa examined his gift. "Man, thanks, kinfolk. This bitch is on point!"

Chino placed the next chain around Joe Bub Baby's neck. Joe Bub embraced him.

"Much love, kinfolk!" Joe Bub Baby told him.

Chino placed the next chain around Rock's neck, then another around Chris J's neck, then Ant's, and then Corey's.

Pam produced a camera. "Let me get a picture of y'all."

The crew gathered around Chino in front of the black BMW. Infa, Corey, and Chris J stood to his left, Rock, Ant, and Joe Bub Baby at his right. The crew had the latest gear on, from Gucci warm-up sets to Kangol hats to Gazelle glasses. They all had their large Triple Crown pieces and gold chains displayed prominently. None of them knew it at the time, but they had just taken the infamous Triple Crown Posse picture. It was a picture that would be splashed across newspapers and in magazines all across the country once the feds came down on them. But for right now, times were good.

"Let's hit the club and pop bottles, kinfolk!" Joe Bub said. "Moët and Cristal is on me!"

The crew headed for the club's entrance. Bystanders stopped and stared, and people stood to the side and let them pass. Many wondered aloud who they were. People knew them as individuals, and even as partners who hung out with one another, but now they were something different. The massive gold necklaces set them apart and told the world that they were special. The Triple Crown pieces told the world that this was a crew that was down for one another, and that they were ballers in the first degree. The Triple Crown pieces put the world on notice that these niggas were not to be fucked with.

Haters in the club paid attention. Dayton, Cleveland, and NY crews as well as the scrubs inside the club all shifted their attention to these local niggas getting paper. The Triple Crown Posse now represented Columbus, and what getting money in Columbus meant. The women paid attention as well.

Women flocked to everyone in the crew except Chino. Pam walked arm in arm with her man, and guarded him like a watchdog. She was ready to whoop any bitch who disrespected her and tried to step up to what was hers. She had hid his gun and risked going to jail for him, she had set up in a dope spot and watched him cook, and she had almost taken a bullet while watching him shoot ball at the basketball court. He belonged to her. She had taken enough risk to claim him for life. Besides, she wore the Triple Crown piece just like the rest of them did. She was a part of the posse, and wearing that necklace made her feel invincible.

The sound system in the club was bumping. The club's multicolored lights were in full effect and the atmosphere was beyond hype. The stereo system was bumping Eric B. and Rakim's song "I Ain't No Joke." It was the perfect song. The posse was no joke.

Chino led his crew up the stairs to the club's VIP section. Joe Bub had his arms wrapped around not one, but two honeys. Chris J had managed to round himself up a pair as well, while Infa chose quality over quantity. His girl looked like she had just stepped out of a music video. She had smooth vanilla skin, and long silky hair all the way down to her waist. She also had a body that could make a grown man scream, shout, and holler for mercy. The rest of the crew hadn't done too bad either. Ant, Corey, and Rock all managed to pick up some nice little pieces.

"Three bottles of Cristal!" Joe Bub told the bartender. She nodded and disappeared. Joe Bub turned to one of his honeys. "There comes a time, in a man's life . . . ," he started singing.

"No, no, no!" Rock shouted. "No Gerald Levert impressions tonight!"

"Hell naw!" Chris J shouted. "We gonna just chill tonight."

The champagne and glasses arrived. Joe Bub poured everyone a glass of bubbly and lifted the remainder of the bottle in the air and toasted, "To the Triple Crown Posse!"

"Triple Crown Posse!" Chino said.

"Triple Crown Posse!" Pam toasted.

"To the Triple Crown Posse!" Infa shouted.

"To the moneymaking, bad ass, take no shit Triple Crown Posse!" Chris J toasted.

"Triple Crown!" Ant said, lifting his glass. "One love, homeys!"

The posse clinked their champagne glasses together in toast. As the night progressed, the champagne flowed, and more and more people flocked around the crew. They had truly become the heroes of Columbus, the new "it" crew. Everybody wanted to be a part of, or know somebody in the Triple Crown Posse. While celebrating the good life, spending money, and toasting their success, they became the talk of the town. Everyone knew where to go in order to get work. The good came with the bad. The ballers in town knew that Triple Crown was where the dope was, but the jackers knew it too. It was the jackers, haters, and rival crews sitting in their corners that began to plot that night. These new niggas weren't going to steal their shine and they certainly weren't going to have all the money to themselves. The plotting and whispers began.

Chapter 16

I'm a Hustla, Baby

Winter was now in full swing, and the streets of Columbus were dusted with powdery February snow. Pam was in full swing as well, but not with her classes. In fact, Pam's winter break had turned out to be a permanent one. With her attendance and grades failing, she was on academic probation.

Her attendance was terrible and had affected her grades even more. She faced looming midterms, which she surely wouldn't be prepared for. Even Erik and Tomiko were giving her grief. She had begun to avoid Tomiko whenever she could and stayed at Chino's most of the day and on the weekends. Pam had to return to her dorm room at night during the week because of a mandatory campus curfew for underclassmen, and that was enough of Tomiko for her. She was usually in there with her ex anyway, bumpin' and grindin' away.

Pam wasn't about to take shit from anyone else when her parents were already discussing her grades with the dean of students. Her mother had threatened to cut off her allowance and to take a trip to Columbus just to put Pam in check. Pam had promised to work hard this semester, but she found ways around it.

She paid other students in her classes to give her their notes to copy and to turn in her homework for her. Pam was beginning to question whether college was right for her. She was head over heels for Chino and had made studying him and his game a priority over OSU. After all, who needed college when your man had money in the bank and plans for a bright future? In Pam's eyes, she was safe in Chino's arms. School wouldn't give her the love Chino had for her.

"Pass me that Pyrex dish," Chino told Infa. Pam's thoughts were interrupted and she looked over at Chino.

"Which one?" Infa replied.

"The long one."

Infa passed Chino a long, three-inch-deep Pyrex dish from the stove. Chino took the dish, opened up a kilo of cocaine, and poured it into the dish. He took a cup of water from the table and poured it into the dish.

"Pammy, pass me that baking soda, honey," Chino told her.

Pam grabbed two boxes of baking soda from the counter and handed them to Chino. He punched open the boxes and poured them into the dish with the cocaine and water. He took a spoon and began to stir carefully.

"Baking soda?" Pam asked.

"Yeah." Chino nodded, stirring, careful not to waste anything. "This is what makes the cocaine harden into a solid slab. Chemically, when you cook it together, all the impurities are removed, and the remaining product hardens into crack. And it also stretches it, so you get more coming back."

Pam nodded. She understood some of what he was saying, but not all. Still, she didn't want to look extra lame in front of Chino's friends.

The crew was gathered at Corey's house to cook up the weekly score.

"Yo, how that shit coming?" Chris J asked.

"Stop asking questions, nigga!" Rock told him. He checked on the other kilo, which was already cooking in the microwave.

Chino stirred his mixture until it reached a thick, pasty consistency. "This one's ready, kinfolk."

"All right," Rock said. He opened the microwave and pulled out the other dish and placed it on the table.

"It looks like jelly!" Pam said. Her eyes were wide with discovery.

"It's supposed to look like that until it cools and hardens," Chino explained.

"Put that shit in the refrigerator," Ant shouted from the front room. He was posted up by the window as the lookout for police and jackers. Niggas in Columbus were notorious for robbing drug dealers. The cops weren't as big a concern, because Corey's house was in a nice area, and his parents never received so much as a parking ticket.

"You can't put it in the refrigerator, idiot!" Chino shouted. "Why not?"

"Because, you'll fuck it up if it cools too fast, dumb-ass!" Rock shouted for Chino. "Let the niggas who know what they doing handle this shit. You just keep looking out!"

Rock took the dish that Chino had been working on and placed it inside the microwave. "You stirred it real good?"

"Yeah, nigga! You seen me stirring it, didn't you?" Chino said.

"I don't want this shit coming back with no holes and bubbles and shit in it," Rock told him.

"Nigga, this shit is gonna come back butter," Chino reassured him.

"Butter?" Pam asked, lifting an eyebrow.

Chino nodded and smiled. "You'll see."

Rock touched the substance inside the other dish. "This shit is hard already."

"We'll let it cool a little bit longer and then cut that shit up," Chino said. "Get the scale out."

Rock went into the cabinet and pulled out a food scale. Chino pulled out two single-edged razor blades and handed one to Rock. Pam watched as they pulled off the brown paper wrapping from the razor blades and then turned their attention toward the hardened substance.

"We gotta time this shit just right," Chino told Pam. "We want it to be hard, but we want to cut it and bag it as soon as possible so that we can get the benefit of the water weight."

"See that scandalous ass nigga you fucking with?" Rock said to Pam, laughing.

Pam shrugged. She didn't understand, but whatever it was, Chino was getting over on something.

Chino took his razor blade and ran it through the large square cookie of crack cocaine, sectioning it off into squares. After making several deep gashes throughout, Chino took the tip of his razor blade and applied pressure to the center of the substance. It snapped right along the fault lines of the gashes he had carved into it. He repeated the process several times, until he had divided it into neat squares. He handed the squares to Rock one at a time and Rock weighed each of them.

"Damn, nigga!" Rock shouted. "You a fucking math genius or something! You gotta show me how you do that shit!"

"Do what?" Pam asked.

"This nigga know exactly where to cut this shit so that each one of these squares ends up weighing exactly twenty-eight grams! That's some creepy-ass shit!"

Chino laughed. "Real street niggas know how to do that shit!"

"That's some old lucky guessing ass shit!" Infa chimed in.

"It's simple arithmetic!" Corey told them. "Three-inch dish. You just cut the square accordingly."

"Oh, shut up, silly-ass nigga!" Rock told him.

"Yeah," Infa said, playfully slapping Corey on the back of his head. "You couldn't do it."

"I'll bet you I could."

"You ain't fucking my shit up!" Chino told him.

The crew broke into laughter.

"How much came back?" Chino asked Rock after handing him the last ounce.

"A key and a half."

"Divide that shit up," Chino said. "Each of y'all take nine ounces, and I'll take the rest."

"Bet!" Rock told him. "Infa, check on that other shit in the microwave."

Infa looked in the microwave. "That shit bubbling. It's done."

"Take it out," Chino said.

Pam thought about where she was and what she was witnessing. For the first time in her life she was inside a cooking house. She had heard about trap houses and dope houses, but never in her wildest dreams did she imagine that crack was cooked inside of nice two-story homes in the suburbs.

She was learning a lot fucking with Chino. Maybe too much. Chino had promised her that being with him would never be boring, and he had certainly lived up to that promise. And she herself knew that it would probably be dangerous messing with someone in his occupation. But now she was all in. Chino had secretly stolen her heart, and now her future, her freedom, even her very life, were in his hands. It was too late for her to pull back, too late for her to leave him alone. She had stood at the precipice and fallen over the deep, dark, and dangerous cliff. The best thing that she could hope for now was that he would catch her. He was now her safety net.

"You better have good hands, Chino," she whispered. "You better catch me."

Chapter 17

Making It Happen

Chino strolled into his apartment followed by Young Mike. They both had arms filled with bags of merchandise.

Young Mike was Chino's go-getter and the crew's adopted mascot. At sixteen, he hustled harder than most niggas twice his age. Young Mike was a street cat, in the truest sense of the word. He had no mother, no father, no family, nobody. All he had was the streets and the people he called his homeboys. Although Young Mike was a for-sure hustler, his biggest trade was boosting and fencing. He could steal the clothes off a policeman without the officer knowing about it. The kid could also sell snow to an Eskimo. He had the gift of gab that came with fencing his stolen materials.

"Chino, what is all of this?" Pam asked, looking at what they had brought in.

Chino lifted a silk kimonolike-gown from one of the bags.

"Oh, that's pretty!"

"You like it?" Young Mike asked. "It's yours, ma!"

Pam reached for the gown, but put it down when Chino

held up a brown leather Prada bag in one hand and a black Chanel purse in another.

"Oh my God!" Pam shouted. "Let me see those!"

With a grin, Chino handed her the purses. Pam bounced up and down examining the bags, quickly making them her own, discarding the paper from inside them.

"What are you gonna do with these?" Pam asked.

Chino shrugged. "What do you think I should do with them?"

"Buy them for someone you love!"

Chino laughed. "I already did that."

"Chino, no!" Pam squealed and wrapped her arms around him tightly.

"What better way to show my love than to spring for some fresh gear?"

Pam kissed Chino all over his face. "Oh, thank you! Thank you! Thank you!" She turned and immediately began rummaging through rest of the merchandise. "Is all of this mine?"

Chino nodded. "Most of it. Some of it is mine and some belongs to Young Mike."

"Where did all of this stuff come from?"

Both men exchanged glances and laughed.

"You know your boy be on his grind," Young Mike told her.

"You stole all of this?"

"Not by myself. I got some other boosters I work with," Mike told her.

"Boosters?" Pam asked. She had heard the term before and she knew it had to do with stealing, but not of this magnitude.

"Boosters. You know, boosting merchandise?" Mike tried to explain. The look on Pam's face told him that she was still unsure. "We go into stores and we steal stuff."

"Why don't you just call it stealing?" Pam asked.

"Why don't people just call boxing, fighting?" Young Mike shot back. "Boostin' is an art, girl. It takes style and talent. You have to know which technique to use, and when to use it."

"Technique?" Pam recoiled, and then laughed. "You got different techniques for stealing?"

"Yeah," Young Mike said incredulously. He couldn't believe how square Pam was. "You steal gum, shoelaces, and shit. Shit you can fit into yo pocket, but with boostin' you getting quality shit, so there's techniques. You got the run-and-grab technique, where you just run into the stores, grab a bunch of shit, and run out. You got the decoy-and-grab, where a partner keeps the salespeople occupied while you grab shit. You got the double stunt, where your partner pretends they having a medical emergency, and while the salespeople are panicking, you grabbing shit. You got the change out, where you take shit into the dressing room, pull off the alarm tags, and wear the shit out like you wore it in. You got the snowman, where you take the shit into a dressing room, put that shit on beneath your clothes, and walk that shit out. You got the pregnant woman, where the female boosters wear a specially shaped backpack in the front beneath their maternity dresses and stuff that joint with merchandise. You got—"

"Okay, okay," Pam said, holding up her hand. "I get it. Damn, y'all are crazy."

Young Mike pulled a black fedora out of a bag and twirled it and placed it on his head. "Crazy, but getting paper."

"So, you sell all of this stuff?" Pam asked.

Chino began trying on a charcoal gray Geoffrey Beene suit.

"Yep!" Young Mike told her. "That's called fencing."

"Fencing?" Pam asked, lifting an eyebrow. "Why can't you just call it selling?"

"That's so lame," Mike said, shaking his head and laughing. "We fence shit. That's how we get paid. Some people hustle, some people fence. I do both, but remember, all fencers ain't boosters. Some fencers are just go-to guys. Niggas like me can get anything, for anybody, for the right price."

"Is that like being a loan shark?" Pam asked.

"Girl, I ain't loaning no money!" Young Mike laughed. "Loan sharks loan people money at crazy interest rates. I just get shit for people."

"Can you get me some Chanel Number Five?" Pam asked. Although she laughed at her request, she was serious.

"All fucking day long, baby girl."

"How do I look?" Chino asked, turning toward them.

"Like the muthafuckin' dapper don of Columbus, nigga," Young Mike told him.

Mike and Chino laughed.

"You look sexy, baby!" Pam grinned, admiring her man in the expensive threads.

"Okay, how much for the suit?" Chino asked.

"Half the ticket price," Mike told him.

Looking at the price tag, Chino negotiated. "I'll give you four hundred for it."

"Nigga, I can add!" Young Mike shot back. "Four hundred ain't half. I said half."

"All right, all right." Chino laughed. "You drive a hard bargain for a homeless muthafucka."

The two men laughed. Turning to Pam, Chino put his hand on the small of her back. "Baby, let me talk to you for a minute." He led her to the bedroom.

"What's up, baby?"

"You know Young Mike, right?"

"Of course! He's right there in your living room."

"He's going to be staying with me for a while."

Pam recoiled. "Why?"

"'Cause he don't have no place to go," Chino explained. "He was living with this girl and her mom, but the mom's new boyfriend kicked him out. He don't got no family, no nothing, and he hustles hard for me."

Pam nodded. "I mean, if he don't have anyplace to go and he's your friend, I understand."

"You gonna be cool with it?" Chino asked. "I mean, if you not comfortable with him being around, then I won't let him."

"I'm good." Pam nodded. "Besides, he's young and needs you. I can tell he looks up to you like a big brother. This is the right thing to do."

"I knew you would understand," Chino said, pulling her close and kissing her. "You have a giant heart, Pooh."

Chapter 18

Keep Movin', Don't Stop

Chino pulled up to the convenience store for a bite to eat in his convertible 944 Turbo. Once inside, he grabbed a strawberry Welch's soda, a bag of Munchos potato chips, a pack of Sixlets, and a box of Boston Baked Beans. As soon as he stepped out of the store, he noticed an ice blue Buick Regal by the gas pumps, full of dark faces, with wide eyes all focusing on him.

When the driver stepped out of the car with a pistol in his hand, Chino recognized him to be one of the city's notorious jackers—a guy named Jo Jo. He had cost the city's dope boys more money than the local police department. Chino went for his pistol. He kept his nine millimeter Beretta in a holster in the small of his back. He drew and dove for cover behind his brand-new Porsche in one swift motion. Jo Jo the Jacker lifted his pistol and the two exchanged fire.

While Jo Jo's bullets raked the side of Chino's new Porsche, Chino aimed his gun and fired, sending his bullets into the driver's side door of Jo Jo's two-door Regal. He could hear a couple of the passengers cry out in pain.

Gunfire came from the Regal as well. Sparks flew off the ground near Chino's hand, and concrete chips flew up off the ground, stinging him in the face.

"Fuck!" Chino cried out. He was happy that none of the concrete flew into his eyes, but still, the shit stung. He lifted his weapon and fired over his Porsche again. This time, there was no return fire. He lifted his head and found Jo Jo running for cover and fiddling with his gun. It had jammed!

Chino opened the door to his car, hopped inside, started up the motor, and burned out.

"Let's go!" the passengers said, shouting at Jo Jo. "He's getting away, nigga!"

Jo Jo raced for his car.

Chino stared into his rearview mirror, and sure enough, the Regal was after him. He needed to find a straight road, fast. He headed for the freeway.

Gunfire erupted behind Chino and a bullet struck his dashboard.

"Fuck!" Chino shouted again. "Muthafuckas!" His Porsche was full of bullet holes. How would he explain that to a body shop? And would the body shop report it to the police? This whole thing was fucked up.

Another bullet struck his dash, blowing open an air conditioning vent. The close call reminded Chino that he wasn't out of the woods just yet. In order to take the car to a body shop, he would first have to survive, and survival meant getting away from the assholes shooting at him.

Usually jackers kidnap you and take you back to your safe and make you give them all your money and drugs before they kill you. Or in a lot of cases, they even let you go, so that they can jack you again. That was Jo Jo's MO. He liked to jack people over and over. Every dope dealer in the city feared him and every dope dealer in the city wanted him dead. They would kill him if they ever got the chance, but the thing is, they never got the chance. He didn't go out to clubs or to the movies or anywhere else. No one knew who he was, where he came from, where his family lived, or anything else about him. He just showed up one day, like a great white shark that had found a new feeding ground, and starting preying on the local dope dealers.

Chino came to the expressway and took the on-ramp. He accelerated to breakneck speed, determined to get away from Jo Jo 'n dem. The only problem was, Jo Jo was a professional jacker, which meant he anticipated car chases. He had been in them before, sometimes chasing drug dealers, sometimes escaping from the police himself, so what Chino did was nothing new. Jo Jo had changed out the stock engine in his Regal for a small-block Corvette engine that he had transformed especially for racing. Despite Chino's best efforts, he wasn't going to lose Jo Jo on a straightaway. Although his car was lighter, Jo Jo's engine was more powerful. Chino's best chance would have been to use the Porsche's superior handling and cut some corners to lose Jo Jo, but getting on the highway had eliminated that option.

More gunfire rang out and a bullet penetrated Chino's front windshield. "Goddamn it!" Chino yelled as shattered glass flew everywhere. He was spooked because only a couple of inches to the left, his ass would have been cooked, but he was getting pissed off.

"Fuck this!" Chino said, grabbing his burner. "Them muthafuckas doing all the damn shooting and I'm ducking like a bitch? Time to play, you black bastard!" He pumped his brakes and brought the Regal in closer.

Seeing that Jo Jo was now up on his bumper, Chino swerved side to side to keep his pursuers from getting a good shot at him. It was apparent that the front passenger was doing the shooting, while Jo Jo drove the car. Chino swerved and hit the brakes, bringing the Regal alongside him. He raised his pistol and unloaded on the driver. He could hear shouting coming from the Regal, just before it began to swerve uncontrollably. He could see someone from the back seat reach over into the front seat and attempt to steer the car as it crashed into a concrete highway divider.

"Yeah!" Chino shouted. "Take that, bitches! Jack this dick, you punk muthafuckas!"

The faint sounds of sirens were in the air and Chino took off. He needed to hurry up and exit. The next exit was one that he was not familiar with, and he took it too fast. Two of the Porsche's wheels lifted off the ground, and the car skidded across the exit, jumped a curb, and landed in a concrete drainage ditch. Chino and his pistol were thrown from the car into a nearby field. His head landed on a large stone and blood poured from his face.

"Pooh . . . ," Chino called out weakly. He could see his Pooh's face in the distance. "Pooh."

Chino slowly lifted himself onto his hands and knees and crawled to his Porsche. He reached into the shattered driver's side window and struggled to grasp the car phone bag in the center console. Using all his remaining strength, he lifted the bag out the window and dropped it on the ground. Lying next to phone, he dialed Joe Baby's home number.

"Hello?" Joe said when he picked up.

"Pammy . . . ," Chino whispered.

"Chino? What the fuck? Where the fuck are you, man?"

Chino closed his eyes. "Joe Bub, I need help. I'm off two-seventy. Fast, my nigga."

"All right, my man, I'm headed out. Sit tight."

"Pooh . . . ," Chino said weakly. "I need you, Pooh . . ."
And then he blacked out.

Chapter 19

They Smile in Your Face

"Revenge is mine, sayeth the Lord," Pam said, quoting the Bible and changing the bandage on Chino's head. "Let the Lord take care of them, Chino."

"Yeah, He can, I'm just gonna give Him an assist," Chino retorted. "The Lord's gonna be MJ and I'm gonna be Scottie. I'm just gonna give an assist."

Pam couldn't help but laugh. She applied peroxide to the wound and Chino winced because he was still in pain.

"Oooooucchh!" Chino cried out. "You did that on purpose."

"Boy, that did not burn. It's only peroxide." Pam held up the bottle to show him. Cleaning off the wound, she continued. "You mocking the Lord the way you are, Christonos, He'll have something that's really going to make you hurt."

"Baby, I'm not mocking the Lord. I just said that I was going to give Him a helping hand."

"He does not need your help, mister."

"I want to help. Me and my nina ross is going to send them

niggas on a trip to the other world. They moms might as well pull them black dresses out the closet."

"Christonos!"

"What?"

"It was by the grace of God they didn't shoot you coming out of that store. It was by the grace of God they didn't shoot you while you were driving on the highway, and it was only by the grace of God did Joe Baby find you before the cops did. Just say your thanks, and move on."

"I'll move on after I kill that bastard. Pooh, this is personal."

"I thought you hit him. I thought that's why they crashed?"

Chino shook his head. "I thought I did too, but I ain't see shit in the *Dispatch*. I've been checking the papers and watching the news, and that son of a bitch ain't been in it. If any of them was dead, then they would have said so. No, those assholes made it, and the fucked-up thing is, I know they had to go to a hospital somewhere. How the fuck they get shot and get medical help without the police arresting their asses is beyond me. I don't understand it. Them niggas got angels looking over their shoulders."

"Chino, you got God looking over yours," Pam told him matter-of-factly. "This is the second time this month you've been shot at and look at you—barely a scratch."

"A scratch?" Chino asked, pointing toward his head. "You call this barely a scratch?"

"At least it's not a bullet hole!" Pam scolded. "Christonos, God had his hands cupped around you protecting you, and now you want to go out and harm someone else?"

"Pam, that son of a bitch has terrorized Columbus for

the last two years. He's got everybody scared as hell. Well, he's fucked with the wrong nigga now. I'm going to kill his ass."

Pam exhaled and shook her head. "Where is he from?"

"Some people say they think he's from Louisiana, but who knows? All I know is that I'm going to put a bullet in his shrimp-smelling, gumbo-eating, jambalaya-looking ass. If that fool is from Louisiana, he's going back to the dirty dirty in a pine box."

"They don't send people across country in pine boxes anymore. This isn't the Wild West."

"Tell them that!" Chino said. "Hell, I thought I was in the middle of the O.K. Corral the way them fools was busting at me."

"Hold still, boy!" Pam said, placing a fresh gauze over Chino's wound. She grabbed some strips of tape that she had peeled off, and taped the gauze over his wound. "There, that should do."

"Thanks, Pooh." Chino pulled Pam close and kissed her. "All I could think about was you."

"Boy, please!" Pam pushed him away from her.

"For real! All I wanted to do was make it back to my Pooh."

Pam folded her arms and pursed her lips. "Yeah, right."

"That's the truth, Pooh. Making it back to you is what kept me alive."

"Okay, Christonos. You know what? You're a smooth-ass talker. I'll give you that much."

"You gonna give me more than that!" Chino said, rising. "You gonna give me some of that suga!"

Chino grabbed Pam, lifted her into the air, and spun her around. She screamed the whole time.

"Boy, put me down!"

"I love you, Pooh!"

"Okay!"

"Okay? Okay, my ass! Let me hear it!"

"Hear what?"

"I love you, Chino."

"Why would I say that?"

"Because you do!" Chino spun her around again.

"Aaaaaah!" Pam screamed. "Put me down!"

"Say it!"

"Okay, okay, if you want to make me say it, then I'll say it."

"I'm making you say it because you're acting like a scary-ass punk. You can say how you really feel to me, Pooh. You don't got to hide your feelings. If you love me, then let that shit be known."

"Chino, what are you talking about?"

"You love me, Pooh, but you're afraid to tell me. You act like if you say it, then I'll somehow hurt you. Well, here's a secret, Pooh. Whether you say it out loud or not, you still feel it. And if I fuck up, then you'll still feel the same amount of pain, whether you said that shit out loud or not. So you might as well say it."

"What if I don't feel that way, Chino?" Pam asked. "You still want me to say it?"

"I know that you do feel that way."

"How do you know?"

"Because I can feel it. I can see it in your eyes. I felt it when you thought I was asleep and you were crying and caressing my face. Because I heard your big-head ass whisper it when you thought that I was still out of it."

"Chino!" Pam shouted. She was embarrassed. He had heard her deepest feelings. "You asshole!"

"I'm not going to hurt you, Pooh." Chino put Pam back down and pulled her close. "I promise you that, Pooh. I'll never hurt you or let anybody else hurt you. I'd rather walk through hell with gasoline drawers on than hurt you. Do you understand that?"

No man had ever professed his love for her. Tears welled up in Pam's eyes. She suppressed a sniffle and turned her head away. She couldn't cry in front of him, or let him know that she had bought into what he had just said. She had to maintain.

"Why do you do that, Pooh?"

"Do what?"

"Resist showing me your feelings?" Chino pulled her hands down away from her face and stared into her eyes. "Pooh, I'm not after you to hurt you. We're on the same team. This is not a battle between us, or a test of wills. We don't have to protect ourselves from each other. We have to protect each other from what's out there. Beyond that door is our enemies. That world is what we are fighting together. I need for you to understand that, Pooh."

"Chino, you just have to understand that I've never felt like this about anybody before. I'm still young. I've never put my trust in anybody like this before. And then you have to understand that you're cute and you have a lot of money, and a lot of girls want to talk to you. I'm scared to get hurt."

"Pooh, I chose you," Chino said, softly. "Those other girls

can say what they want to say, do what they want to do, but that don't mean shit to me. I'm here, Pooh, because I want to be here, and because I couldn't help it if I tried. I'm in love with you, girl. You have my heart. I couldn't help it, or change it, and I don't want to. I like it like this, Pooh. I love being in love with you."

Chino lifted her hand and kissed her fingers one by one. "I love being wrapped around this cute little finger of yours."

"Oh, God!" Pam said, throwing her head back. "Chino, you better not hurt me! Do you hear me? You better not ever hurt me!"

"I'll hurt me before I hurt you." Chino pulled her close and kissed her. "Now come on and ride with ya man."

"Where are we going?"

"To the Benz dealership. Them fools fucked off my Porsche, so now it's time to step it up and go top dog."

"Boy, being flashy is how they found you in the first place," Pam warned. "When are you going to learn?"

"That's right. That Benz is going to draw the niggas like moths to a flame." Chino smiled, pulled out his new handgun, and cocked it. "But this time, they ass is going to get burnt for real!"

Chapter 20

Money to Burn

Chino pulled up to the spot in his brand-new, porcelain white Mercedes Benz 560SEL. It had a full AMG kit and porcelain white and chrome AMG rims. The interior was white, with black piping around the seats, and a dark zebrano wood trim. It was truly a sight to behold.

"What the fuck?" Ant said the moment Chino pulled into the spot. Chris turned to see what Ant was talking about.

"No this nigga didn't!"

Rock looked up and saw what the others were looking at. His mouth fell open when he saw the car, and he tapped Joe Bub Baby on the shoulder. Joe Bub looked up from the ground where he was shooting dice.

"Fuck me!" he shouted.

Infa stood staring at Chino and shaking his head. "This nigga is crazy!"

Chino blew the horn and climbed out of his Benz. "What up, my niggas?"

He and his new car were quickly surrounded.

"Nigga, what the fuck are you thinking?" Joe Bub asked. "A Benz? A five-sixty at that?"

"Didn't you just barely get away from Jo Jo and them niggas?" Chris J asked. "And now you go and knock off a Benz? What are you asking for—death, nigga?"

"Fuck them niggas!" Chino shouted. "Them niggas can't control what I buy. Fuck them hoes! If they want to try it again, bring it on!"

"I can't believe you, my nigga," Corey said. "If it was me, I'd a bought another Porsche. A faster one than the one I had."

The crew burst into laughter.

"Shut yo silly ass up!" Rock told him. He turned to Chino. "This bitch is clean, kinfolk!"

"I was gonna go and buy one of these bitches," Joe Bub declared, "but now, since you got a white one, I'ma have to get me an ice blue one."

"Like that one we seen the other day?"

"That's the one!" Joe Bub confirmed to Ant.

"That bitch was clean," Ant told them. "It was ice blue, sitting on some chrome AMGs, with a cocaine white interior."

Corey's eyebrows rose. "Why do niggas always describe white as being cocaine white? Nigga, just say white!"

"Fuck you, nigga!" Ant retorted.

Again, the crew laughed.

"I don't know if I would have did this, kinfolk," Infa told Chino. "I would have laid low for a minute."

"Fuck them niggas!" Chino said. "This is our muthafucking town! I know we ain't gonna let some out-of-town ass niggas intimidate us like that."

"Don't listen to this nigga!" Rock said, pointing to Infa. "He's one of them tuck-in-his-chain ass niggas!"

Again the crew burst into laughter.

"Man, I'm just being real. Let's find them niggas first and put some work in on they ass."

"Man, them niggas is lying up somewhere, recuperating from them bullet holes I put in them," Chino said. "Let them hoes know that a Cleveland nigga don't bar nobody!"

Rock shook his head to clear the memory of all the shit that had gone down and looked at Chino. "So, how you feeling, kinfolk?"

"Shit, better."

"You sure?" Chris J asked.

"Yeah, nigga!" To prove it, he put his dukes up and started shadowboxing in Chris's face. "I'm good. Ready to dance."

Chris J waved Chino off. "Not even on your best day, nigga. You couldn't fade these hands. These are lethal weapons."

"Nigga, this is one bad-ass pussy machine," Corey said, peering inside the Benz. "Hoes are gonna be throwing their panties at you now."

"I can't wait to pull up to the club in this bitch and watch them haters' eyes pop out," Chino said.

"Them Cleveland niggas is gon' be hating!" Infa said. "So is them Youngstown niggas, and them Cincinnati niggas."

"And a whole bunch of Columbus niggas!" Rock confirmed, glancing toward Joe Bub.

"So, what you niggas doing?" Chino asked. "Y'all ain't balling?"

"I'm taking these young niggas' money in this crap game," Joe Bub Baby declared. "You can get some too if you like."

"You ain't said nothing, nigga," Chino told him. "High made gets the baby teeth."

"You can have the baby teeth first!" Joe Bub handed Chino the dice.

"You done fucked up now!" Chino shook the dice vigorously in his hand.

Joe Bub Baby shrugged. "Your luck ain't been too hot lately, so I ain't worried."

"Wrong!" Chino rolled the dice. "I'm still here, nigga!"

The dice hit on a five and a two.

"Bust that ass!" Chino shouted.

Joe Bub tossed a hundred-dollar bill at Chino and threw another on the ground. Chino grabbed the dice and rolled again. This time a four and a three came up.

"Bust his ass, baby girl!" Chino shouted.

"Damn!" Joe Bub shouted. He threw down another C-note.

Chino picked up his winnings and rolled the dice again. "C'mon, baby girl!" This time he rolled a six and a one.

"Fuck!" Joe Bub yelled. He kicked the dice through the parking lot. "Old jinxy-ass monopoly dice!"

"That's Corey's jinxy-ass shit!" Ant said laughing. "Stop taking the dice out of your family's board games, nigga!"

"Nigga, you took them out the board games, ole Monopoly-playing muthafucka." Everyone laughed. "Besides, you thought they was lucky when you was winning!"

Joe Bub pulled a different set of dice out of his pocket and handed them to Chino, who gave them a questioning look.

"What I'm gonna do with these red ass dice?"

"Nigga, these dice are like chum!" Joe Bub said, laughing.

"What the fuck is some chum, nigga?" Rock asked.

"Corey, explain to this nigga what chum is."

"Chum is blood and fish parts," Corey explained. "They bring sharks closer to the boat so muthafuckas can get 'em."

"That's right!" Joe Bub wailed. "These red dice is like chum. They bring niggas like you who think they sharks right to Joe Baby, and that when I fuck you up!"

"Old Discovery Channel–watching ass nigga!" Rock joned. "Speak English, muthafucka!"

"Take yo ass back to high school!"

"Fuck you, nigga! The streets is my high school, and now I'm the teacher in this bitch!"

Joe Bub looked at Chino. "Roll the dice."

Chino took one look at the dice and tossed them in the direction that Joe Bub had kicked the other dice.

"What the fuck you doing!" Joe Bub shouted. "Them is my lucky dice!"

"The other ones were my lucky dice!" Chino told him.

"Man, fuck this game!" Chris J said. "I'm broke now anyway."

They all got up and started walking toward Chino's new ride.

"Let's ride!" Infa said, walking around the Benz to the passenger seat.

"Who said you got shotgun?" Chris J asked.

"Because I'm the best-looking nigga out here. Ugly muth-afuckas ride in the back. You niggas scare the bitches off!"

"Old bucket-head-ass nigga!" Chris shouted.

Chino climbed into the driver's seat. Corey, Chris J, and Rock climbed into the back, while Infa hopped into the front passenger seat. Chino turned up the stereo, and the Triple Crown Posse hit the streets of Columbus to be seen in the new Benz.

Chapter 21

Keeping Score

"Face, nigga!" Chino said, swishing the basket in a jump shot over Rock.

"That ain't shit! We gon' win this muthafucking game. Y'all can't win again! C'mon, y'all!"

"If Chino quit fouling!"

"Aw, nigga, what the baby gon' do?" Chris J shouted at Joe Bub Baby.

Rock dribbled the ball down the court, Infa picked him up, and Rock passed the ball to Ant, who passed it to Corey. Young Mike stole the ball from Corey and ran down the court. He tossed it to Infa, who tossed it to Chris J, who tossed it back to Young Mike for an easy layup.

"Foul, nigga!"

"How in the hell you gonna call a foul way the hell back there?" Infa asked Joe Bub.

"Young Mike fouled when he stole the ball!"

"How in the hell you gonna call that?" Chino challenged.

"Corey didn't even call it!" Infa shouted.

"And that shit is late as hell!" Chris J added. "You gonna call a foul after a nigga done went down the court and made the basket and shit. Damn, you still gonna be calling fouls when a nigga at home eating dinner and shit?"

Chino, Rock, Infa, Young Mike, and Chris J laughed.

"Man, fuck you!" Joe Bub told him. "Y'all niggas be cheatin' and shit. Chino fouling every time he come down the court."

"Man, ain't nobody fouled you!" Chino said, waving Joe Bub off.

"Man, are y'all gonna cry or are we gonna play ball?" Rock shouted, getting irritated at what the guys were doing.

"Let's play ball!" Infa shouted.

Ant took the ball out, and Rock dribbled it downcourt. He got caught on a back slash running toward the basket and rocketed the ball to him for a quick layup.

"Deuce, niggas!" Corey shouted.

Chino took the ball out, passing it to Infa. Infa passed it to Young Mike, who had the best handles on the court. He was even better than Rock when it came to handling the pill. Young Mike drove to the basket and kicked the ball back out to Chris J, who passed it to Chino, who was trailing. Chino pulled up for a quick three and swished the ball.

"That's a foul-ass screen!" Joe Bub Baby shouted. "That was some bullshit, Chris!"

"What?" Chris asked, turning up his palm. "I ain't moved."

"Yeah, whatever!" Joe Bub said.

Ant took the ball out, and again Rock dribbled down the court. He pulled up at the three-point line and swished the ball.

"Face, niggas!" Rock said, beating his chest.

Young Mike took the ball out, passing it to Infa, who dribbled it downcourt. He passed the ball to Chino, who passed it to Young Mike. Young Mike caught Chris J and gave him an alley-oop. Chris J slammed the ball so hard the backboard shook.

"Yeah, niggas!" Chris J shouted. "Get with that!"

Corey took the ball out, and Rock dribbled it down the court. Beneath the net, Joe Bub Baby and Chino were fighting for position. Joe Bub grabbed Chino's arm and slung him to the ground.

"What the fuck is up with you?" Chino asked.

"What the fuck are you doing?" Rock asked Joe Bub Baby.

"Man, fuck that nigga!"

Chino got up off the ground and dusted himself off. "Fuck you, nigga!"

"Joe Baby, you on some bullshit today!" Ant said.

"For real!" Corey agreed.

"What's up, kinfolk?" Infa looked from one man to the other.

"Ain't nothing wrong with me!" Joe Baby shouted. "Ask that fouling-ass nigga right there!"

"I ain't fouled you!"

"Old punk-ass nigga wanna foul everybody but think can't nobody touch him! You ain't gold, nigga!"

"It's obvious you going through some things right now, so I ain't even trying to go there with you," Chino told him. "But I ain't gonna be no more punks."

"Man, let's bounce," Ant told Joe Bub Baby.

Joe Bub pushed Ant's hand away. "Naw, this nigga thinks

he's God or somebody! Like everybody's suppose to bar him or something. Don't nobody bar your status, nigga! Hell, getting over on muthafuckas and shit!"

"What?" Chino asked. "What the fuck you talking about?"

"I'm talking about getting over on your homeboys and shit!" Joe Bub shouted. "We want to drive Benzes and shit too! Break us off! Show us a good ticket! Nigga ain't paying nothing and charging us an arm and a leg!"

Chino couldn't believe what he had just heard. All he had done for Joe Bub, and he had the nerve to complain. "I'll tell you what," he looked at the man, "just pay me the rest of my money and get your shit from somewhere else!"

"Nigga, get it like Tyson got the belt!" Joe Bub challenged.

"What?" Within seconds, Chino charged Joe Bub, knocking him to the ground. The two of them wrestled on the ground. Chino got loose and swung, striking Joe Bub in his jaw. Joe Bub swung and struck Chino in the side of his face. Rock, Infa, Ant, Chris J, and Corey rushed over and pulled them apart. Chino charged at Joe Bub Baby again, tackling him. The two of them exchanged blows until they were once again pulled apart.

"That's it, nigga!" Joe Bub snarled, touching his bloody lip. "We through. We don't have shit to say to each other no more!"

"I want my money, nigga!"

"Yo, you can have that bullshit! I'll send that shit to you by Ant!"

"Bet!"

"Bet!"

"You niggas better get your own shit, and your own connects!" Joe Bub shouted. "You can't come up with this nigga's foot on yo necks! He's winning all the way around and ain't sharing none of the love! We struggling to score two keys, and he's rolling in a hundred-thousand-dollar Benz and flossing and shit!"

Ant pulled Joe Bub away, leading him to his car.

"Get your own shit, my niggas!" Joe Bub continued.

The crew was left staring at one another in silence. Finally Infa broke the ice.

"Fuck that hating-ass, Gerald Levert wannabe-ass nigga!"

The crew burst into laughter, but inside, each of them felt different. Chino felt the most awkward. He wondered if Joe Bub had said what the others were thinking. Were his boys really jealous of him? Had they been discussing his money behind his back? Suddenly he felt that he had to leave. In the back of his mind, he wondered who he could still trust. Rock was loyal and so was Chris J and maybe Infa. He knew Corey was a follower, and Little Mike's loyalty was without question, and for sure, he could trust his Pooh. She was the one person in the world that he knew for a fact had his back. He needed to find her, lay his head in her lap, close his eyes, and rest. The only problem was that Pooh was still living on campus. She would be stuck in the dorm because of the curfew. Her living situation was bullshit, and it would have to change. He needed his Pooh. And when he needed to get to her, she would have to be able to be gotten to. He would change all that. Besides, he needed new digs anyway. That punk-ass nigga Joe Bub knew where he laid his head. He needed a new pad, in order to keep the wolves at bay.

Chapter 22

Wife Me

"What are you doing?" Pam asked.

Chino continued to lead the blindfolded Pam up the stairs, carefully guiding her so that she wouldn't hurt herself. "Just keep walking."

Chino pulled out his keys and opened the door to his new apartment. "Step inside."

Carefully doing as he asked, Pam spoke. "Can I look now?"

"Yeah." Chino removed the blindfold.

Pam gasped as she gazed around the room. "This is beautiful!"

"This is our new place."

Pam quickly turned toward him. "Our place?"

Chino nodded. "I want you to move in with me, Pooh. I got us this condo. It has amenities, and a view overlooking downtown. At night, you can see the lights in City Center, and they look beautiful."

"You want to live together?"

"Yes, Pooh. I don't want you to have to worry about a curfew, or about your roommate, or where you're going to sleep if her man comes over. I just want you with me. I want to wake up with you in my arms every day. I want to go to sleep feeling you next to me."

Pam strolled to a massive wall of windows and looked out over the city. It was dusk outside, and the city's night lights were coming alive. "I don't know if I'm ready for this."

"Ready for what?" Chino asked. "Ready to move in with me? Nothing changes, Pooh. There's still no pressure. I just need you here with me. Like I said, it's me and you against the world, baby girl. I want you safe here with me, and I need to be able to come home, crawl up in bed, and have you rub my head and let me know that everything is going to be all right."

Pam nodded. She understood completely what he was saying. It was her and him against the world. If they were going to do battle against that world together, then it only made sense for them to share a castle together. Moving into a luxurious condo wasn't the worst thing in the world that could happen to her. In fact, moving out of that noisy dorm would afford her the chance to get more studying done. No more having to gather her books and head over to the library for some peace and quiet. No more worrying about coming home and finding the secret signal telling her that her roommate was inside getting busy.

"Check this out, Pooh!" Chino said excitedly. He pointed toward the kitchen. "It has one of those giant metal refrigerators that you like."

"Stainless steel," Pam said, correcting him.

"It's got a view and three bedrooms and two living rooms and three bathrooms," Chino said. "This is the place for us to start our life together, Pooh. Say you'll do it. Say you'll move in with me."

Pam hesitated at first, then nodded.

"Yeah!" Chino shouted, lifting her into the air and spinning her around.

"I wanna check everything out."

Chino set her back down and waved his hand around the apartment. "After you."

Pam turned and slowly began to explore her new digs. She walked through her kitchen, through her dining area, through her living room, and into one of the secondary bedrooms. "This is pretty big."

"It's bigger than the rooms in my old apartment," Chino told her.

"It's bigger than my dorm room," Pam said. She continued to explore, walking through a Jack-n-Jill bathroom into another secondary bedroom. She explored the bedroom's walk-in closet. "Dang, this is big!"

"I want to use one of the extra bedrooms as a weight room," Chino said. "I want to get my buff on."

Pam looked at Chino, shook her head, and walked out of the bedroom. Down the hall she opened the double doors to the master bedroom. She found a surprise. Chino had scattered rose petals all over the floor.

"Chino!" Pam said, placing her hand over her heart. "What is this?"

"I don't know." Chino shrugged.

Pam was all smiles as she followed the trail of rose petals into the master bath. There was a large Jacuzzi tub inside the master bath. The rose petals led to the tub, and several bouquets of roses sat in vases surrounding the tub. Sweet aromatic candles were lit and arranged throughout the bathroom. A silver wine chiller sat on the edge of the Jacuzzi, with a bottle of Moët chilling inside it. A crystal dish filled with strawberries that had been dipped in chocolate also sat on the edge of the Jacuzzi.

"What is all of this?" Pam asked.

"I wanted us to celebrate our new place and our good fortune, Pooh. We've been blessed."

Pam kicked off her boots, unbuttoned her blue jeans, and dropped them to the floor. She pulled off her hoodie and her T-shirt and tossed those as well. Next came her socks, and then her panties. She turned and wiggled her shoulders, indicating to Chino that she wanted him to unfasten her bra.

Chino was shocked at her boldness. This was unusual for his shy little Pooh. Her coming out of her clothes like this was way out of the ordinary. He swallowed hard as he unfastened her bra. Pam climbed into the warm bubble bath.

"Are you going to just stand there?" she asked, waving her finger at Chino, motioning for him to join her. "This tub is more than big enough for two."

Chino kicked off his Timbs, jeans, and his hoodie. He quickly tossed off his boxers and wifebeater and hopped into the tub, sending bubbles everywhere. Pam laughed.

"You're so silly!" she told him.

"Ever watch Captain Nemoy?" Chino asked.

"Captain Nemoy? What's that?" Pam asked, flicking water in Chino's face.

Chino slid beneath the surface of the water, blowing bubbles as he continued to try to talk. "They did some wild shit beneath the sea . . ."

Chino bit Pam on her toe.

"Ahhhh! Chino, stop!" Pam said laughing.

Chino came up from beneath the water. "Did you see that?"

"See what?"

"There's a shark in here."

"Boy, stop!"

Chino started making the noise from the movie *Jaws*. "He's going to get you. Just when you thought it was safe to go back into the water."

Pam laughed again. "Chino, you are silly. You know that? You are really crazy."

"Crazy in love with my Pooh."

"And your Pooh is crazy in love with you."

"Wow."

"What?"

"That's the first time you ever said that."

"What?"

"That you love me."

"Did I have to say what was obvious?" Pam asked. "That would have been like me saying the sun came up today."

Chino looked at his innocent Pooh. "C'mere."

Pam turned and lay against his chest while he began to massage her shoulders.

"Uhmmmmm," Pam moaned, becoming relaxed.

"You like this?" Chino whispered in her ear.

"Yes," she said softly. A silent moment passed between the two of them, until Pam spoke again. "Tell me that it's always going to be like this."

"I can't say that."

"Why not?" Pam turned her head to look at Chino. Her heart started beating fast, as she wondered if something was wrong.

"Because it's going to get better than this," Chino said softly, kissing her on the lips. "Pooh, we're on our way up."

"You talked to Joe Bub yet?"

"Fuck him!"

"Make it right with him, Chino."

"Why should I?"

"Because he's one of your oldest friends. Money comes, money goes, true friends are forever."

"He's the one that let money come between us. He's the one who's jealous."

"Take it from me, Chino. You don't want to have a room full of money and no one to share it with. You can't talk to your money, shoot ball with your money, or count on your money to have your back if shit goes down."

Chino nodded as he listened to Pam. She was right. He knew where he stood with his friends, and where his friends stood with him. Rock was solid, and so was Chris, Infa, Young Mike, and Ant. He and his boys were solid. It was just that Joe Bub Baby had let jealousy cloud his judgment.

"That nigga know he was in the wrong and he will come back around again. And if he don't, then fuck him." Chino was adamant. In fact, money was one of the few things in this world that told the truth. It was money that talked, and bullshit that walked. "Let that bullshit-ass nigga beat his muthafucking feet."

Chapter 23

Expensive Taste

Pam strolled through the furniture store examining the prices on the furnishings. "Damn, Chino! They want three thousand dollars for this sectional! And they want three thousand dollars for that three-piece living room set."

Chino shrugged nonchalantly. "You want nice leather, you have to pay for it. What comes with that three-piece set?"

"A sofa, love seat, and easy chair. The chaise is another eight hundred bucks."

"I like the sectional," Chino said, wrapping his arms around her. "We can curl up and watch the projection screen TV."

"I can't believe you paid almost ten thousand dollars for that thing!"

"I always wanted one of those, Pooh. Ever since I was a kid."

"And that laser disc player?" Pam smiled. "You always wanted one of those too?"

"They didn't have anything like that when I was growing

up. We just had rabbit ears and I was the damn rabbit." He laughed. "You wanted to watch a movie, you had to sneak through the back door of the movie theater."

Pam laughed.

"You ever did that before?"

"Nope."

"Don't tell me you never snuck inside of a movie theater before?"

"I said no!"

"Aw shit! We gonna have to sneak inside of a movie theater, Pooh."

"I am not sneaking into any movie theater, boy!"

Chino slapped Pam on her behind. "You're going to have to start living a little, girl. We gonna sneak inside one of these days, you watch. I'm going to make a gangsta out of you yet."

"A gangsta?"

"Yeah, we gonna be like Bonnie and Clyde."

"Didn't they get killed?"

"They lived, Pooh. They lived life for real."

"They were criminals."

"And what am I, Pooh? Am I just a criminal to you?"

Pam shook her head. "You know what I mean. Stop putting words in my mouth."

"We gonna live life to the fullest, girl. We ain't gonna be scared of nothing. That's what it means to be a gangsta. Gangstas ain't scared of shit. Gangstas go for theirs. Nothing stops them, and they don't let nothing get in their way."

"I can live with that," Pam agreed.

"What do you think about this, Pooh?"

Pam examined the dining room set Chino was pointing at. "It's kinda old-fashioned."

"Old-fashioned? I like it. It's classic. Like something you would find in rich white folks' houses. See, white folks know the secret. They buy traditional shit, not trendy shit. They shit still be looking good twenty years from when they bought it and then they pass shit down for generations. That shit becomes valuable family heirlooms. That's how we need to roll, Pooh."

"Chino, that looks like something my grandmother would pick out. It's dark cherry wood, with a dark cherry wood china cabinet. What about this one?" She looked toward something less traditional.

"That's made out of glass and chrome!" Chino said. "What kind of china cabinet is made out of chrome and glass?"

"I like modern furniture!" Pam protested.

"What about this one?" Chino asked, pointing toward another dining room set. "It's a good compromise. It's light-colored, birch wood. It looks modern and classy at the same time."

"How is this going to match with a green leather sectional?"

"How about we get the beige leather sectional, or the burgundy one?" Chino asked.

"I like that lime green one."

"We got two living areas. We can put the lime green one in one room, and the beige one in another."

Pam nodded. "Ooooh, this vase would look pretty with that sofa. And I like that bombé chest too!"

"We can get both of them, the dining room set, and both of those sectionals."

"We need some end tables, lamps, and coffee tables."

"What about the stone coffee table and end tables? The ones shaped like elephants, with the glass table tops."

"Ooooh, I like those!" Pam told him.

"We need to go by a gallery and pick up some art. African-American and African art."

"What do you know about African art?"

"I like sub-Saharan masks and shields and carvings."

Pam smiled and touched Chino lightly on the cheek in amazement. "You keep surprising me."

"We need some bar stools too."

"I like those metal bar stools with the leather seats."

"Hello, may I help you?" a salesperson asked.

Pam stared at Chino.

"Yeah, we'll take those two sectionals over there, that bombé chest by the entrance, those two giant vases right there, and that dining room set over there."

"Wow!" the saleslady exclaimed. "Have you applied for credit with our credit department yet?"

"Chino, don't go there," Pam whispered.

"It'll be cash," Chino told the saleswoman. He used every bit of self-control he could muster to keep from telling her off. "You know colored people don't have no good credit."

"Chino!" Pam shouted.

"Sorry, I couldn't help myself." Chino smiled. "She assumed that we needed credit, baby. Like we didn't have the money to pay for this shit right now."

"My apologies, sir," the saleswoman told him. "Usually when customers make such a large purchase, they finance it and make monthly payments."

Chino shook his head. "Forget about it. We just need it delivered as soon as possible."

"I can write up your ticket over here." The saleswoman pointed toward a counter.

"Oh, you gonna give me a ticket?" Chino asked. "I usually get my tickets in New York."

Pam elbowed Chino, and both of them laughed. The saleswoman looked lost. Chino pulled out a ten-thousand-dollar stack of one-hundred-dollar bills and handed it to Pam. "Take care of the bill, Pooh. I gotta run to the little girls' room and tinkle."

"Boy!" Pam said laughing.

The saleswoman looked at Chino strangely.

Chino headed toward the restroom, and Pam placed the stack of bills on the counter. She had never held that much money in her life. She loved having the salespeople's full attention. She loved the power she felt having that amount of money. Whatever Chino did, and however he did it, he must have been very good at it. The money that he had made her curious. Now more than ever, she was intrigued with the drug world, and the enormous amount of money that the drug game generated. She wanted to learn more.

Chapter 24

Diamonds Are Forever

"She is really going to love this!" the saleswoman said excitedly. "Your soon-to-be fiancée is one lucky lady!"

Chino held the ring in the air and examined it once again. It was a three-carat, round, VVS diamond, sitting in a platinum base. It was an engagement ring for his beloved Pooh. They had moved in together. He had given her a comfortable home, and now it was time to take that final step. He would ask Pooh to marry him.

That he loved Pam was without question. She was everything that he was not. She was good-hearted, innocent, and square. He was hood and grimy and street. Pam made him a better person, making the world seem like a better place. His Pooh gave him hope, and she gave him the final piece of his dream. He wanted a house in the suburbs, and he wanted a son to carry on his legacy. Pooh would be the perfect wife, the perfect homemaker, and the perfect mother for that son. Would she say yes?

She could stay in college. He would take care of her. They

would have their house, their children, their two cars, their dog, and the life that he dreamed of. He would open his own business, maybe even go back to college himself. He was definitely going to get out of the game. That was what it was all about, getting what you needed and getting out, as Fabian had said. That was the race he was in. Getting his before the police got theirs, or better yet, getting the hell out of town before his karma caught up to him.

"Are you sure this is the right size?" the saleswoman asked.

Chino nodded. "Yeah, I bought her a ring a couple of months ago, and this was the size."

"The absolute worst thing in the world is receiving an engagement ring and not being able to wear it right away because it doesn't fit right," the saleswoman explained. "Then she would have to wait while it was sent off to be resized. The wait would be excruciating!" She rolled her eyes upward and gave a distressed look. Chino and the saleswoman shared a laugh.

"Gosh, she is so lucky. And you look so young! I wish that my husband could have afforded a fourteen-thousand-dollar engagement ring when we were your age."

Chino pointed at a watch in the display case. "Let me see that watch right there."

"Which one?"

"The gold Rolex." He pointed. "The Oyster Perpetual model."

"Good choice." She pulled the watch from the case. "It comes with a self-winder too."

Chino took the watch and tried it on. "How much for this one?"

"Ten thousand dollars."

"And if I wanted to add a diamond bezel?"

"We're running a special right now. You can get the diamond bezel and diamond face for an additional five thousand dollars."

"Y'all install it?"

She nodded. "We have an in-house craftsman that does it. You can pick it up in three days."

"I'll take it," Chino told her. "And the special with the diamond face and bezel."

"Good choice," the saleswoman told him. "And the ring?"

"Most definitely, yeah." Chino nodded.

Chino counted out thirty-two thousand dollars and handed it to the lady. "Seven percent tax, right?"

"Yes," she said, still adding the numbers on her calculator. She glanced up at Chino surprised, after she finished her calculations. "Wow, you hit the nail right on the head!"

"Counting money has always been my specialty." Chino smiled.

"Are you an accountant?"

"Something like that."

The saleslady placed Pam's ring inside a small purple felt box, then inside a small plastic bag, and placed the bag on the counter. "Your watch should be ready in three days, but you can call tomorrow and check on it after four o'clock. There's not many people in front of you, so he may be able to get to it tomorrow afternoon. Just call and see."

"Thank you," Chino told her, taking his receipt and bag from the counter.

Chino headed out of the jewelry store toward his car, when he noticed three people walking toward him.

"Fuck!" Chino said when they became visible.

He had learned his lesson from the last time, so this time Chino raced and dove behind another car. He wasn't going to hide behind his Benz and get it shot up. Within seconds, gunfire erupted in the parking lot. Innocent shoppers scattered into the stores trying to find cover.

"Fucking bitch-ass niggas!" Chino shouted. He pulled out his pistol and returned fire over the Nissan Maxima that he was hiding behind. "I thought I killed you, Jo Jo!"

Jo Jo and two members of his crew had been walking up to the jewelry store as Chino was heading to his car. They recognized each other at the same time, and both went for their weapons. The good thing was Jo Jo hadn't been there to jack him, they had just run into each other by accident. The bad thing was it didn't matter. Whether they came to jack him or not, their bullets were still just as deadly.

Chino worked his way around to the back of the brown Maxima and peeked around the rear bumper. Jo Jo and his boys were hiding among the parked cars. He didn't know whether they were going to try to get away or to jack him now. He had become a target of opportunity. And then an idea hit him.

Chino got down on his hands and knees and looked stealthily beneath the cars in the parking lot. He saw feet gathered together about forty yards away. He had to make them get out of there before they split up and came at him from different directions. And then there was the little matter of the police, who would be coming soon.

Chino lay on his belly and carefully took aim. He unleashed the fury of his pistol on his targets, watching as the sparks flew off the concrete near their legs. He saw two of them fall and heard voices crying out. Now would be the time to make it back to his car and get the hell out of the shopping center before the police arrived.

Ducking behind vehicles, he made his way back to his Benz. He didn't want to climb inside unless he was sure they weren't looking. Although he knew that they knew what he was driving, he still didn't want to risk its getting shot up. He dropped to his stomach again, looking intently beneath the cars. He couldn't see anyone.

"Fuck it!" he said, rising to his feet. He noticed that others in the parking lot were starting to stand too, and they were all looking in the same direction. Chino quickly turned to see what they were staring at. He could see someone being helped into a green Mustang 5.0. He wondered if he should run over and finish them off or make his own escape. His Mercedes would allow him to leave without suspicion from the innocent bystanders who were now fleeing. No one would suspect the driver of a Benz to be involved in a mall shooting.

Chino climbed into his car, cranked it up, and backed out. As bad as he wanted to kill Jo Jo, he knew that he wouldn't be able to get away with it. It was broad daylight, and everyone was watching. That muthafucka had gotten away once again, but next time, he wouldn't be so lucky.

"Either me or you, Jo Jo," Chino said, pulling out of the parking lot. "Next time, one of us ain't leaving the scene. One of us is being put on a slab." The next time, someone was going to die.

Chapter 25

Bonnie & Clyde

Chino led Pam across the parking lot and stopped just in front of the window of an empty store.

"What is it? Pam asked, cupping her hands around her eyes, looking in the window. "It's empty."

"It's empty for right now. But close your eyes and imagine it full of people. People getting their wig done in our very own beauty shop."

"What?" Pam turned toward him excitedly. "Are you kidding me?"

"Nope." He pulled a key out of his pocket, stuck it into the lock, unlocked the door, and led Pam inside. "What do you think?"

Pam looked around and grinned. "Chino, I love it! It's perfect!"

Chino and Pam walked through the empty store and took everything in.

"I could put my hair dryers against this wall, and my sinks

against this wall. We could line up the chairs over here for the beauticians."

"We could put the lounge area over there," Chino said, pointing, "and we could put a play area for kids over in the corner."

"Ooooh, that's a great idea!" Pam grinned. "We can put toys and children's books, and coloring books, and blocks and shit in the corner for the kids."

"Not too much though," Chino warned. "We don't want people dropping their bad-ass kids off here and jetting for a while like we some damn day care."

They both laughed.

"What do you think about a barbershop on that side?" Pam asked.

"Of course, boo. Let's do it all. We ain't leaving no money behind. We need to cut hair, do hair, nails, pedicures, manicures, the works. Shit, if we wouldn't get in trouble, I'd say throw a massage parlor in the back too."

"Nuh-uh," Pam told him. "We know what goes on in those things." She looked around eagerly and a smile crossed her face. "Oh, Chino, I really want this to happen!"

"What are you talking about, Pooh? This is going to happen." Chino emphasized the word *going*. "We are going to open this shop, and you are going to manage it. Do you think you're up to managing a shop?"

"Yeah. This is something that I've always wanted to do! I've always wanted my own business."

"Well, now you've got it, but remember, the purpose of the shop is twofold, baby girl. We are going to really do hair and run a business, but we are going to inflate the numbers so I can wash my money through the shop."

Pam nodded. She understood, but what Chino was saying wasn't important at the moment. This was her chance to build her dream shop. The shop that she always wanted to go to when she got her hair done. Everything would be just perfect. "I want this to be the best shop in the world! I want it to be luxurious. Almost like a spa experience."

"Maybe one day we can get the space next door and turn it into a full-blown spa and beauty salon."

"That would be fly. We could cater to the sisters who don't feel comfortable going to those white spas."

Chino looked at his watch. "I'm glad you like it, Pooh, because the contractor should be here any minute."

Surprised by what he had just said, Pam crossed her arms across her chest and pouted. "What if I didn't like it?"

"Ah, baby girl, I knew you would."

"Yeah, what makes you so confident about that?"

Walking toward Pam, Chino put his hands on her hips and pulled her toward him. "Pooh, do you know how long and hard I looked for a place like this? Everything else that I ran across, I knew you wouldn't like. I know my Pooh and she has class. Everything you visualized in here"—he nodded with his head—"I did too."

"You know me so well." Pam winked and kissed Chino on his lips. Breaking away from his grasp, Pam became even more hype. "Chino, I want this to be top-notch. I want coming here to be an experience, one that's different from all the other salons. I want jazz music playing over a stereo system. I want to serve beverages like coffee, tea, soda, juice, and bottled water.

I want mirrors all along this wall and this wall, and I want a lot of chrome. I want it to be really modern and futuristic."

Chino nodded. "We can hook that up. We're gonna need a name for this futuristic and luxurious shop. I was thinking of calling it Pam's at first."

Pam shook her head. "Oh hell no! It has to be something flier than that!"

Chino grabbed her, pulled her close, and wrapped his arms around her. "How about we call it Pooh's?"

"Boy, please!" Pam pulled away and turned to face him. "Be serious!" Mocking a fake customer, Pam jibbed, "Girl, where you get yo hair done? I got my hair done at Pooh's." They both laughed. It sounded ghetto as hell.

"Okay, since that's out, how about Divas?" Chino suggested.

"Divas. Hmm . . . ," Pam said, mulling it over. "Maybe. We'll keep that one in mind."

"How about D'Elegance, like the Cadillac?"

"I think not!"

"How about Eloquence?"

Pam shrugged and pursed her lips. "Those are stripper names, Chino!"

Chino burst into laughter because she was right. "Okay, how about Turning Heads?"

"Turning Heads?" Pam smiled. "I like that. I like it a lot."

"How about Lasting Impressions?" Chino spit out.

"Yeah, but those names are kinda ghetto. I wanted something more classy."

"Call it A Touch of Class," Chino suggested.

"That's real ghetto!" Pam said. "I want it to be classy and

sassy and urban, but without being ghetto . . . something eloquent."

"That's it!" Chino grinned from ear to ear.

"What's it?"

"Eloquent. We'll call the shop Eloquent."

Pam pondered for a moment. She liked the name but there was something missing. "Not just Eloquent. It needs to be jazzier than that."

"What if we just played on that word?" Chino suggested. "What if we called it L O Quent?" he said, pausing between the syllables.

A smile spread across Pam's face. "I like it. L O Quent," she repeated. "In fact, I love it! That's what we'll call it! L O Quent Beauty Salon."

A car pulled up to the shop and stopped. It was a blue Cutlass Supreme with black faces inside. Out of pure instinct, Chino whipped out his strap.

"Chino!"

"Hold on, baby!" he said, waving Pam out of the way.

"It's just a group of females!" Pam shouted, seeing the girls exit the car, laughing and walking toward a Chinese takeout restaurant two stores down.

"What?" he asked. He heard her, but didn't.

"They were females."

Chino looked out the window and saw the last of the girls enter the Chinese food place. After a deep sigh, he tucked his pistol back into the small of his back and pulled his shirt down over it.

"What's wrong with you?" Pam asked.

"I ain't taking no chances, baby. I ain't gonna get caught slipping."

"Chino, look where we're at. We're in a nice area. Can you just, for once, leave that stuff behind us? For me? Please?"

"That stuff is getting us where we need to be, Pooh. That's a part of me. My life."

"I understand that, Chino, and I'm not knocking it. Just look around us. If anything were to look shady, don't you think it would have been noticed before now?"

Chino nodded. Pam was right. They were in a nice area and it was doubtful that Jo Jo or anyone else would prowl this area looking for dope dealers to jack. Although he had run into Jo Jo at an upscale shopping center last time, that had purely been an accident.

"Chino, look at me," Pam said softly.

Chino turned and looked into her eyes.

"We are trying to make a better life for ourselves," she explained. "We have a new apartment, we are opening up a business, and pretty soon you'll be able to leave that lifestyle behind. We are making a fresh start, baby. We are creating a whole new world for ourselves, but in order to do that, you are going to have to take the first steps of leaving the old world behind. A new life, Christonos. That's what we are building."

Chino nodded, walked to the glass window, and gazed out. Pam had so much hope for this new world that they were building that he couldn't tell her the truth. He couldn't tell her that once you have a reputation for being a baller, you'll always have it. Even if you no longer sell dope, people will assume it's because you got enough to get out of the game. And if you've got enough money to retire from the dope game, then that just makes you an even bigger target for jackers. Chino knew he would always have an X on his back in Columbus and the only way out would be to leave, and that's what he planned to do—wash his paper through the salon and then get them the hell out of Columbus. Chino just hoped that he wouldn't die trying.

Chapter 26

Soul Mates

Chino's hands shook a bit as he held the door open for Pam. Pam loved shrimp, especially shrimp scampi, so he had brought her to Red Lobster. She had an affinity for the garlic butter and the biscuits that they served with the meals. He had asked her to dinner for a special purpose—to present her with the ring. Things had been going well for them. Winter had quietly morphed into spring, and Columbus was alive and bustling again. Although they still had Young Mike living with them, living together was wonderful. Chino loved coming home to his Pooh. He loved having someone in his arms at night, and he loved having someone around to talk to all the time. Despite all the protesting from Pam's parents, she had stood up to them and told them she was done with school and had been managing the startup of L O Quent full time.

Waking up to breakfast, coming home to a hot lunch and a hot dinner was something that Chino quickly got used to. Pam had proven that she was wifey material and now he was about to wife her. He tapped at the ring in his pocket as the hostess seated them in a secluded corner booth and handed them their menus. Their waitress came almost immediately and took their drink orders.

The beauty shop was coming along well. L O Quent was going to open on schedule, and so far, the buzz that they had been generating across the city was all good. Even the *Columbus Dispatch* wrote an article about the new upscale salon. Things couldn't have been better, and yet, somehow, he felt that they were about to be. Locking down Pooh would secure everything for him. She was a major piece of the puzzle in the life that he was trying to create for himself. Pooh—wife, future mother, salon manager, business partner, life partner, best friend. She played so many roles in his life, and he had even more in store for her. Soon she would merge all the titles into one, and he would just refer to her as his everything.

"I'm definitely ready to get my grub on," Pam told him. "You are going to have to forgive me and forget about what I'm about to do to this shrimp."

Chino laughed. "Girl, you sound like you're about to eat up some shit."

"Are you ready to order?" the waitress asked, setting down their drinks.

Pam nodded. "I'll have the butterfly shrimp and shrimp scampi."

"Mashed potatoes, baked potatoes, fries, rice pilaf, or steamed broccoli?"

"Mashed potatoes."

"What type of dressing would you like on your salad?"

"Caesar."

"Very good, ma'am." The waitress turned to look at Chino.

"I'll have the lobster and steak."

"How would you like your steak?"

"Well done. I don't wanna see any blood or red or none of that gross vampire type of shit. I want the cow dead. Capital D-E-A-D."

The waitress and Pam laughed.

"Mashed potatoes, baked potatoes, fries, rice pilaf, or steamed broccoli?"

"Mashed."

"Dressing?"

"Caesar."

"Great. Is there anything else I can get you?"

"Yeah, we want a bottle of Chablis."

"You got it!" the waitress said, disappearing.

"Wine?" Pam leaned forward. "I'm surprised she didn't ask for your ID."

"I look like I'm older than what I am," Chino whispered. "Plus, all you gotta do is get 'em laughing."

"Is that the strategy that you used on me?" Pam asked. "Just get me laughing?"

"That's the strategy, ma! And guess what?"

"What?"

"It worked."

Pam nodded. "Uh-huh."

"I was thinking that I would do this after dinner, but instead, I'll pop the question right now."

"Pop the question?"

Chino nodded. He stood and then dropped to one knee next to where Pam was seated. He took her hand in his and stared into her eyes. "Pam, will you marry me?"

"Is this some kind of joke, Chino?" Pam said, looking serious. "If it is, it's not funny."

"What do you mean?" Chino asked, nervously. "Why would I joke like this? I'm serious, Pooh. I want you to marry me."

"And that's why you brought me here today? To ask me to marry you?"

"You said that this was your favorite restaurant. What better place than your favorite restaurant to ask you to marry me?"

"How about something more romantic, more intimate, more . . . I don't know . . ."

"Pooh, what's the matter?" Chino asked. "This is not about the restaurant. Don't make no lame-ass excuses. If you don't want to marry me, then just say so. Nothing is going to change. I'll just have to wait until you're ready."

Pam shook her head. "Uh-uh, don't put this off on me. It's not that I'm not ready, Chino. This is not about me, this is about you. Are you really ready for that kind of commitment? Do you know what a marriage entails? Are you ready, at your young age, to commit to one woman and only one woman? Can you honestly say that, Christonos? One woman?"

Chino nodded.

"No, say it like you mean it!" Pam said forcefully. "Because if you hurt me, Christonos, I will kill you! I will kill you! Are you ready to take it to that level?"

"Pam, I love you," Chino said softly. "I keep telling you, I would never hurt you. Never. I'm ready for that kind of commitment, Pooh. You're the one and only for me. You're all the woman I need, Pooh."

Pam smacked her lips and tilted her head to one side.

"Pooh, what can another woman give me that you can't?"

"Variety. She can stoke your little ego. She can—"

"Do nothing for me," Chino interrupted her.

"Christonos, I don't know," Pam said, shaking her head.

"What don't you know?"

"I don't know if you know why you want to get married. I don't know if you really understand what a marriage is about. I don't know if you really want to do this. Don't just do this to fulfill some little fantasy of yours. It has to be for the right reasons, not out of some deep psychological need because of a deprived childhood."

"Pam, listen to me," Chino said, clasping her hand once again. "I want to marry you. I want to marry you because I love you. I love you because you keep it real. I want to marry you because you bring out the best in me. I want to marry you because you bring into my life a whole other world. You are the best half of me. You complete me. Until I met you, I didn't really understand the term 'my better half.' After I met you, I understood it completely. You are everything good that is in me. You are everything good that I want to be. I need you in my life, like I need air. I need you because I need to breathe. You are my life now, Pooh. My life without you is like I'm missing a lung, a kidney, half a heart. You are that much of me. I need you. I need you for the rest of my life."

Pam lifted her hand to her face and wiped away her tears. No one had ever said anything like that to her before. Chino really did understand marriage. He put into words what she had witnessed with her mother and father her entire life. They were one. They operated as one, acted as one, completed each other's sentences. She had always dreamed that she would be lucky enough to find a love like that one day. And now there existed the possibility that she had found it.

Chino reached into his pocket and pulled out the small purple felt box that held Pam's engagement ring. He held the box up toward her and flipped the top open. Pam gasped.

"Chino!" she cried out. "Oh my God! It's beautiful!"

Pam snatched the ring and placed it on her finger. She held the brilliant diamond up toward the light and watched it sparkle like the north star.

"It's huge!" She laughed, wiping tears away from her eyes and sniffling. She hugged him. "Oh, Chino! I love you so much. I'm sorry for doubting you. I love you too, boo. I love you for understanding. I love you for waiting. I love you for putting up with my crazy-ass and my mood swings. I love you for laughing, and singing to me, and ice-skating, and fixing me chicken soup, and feeding me, and giving me flowers, and for making me laugh. I love you for so many reasons. I love you because you bring life to me. I was living before I met you, but now I have a life. You make the flowers smell prettier and colors look brighter and the stars in the sky shine more brilliant. You are my life too, boo. My breath, my love, my heart, my everything."

"Does this mean yes?" Chino asked, lifting an eyebrow.

"Are you crazy? Of course it means yes!" Pam leaned over and fell into his arms. Together they lay on the floor of the Red Lobster and kissed, as if they were the only two people in the entire universe.

Onlookers applauded.

Chapter 27

Mother Knows Best

"Hello?"

"Hello, Mom?" Pam asked.

"Hey, Pammy!" her mother said excitedly.

"Mommy, it's so good to hear your voice."

"No, it's great to hear your voice," her mother replied. "How are you, sweetheart?"

"I'm good."

"Are you?"

"Yeah," Pam told her. "How have you been?"

"Fine, sweetie."

"How's Dad been?"

"Worried about you."

"Worried about me? Why?"

"Pammy, you know Dad and I want you to be safe. Chino is almost as young as you, and I don't think you're ready to be living with a boyfriend."

Pam exhaled. Her life had changed dramatically. She had quit her job, moved into an apartment with a guy, lost her virginity, and dropped out of college. But she saw where Chino was leading her, and that was to opportunity and the American Dream. Why couldn't her family see this?

Becoming frustrated with how the conversation was going, Pam protested. "Mom, I'm not in high school anymore."

"Pammy, I'm not trying to be an enemy. I'm . . . I'm so disappointed . . ." Her mother trailed off and quietly sucked in air to control her sobbing.

Disappointed was a word that Pam hated to hear come out of the mouth of either of her parents, particularly if it was aimed at her. She had worked hard her whole life to keep her parents happy. Pleasing them was what she strived for. It was what pushed her to graduate from high school at the age of sixteen. It was what had kept her in advanced placement classes, in honors classes, and on the honor roll.

"Mom, I'm sorry." Pam's voice had a tinge of sadness in it.

"Sorry? Sorry, Pammy, 'sorry' is not going to cut it."

"Mom, I know. I'm working hard at the salon and I'm going to prove myself to you."

"Pammy, there is something going on with you, and your father and I want to know what it is. What is going on up there?"

"Nothing."

"Nothing?"

"So, what are you saying?" her mother asked. "Are you saying that we have to drive to Ohio to see what's going on with you?"

Getting away from her protective parents had been her

reason for leaving Detroit and heading for Ohio. To have them start coming to Ohio was the last thing she wanted.

"No, Mom. You don't have to do that."

"Are you sure?" her mother snapped. "Because I can't tell! Right now, it seems like you need some guidance. It seems like you need someone to help you get back on the right track."

"Mom, I'm okay. Really."

"Is it Chino, Pammy? Have you gone up there and let some boy control your life?"

"No, Mom, I haven't."

"Then what is it?"

"I've just been busy with so many things."

"So many things?" Her mother laughed. "Like what? Which, by the way, brings me to another subject. Your father went to put money in your account, and it was empty. He got a bank statement, and you haven't had any deposits from your job in quite some time."

Pam exhaled. Her parents would find out sooner or later.

Chino was now her fiancé. In fact, she had called to break the news of her engagement to her mother. She had hoped that the conversation would be different, but this was the conversation that she had been presented with. The best that she could hope for now was to gain control of the situation and present her news in a positive light.

"Mom, Chino is like my best friend. He wouldn't ever hurt me. Actually, he's more than my boyfriend, Mom."

"More than your boyfriend? Pammy, what are you trying to say?"

Pam swore that her mother had stopped breathing. She

wanted to laugh, but the subject was so serious that she knew she needed to deal with it in a serious manner.

"Chino has asked me to marry him."

"Marry him?" her mother exploded. "Pammy, are you serious? You're a child! You can't get married. You're still in school! What is this young man thinking?"

"Mom, calm down."

"I will not calm down!" she snapped. "This is ridiculous! What are his parents saying about this?"

"He hasn't told them," Pam said softly. "Actually, his mother is dead, and he hasn't talked to his father—"

"Hasn't talked to his father? What kind of young man proposes to a woman without even consulting his family about it? Or your family? What is going on with his father? And what does this young man do for a living? Obviously, he can't be in college, if he's supporting you and him at the same time. Has he graduated from college already? Oh, my baby! If he's finished school, then he's a grown man already, and that bastard is preying on my baby!"

"Mom! Calm down! No, Chino isn't in school. He takes care of me through his job. And no, he is not preying on me, we're only a year apart," Pam lied.

"So, both of you are still wet behind the ears, and you're talking about getting married? Pam, marriage isn't what the fairy-tale books make it out to be. Marriage is hard work. It's a commitment, Pamela." Pam rolled her eyes. When her mother called her anything other than 'Pammy,' she knew Mom was pissed. "It means being responsible for another adult's life! Do you think that both of you are ready for that?"

"I'm not a baby anymore."

"What's that supposed to mean?" Mrs. Xavier blew up again. "You're seventeen! Are you having sex? Is that what you're saying, Pamela Xavier? God, I knew it was a mistake letting you go so far away for college! Listening to your father! I knew better!"

"No, Mom, I'm not having sex and I am okay!"

"We should drive up there and put an end to this nonsense!"

"No, Mother, don't. I'll be there soon."

"You'll be here for Christmas, right?"

"Yeah," Pam lied.

"Bring this young man with you. Perhaps your father and I can talk some sense into him. Both of you are so young."

"I will, Mom."

"Okay, call me soon, sweetheart. Your father and I are here for you and we love you dearly."

"I love you too, Mom," Pam said. She hung up the telephone and lay back on the bed. She loved her mother, but parents were parents, and they could be overdramatic and nerve-wracking. She would always be their little girl, no matter how old she got. But still, she wished that they would let her grow up just a little.

Chapter 28

More to Life

Pam pulled her legs close and rested her chin on her knees. The wind was blowing gently, providing a nice cool breeze off the Scioto River. Summer had turned into fall again, and Pam would be eighteen in a few months. Chino's game was getting better and better, and the salon was up and running. Soon they would be free to move anywhere and do anything they wanted. Pam breathed in deeply and was overcome with an overpowering feeling: she was happy.

She watched as Chino ran along the bank, chasing one of the large white ducks that called the place home. Watching Chino play around made her wonder what kind of father he would be if—or better yet, when—they had a family. He was certainly a good provider. He had given her everything that her heart ever desired. Although he would have to quit his profession before she finally walked down the aisle with him, they hadn't had that conversation yet. She would deliver the ultimatum: stop selling drugs so we can move forward, marry, and start a family.

Pam thought about the families she knew that had absent fathers. She was determined that that was not going to be the fate of her family. Her children were not going to learn about their father through pictures, or get to see him only on visitation days, or have to say good-bye to him at the end of an eight-hour supervised visit. That was not going to be her touching a jailhouse glass and wiping tears from her eyes.

No, if Chino really wanted it all, he would have to take steps to make sure that he was going to be around. And the way to do that would be to stop all his illegal activities. She didn't know how Chino was going to take the conversation, or how he was going to react. Sure, she should have given him that ultimatum when he proposed, but she had been caught up in the moment. She had been so happy that the only thing she could see at the time was their future together. She could only see the white house, the picket fence, the 2.5 kids, the two cars, and the family dog. She wasn't thinking about the slammer, the bars, the long drives to a remote prison farm.

Watching Chino run around and act a fool told her that he would be a great father.

There were so many questions that had to be answered, so many variables. Chino could act a fool, and he could make you laugh, and he could make your heart soar with emotion. He could bring tears of joy to your eyes, or tears of laughter. He could be charming, witty, sarcastic, spontaneous, adventurous, and so many other things. He was always a breath of fresh air, but what would it be like raising a family with him?

Pam burst into laughter as Chino squatted, flapped his arms, and got in line behind a team of marching ducks.

"If it walks like a duck, quacks like a duck, and looks like a duck, then what?" Chino shouted to her.

"Then it's a crazy-ass fiancé who needs a paddy wagon!" Pam shouted back.

Chino quacked and quacked, picked up one of the ducks, and headed toward Pam.

"Don't bring that thing over here!" Pam shouted.

"Oh, you scared?" Chino asked with a smile.

"That thing might bite!" Pam got on her feet to run if need be.

"How is a duck going to bite you, girl? It's a duck, not a pit bull!"

"It's got teeth!" Pam said, backing away. She scanned her surroundings, looking for a safe place to run to.

"Ducks don't bite," Chino said laughing. "C'mere!"

"Chino! Ahhhhh!" Pam screamed and took off running.

"C'mere, girl!" Chino shouted, chasing Pam around with a quacking, flapping duck.

Pam ran until she became tired. She stopped, exhaling heavily. "Chino, if you put that duck on me, I swear I'm gonna cut your nuts off while you sleep."

"Girl, it's not going to bite you," Chino told her, seriously. "Do you think that I would let something hurt you?"

"Get that thing away from me, Chino."

"Pam, you have to face your fears."

"My fears, I can face. I just don't wanna face that damn duck."

"Pam, I want you to meet Psycho, my killer duck."

"Chino, I will fuck you and Psycho up!"

"That's it, Pam. You shouldn't have threatened him."

Chino held the duck up to his ear. "What was that, Psycho? You want to fly into her hair?"

"Chino, no!" Pam shouted. She covered her head and took off running again.

Chino put the duck down and rolled on the ground laughing. The duck raced off into the river. Seeing this, Pam walked up to Chino and kicked him.

"Asshole!"

"You should have seen the look on your face, Pooh!" Chino said, laughing hysterically.

"You think that's funny?"

"Pooh, you took off running like you were Flo Jo!" Chino told her. "I'll put you in the Olympics, put my killer duck behind you, and sit back and rake in the endorsements."

"That's not funny!" Pam said, laughing.

"I can't believe you threatened to cut off the family jewels."

"I would have chopped the suckers right off."

"Then how would we have fertilized your eggs?"

"Ain't nothing getting to these eggs, mister. None of your crazy-ass sperm anyway. My eggs will grow up scrambled, just like their daddy!"

Chino laughed. "Aw, c'mon, Pooh. Come sit down here with your man."

Pam dropped down to the ground and sat next to Chino. "You just answered a bunch of questions for me."

"Oh yeah, like what?"

"Like how you would provide for us if you weren't hustling. I now have the answer."

"What answer is that?"

"You get a crazy check. I know you have to be getting a disability check from the government."

Chino placed his finger to his lips and shushed her. "Don't be telling my business, Pooh."

Pam nodded. "Yeah, you're crazy, and the bad part about it is that our kids are going to love the ground your mentally retarded-ass walks on."

Chapter 29

Loving You

Pam stepped out of the shower and strolled into the bedroom to find Chino waiting for her with a gift box and rose petals sprinkled on the bed.

"What's this?" Pam asked with a smile.

"I don't know," he told her in a singsong voice. "It was here when I came in the room. Open it. Let's see what it is." Pam eyed him suspiciously. She knew it was some type of jewelry because it was in a felt box.

"Open it," Chino urged.

"Uh-uh, I ain't touching that. You said you didn't know what it was and it was there when you came in the room. I'm sorry, I don't open boxes just laying there," Pam called Chino's bluff, with a smile, and started drying herself off. "Even if it is in a felt box."

Chino snatched the towel out of her hands.

"Chino!" she shouted. "Stop it! What are you doing?"

"Open your gift, girl!"

"Oh, so now it's a gift?" Pam looked at Chino and laughed. She held out her hand. "Give me the towel. I'm soaking wet."

Chino nodded toward the box. "After you open that."

Pam exhaled and reluctantly sat naked on the bed. She picked up the felt box and pulled off the top.

A gasp escaped Pam's lips. "Chino! It's beautiful!" A gorgeous diamond tennis bracelet sparkled inside.

A smile shot across Chino's face. "I knew you would like it, Pooh."

"Like it?" Pam leapt to her feet and wrapped her arms around Chino. "I love it!"

"Here, let me put this on you," Chino told her.

Pam handed Chino the bracelet.

"Not that." Chino smiled seductively. He picked up a bottle of cocoa butter lotion that was on the nightstand next to the bed. "I meant this. Let me put this on you."

Pam laughed. "Silly!" She turned her back to him and rolled her shoulders. "Put it on me, big daddy."

Chino squeezed some lotion in his palm, rubbed his hands together, and then gently massaged the lotion into Pam's back. He deeply rubbed her shoulders, down her back, then walked his fingers up her spine.

Instinctively, Pam leaned back into Chino's touches while he leaned forward and placed his lips on her neck. Chino then began to trace just below her earlobe with his tongue. Pam hunched up her shoulders and tried to block his tongue by pressing her shoulder and neck together.

Breathing heavily in Pam's ear, Chino asked, "What's wrong? You can't take it?"

"It tickles."

"Lay down, Pooh. Let me put some lotion on your legs."

Pam did as she was told, lay back on the bed and teasingly lifted her smooth caramel leg into the air. Chino walked his eyes down her legs and swallowed hard. Her firm, muscular legs had him excited. He could feel himself growing larger with each passing second.

"You wanna put some lotion on these legs, Chino?" Pam asked, rubbing her legs seductively.

Chino nodded and again swallowed hard. His wide eyes followed her hands up and down her smooth legs.

"C'mon then." Pam wiggled her finger, motioning for him to come to her. Chino squeezed more lotion in his hand and rubbed from her thick thighs to her petite, manicured feet.

"Damn, girl. You got sandpaper feet!"

"Chino, please!" Pam laughed and kicked him. "You know my feet are smooth."

Chino kissed each of her toes. "Yeah, Pooh, your shit is on point. They smoother than a baby's ass."

Chino placed her big toe in his mouth, then moved down the line, sucking each toe in turn. Chino's touches, kisses, and thick tongue were more than Pam could take. She felt like she was about to explode between her legs . . . and then she did.

"What's the matter, Pooh?" Chino asked softly. He knew from the look on her face and her heavy breathing that she had an orgasm.

"Nothing." She tried to catch her breath.

Chino laughed. He continued to work his tongue up her feet, past her calf, up her thigh, to her erotic zone. Pam clasped the back of his head in anticipation of what he was going to do next.

"What you got for me, Pooh?"

"What do you want?" Pam responded in a whisper.

"I don't know." Chino shrugged. "Tell me what you got for me."

Pam placed her hand on her coochie and parted it. "This."

"Hot damn," Chino moaned. "Diamonds and pearls are a man's best friend."

"Diamonds and pearls?"

Chino grabbed the tennis bracelet and laid the cool strip down the slit of her pussy, alternating his licks on both sides of the tennis bracelet and her pearl tongue. Pam's body welcomed Chino. She gasped and moaned with each lick, arched her back, and grabbed hold of Chino's head.

"Wha . . . what are you doing?" Pam said through tightly clenched teeth.

"Damn, Pooh." Chino continued to feast. Instantaneously Pam stretched her legs and cried out in pleasure as she exploded again.

"Chino, you already know."

"Know what?" Chino gently pulled the tennis bracelet across her clit, giving her a heavenly sensation. Chino parted her vagina and stuck his tongue inside, stroking her deeply.

Pam moaned repeatedly.

"Chino!" Pam screamed. It was a move that always drove her crazy. She held his head and gyrated her hips. Chino could feel her going stiff and hear her purring. He looked up at her to find her face twisted with one eye open. She was gushing like Old Faithful.

"You cummin', baby?" Chino asked.

Pam couldn't answer. Chino laughed.

"I guess that's my answer."

"Why do you do that to me?" Pam asked.

"Because I love seeing that look on your face when you cummin'," Chino told her. "You gonna have to be careful, girl."

"What do you mean?" Pam asked between heavy breaths.

"You gonna shoot my baby outta there one of these days."

"Ain't no baby up in here."

"Not yet," Chino said, kissing her belly. He gently licked at her pearl tongue with a soft circular motion. Pam moaned. "But we are going to put a little Christonos up in here one day."

"Really?"

Chino sucked her labia again. "Yeah."

Pam moaned and gripped the back of his head. "So is that what this is about, Chino?"

"What are you talking about?" Chino asked, still licking and sucking.

"You're after my eggs?"

Chino laughed. "Can I get a half a dozen?"

"A half dozen? Are you crazy?"

"I can't get a half dozen eggs?"

"Do I look like a chicken farm?"

Chino stuck his tongue deep inside her and licked around. Pam gasped.

"Can I get at least one good egg then?" Chino asked.

"That depends."

"On what?"

"On whether you're going to take care of it or not," Pam told him. "I don't pass out eggs to just anybody."

Chino laughed and nodded. "I promise that I'll take good care of your egg, Pooh. Are you going to take good care of my seed?"

"Your seed?"

"Remember this, Pooh, it's my seed. The sperm swims to the cell and works its way inside so that it can be safe. The egg don't swim to the sperm. Life comes from a man, it just comes through a woman."

"So, I have to carry your baby for nine months, have swollen feet, an aching back, and be peeing every five minutes, and all I am is a bun warmer?"

Together they laughed.

"I'll be there going through it with you, Pooh."

Pam felt herself building to another climax.

"Are you going to give me an egg, Pooh?"

"I'll give it to you, Chino!" Pam said, cumming again. "I'll give you whatever you want."

Chino began to lick slowly.

"But you better be there for him, Chino!" Pam said breathing heavily. "You better take care of us."

"I will, Pooh. Don't I take care of you now? I won't leave his side, from the day he's born, till the day I die. I'll always be there for him and for you, Pooh."

Pam nodded.

"I guess I'll have to go and buy one of those video cameras, so I can tape the delivery."

"You going to be in the delivery room with me?" Pam asked.

"I wouldn't miss it for the world, Pooh!"

Chapter 30

Untouchables

Ricardo and Jesús were two of Dragos's most reliable soldiers. He used them for really important jobs, and for jobs that were too complicated or too messy for his ordinary soldiers. He used them this time to deliver a special ticket to Ohio. Instead of the usual twenty keys this week, he sent Chino forty. He was doubling everyone's ticket, because two of his major clients in North Carolina and Virginia had gotten popped. That had left him holding an unusual amount of product. His clients in Virginia and North Carolina had enormous tickets, and now those two tickets had to be divided among the remaining clients in order to get rid of the enormous stockpile of cocaine that he had been left with.

"Damn! What y'all doin?" Chino said, as he watched Ricardo and Jesús unload kilo after kilo. "I only move twenty."

Ricardo shrugged. "The boss's orders. Everyone gets double."

"I ain't never moved this much in a week!" Chino complained. "And then next week, he's gonna want us to move the same?"

"Probably," Jesús said, nodding. "The boss has a major problem right now."

"Damn," Chino declared. Normally he wouldn't complain about getting so much dope; no one would. It was just that he had no idea how he could move so much stuff in such a short amount of time. He was already pushing his max right now at twenty. He would have to move into other people's territory, start stealing clients, start pushing his crew to do more. He was already pushing two keys a week off on them, some were moving three, and he was pushing Chris J and Infa to move even more. But that would mean that they would be stealing other people's clients too. And if they were all stealing other people's clients and moving in on other people's turf, that could spark a drug war. Crew against crew, if they were lucky. But crews ran deep, and if they were working for niggas from another city, that could spark a city-against-city war. The last time Columbus went to war against Cleveland, the body count was crazy. No one wanted one of those again. Wars fucked up everybody's business and ruined way too many people's lives, but Chino could see no other way to expand. Was he truly the Prince of Columbus, or was he just bull-shitting?

Chino knew that he had dreams, big ones, but he also knew where he wanted to be a year or two from now. He wanted to be done, and if pushing this much weight until Dragos got out of his jam was how he had to accomplish that, then so be it. He had to keep his connect happy. Besides, things would probably go back to normal after a couple of enormous shipments. It would mean more work for him, but it would also mean a lot more money. Who couldn't use more money?

It would bring him to his goal just that much faster. But then again, it would also bring more attention.

Chino weighed the good and the bad. More bread, good. More attention, bad. More attention would bring more jackers and more haters out of the woodwork, bad. It would also expose him to greater danger, because he would be fucking with more people, even worse. And everyone in the game knew that the more people you fucked with, the greater the chance of one of them being a snitch, and getting caught up in a conspiracy wasn't something that he wanted to do. Columbus had its share of people working for the man, just like any other major city. People snitched because they were haters, people snitched to get rid of the competition, people snitched just because they wanted to be good citizens, and they snitched because they wanted to be the police. The majority of muthafuckas who snitched were trying to save their own rotten skins. Muthafucka snitched for a variety of reasons. And then there were the undercovers.

There were many of those and they came in all shapes, colors, and sizes. The fattest, stinkiest, most grimy-looking muthafuckas turned out to be narcotics detectives. Chino had seen one fool with a giant scraggly beard that looked like it had lice in it, and who had slept on the street for a week, turn out to be a detective. The scariest fool he had run into was a cat that looked like he was an eighteen-year-old baller. The cat had fat gold chains, rolled in a Benz, and was always in the club hollering at bitches. That fool wound up as the officer testifying at his partner's drug trial. You had to really watch your ass in Columbus, 'cause the police had taken out all stops in their war on drugs.

"Damn, kinfolk, what are we going to do with all of this?" Chris J asked.

Chino shook his head. "I need for you to take six keys and move 'em."

"What?" Chris asked.

Chino nodded. "Rock, I need for you to move six, and Infa, I need for you to move about six or seven. Ant, I need for you to move six, and Corey, I need for you to move four."

"Man, kinfolk, give me ten of them hoes, and I get them off!" Young Mike told him confidently.

"Ten?" Rock asked.

"Nigga, you can't move no ten birds in a week!" Infa told him.

"Watch me, fool!"

"Man, don't you give that youngster no ten birds!" Rock told Chino.

"I can move them hoes, kinfolk!" Young Mike reiterated.

Chino looked into the youngster's eyes. There was straight confidence and no fear in them. He nodded. "You got that."

"Bet!" Young Mike told him.

"Chino, Dragos knows that he's asking a lot of you to move this much product, but he still ain't taking no shorts," Ricardo said, after hearing the conversation.

Chino looked at Young Mike, and then back at Ricardo. "He's like my little brother. He lives with me."

Ricardo nodded.

Chino knew what Young Mike was going to do. It was basically the same thing that they all were going to have to do, which was beat the streets. They were going to have to push dope in uncharted territory. Other people's territory. Young

Mike was going to grind in other people's hood and be all up in the projects. And he was going to get the job done. He just hoped that the kid didn't get himself killed in the process.

Chino pulled out a gym bag filled with money and handed it to Ricardo. "Give this to Dragos. This is last week's ticket, and for what I thought was going to be this week's ticket. I was just going to pay him in advance, but now it appears that I owe him for another twenty."

"This is going to make him real happy," Ricardo said, holding up the gym bag.

"Chino, how in the hell are we all gonna move this much shit?" Rock asked.

"We gonna have to do the best that we can," Chino told him. "We can move it. Besides, I already gave him half the money for this ticket, so if we come up a little short, then that's okay. If it takes us an extra day or two to finish up, then so be it."

"And then another major ticket?" Chris J asked.

"By then, we'll have built up enough clientele," Ant said.

"Man, this is a dream, niggas!" Infa told them. "Most niggas only dream about getting this much yayo, but we got it! You niggas is acting like it's a funeral. Let's ball till we fall, niggas!"

Infa got a point, Chino thought. They were acting like it was the end of the world, but they should have been celebrating instead. They finally got a major ticket, and they were acting scared. It was do or die. Time to see what they really were about.

Chapter 31

Don't Ask, Don't Tell

"Fuck me, daddy! Fuck me!"

Corey pulled her hair as he pounded her doggy style. He had her on the couch in his parents' den, going at her like I-95 going south. Tish was a crack addict he picked up in the hood. He gave her two twenty-dollar rocks in exchange for unbridled sex. It wasn't his first time, nor hers. In fact, she was one of his favorites, and he was one of hers. Corey always paid well, had a nice thick dick, and he never beat her or tried to cheat her. She even found herself liking Corey and looking forward to their twice-weekly rendezvous.

Corey liked Tish because she was discreet and didn't put his business in the streets. He didn't want all the homeys to know that he was regularly dicking down a dope fiend. They wouldn't let him hear the end of it if they found out. The only one that knew was Chris J, and he was lying back on the couch while Tish sucked his dick.

"Oh, Corey! Oh! Oh!" Tish cried out.

Corey was rock hard and giving her all that he had. He

was pounding her as hard as he could, trying to get his rocks off. Chris J pushed her head down on his dick to silence her.

Tish gagged. "Chris, stop it!"

"Shut up, ho!" Chris J told her. "Suck this meat."

"It's too big," she whined. "When you push my head all the way down like that you choke me."

"Well, stop hollering, bitch!" Chris said. "Don't nobody want to hear that shit!"

"Oh!" Tish cried out. She tried to stifle her moans but couldn't. Corey was hitting that pussy just right. "Oh! Oh!"

Corey pulled off his shirt and tossed it across the room. He slapped Tish on her big, firm, yellow ass.

Tish was fine as hell. She was one of those girls that used to run track and play volleyball in high school. She was popular and all the guys at school wanted to get with her. Even after high school, she had kept her athletic shape, firm stomach, thick, firm thighs, and a big firm booty. Her life had changed when her mother was diagnosed with cancer. Tish was forced to leave college and take care of her. Her mother's death left her in debt and depressed, and she began drinking. Once the alcohol stopped taking away her pain, she turned to pills, and then to cocaine, and finally crack. She had only been an addict for six months and wasn't as hulled out as a lot of the other geekers. She could fix herself up and look decent. As a matter of fact, Corey had taken her to the movies across town a couple of times, like they were actually a couple. She could be cool when she wasn't smoking, Corey realized. He had even begged her at one time to stop smoking, and offered to help her. His efforts and pleas came to naught when he saw her on the corner high, trying to score more crack from a dealer that he was supplying.

"Oh! Oh! Oh, Corey!" Tish cried out in rhythm with his thrusts.

Chris J shoved his dick in her mouth again, muffling her cries. "Suck, bitch!"

Tish grabbed Chris J's dick and went to work on it again. Corey had her crying out every once in a while, but she decided to concentrate on Chris J. While Corey wouldn't whip her ass, she knew that Chris J would have no such reservations. He had slapped the shit out of her twice before.

"Take this dick!" Corey shouted. He slapped Tish on her ass, turning it bright red.

Tish glided up and down on Chris J's dick, sucking and licking alternately. She lifted one of his balls into her mouth and sucked on it, and then sucked on the other one.

"That's right," Chris J said, enjoying what she was doing. "Lick my balls, bitch!"

Tish stroked Chris J's massive tool and sucked as hard as she could.

"Got damn!" Chris cried out. "Hold on! I'm gonna cum, bitch! Hold on!"

Tish looked up at Chris.

"Get up!" Chris J ordered. "I wanna fuck this bitch before I cum."

Corey and Chris J changed positions.

"No!" Tish cried out. "No!"

"What the fuck are you talking about?" Chris J asked angrily.

"You're too big, Chris," Tish pleaded, trying to reposition herself. "Here, let me lay down. But not from the back."

"Bitch, turn around!" Chris shouted.

"No, Chris, please! I'll lay down!" Tish whimpered. She tried to lay down again, but Chris J grabbed her. "We paid you, so you gonna fuck how we tell you to fuck! So turn around and suck my boy's dick."

Tish reluctantly turned around and bent over. She nervously began to suck Corey's piece. Chris J moved in behind her and inserted himself into her. Tish tensed up.

Chris J was six feet, four inches and wore a size thirteen shoe. His dick stayed true to the big foot myth: it was just about as long as his shoe size, just a half an inch shorter at twelve and a half inches. He was a legend in the city, and females from all around vied to see if the legend was true. It was said that he caused miscarriages, internal bleeding, and had even hospitalized a girl or two. Rumor had it that he could fuck for twelve hours straight before busting a nut, and that he had the energy of the Energizer bunny, the thrust of a Titan rocket, and the explosive power of a nuclear missile. A lot of females were actually scared to talk to him once they realized who he was, but then there were those who loved a challenge.

"Chris, please . . . ," Tish pleaded.

"I ain't gon' hurt you!" Chris J shouted. He worked her gently, sliding in and out of her pussy. She closed her eyes and grunted each time he went in. She could feel every single vein in his thick meat. Despite her fear, she came within two minutes of his being inside her.

"Oh, Chris." She shuddered.

"Now you like it, huh?"

Tish focused on her breathing as Chris slid in and out of her.

"Suck my dick," Corey said, pulling her head down.

Tish began to work on Corey's shaft as best she could. Slowly, Chris J was beginning to work her, going a little deeper each stroke. She found herself gripping Corey's arms and squeezing him. Her eyes pleaded with him for understanding. Corey even felt sorry for her a little bit. He'd let Chris do his thing and then he would worry about getting his nut after he was done. He had definitely had second thoughts about picking her up while Chris was in the car with him. He thought that Chris would let him get his freak on and just play some Intellivision or Atari, but Chris had other thoughts. He wanted a piece of Tish too, and of course Corey had to let him in on it, otherwise the crew would think that he had feelings for her, which in a way he did. Even though she could never be his woman, he still didn't want the streets to dog her out real bad. A knock came at the door. It saved Tish from more of Chris's assault.

"Damn!" Chris cried out. "I was gonna bust a nut on this ho's back!"

Corey rose and went to the door while Chris and Tish hurriedly got dressed. Corey buttoned up his shorts and opened the door. It was Chino.

"What's up, kinfolk?" Corey asked.

"What are you doing?" Chino asked. "I got niggas blowing up my shit, saying that they can't get in touch with you!"

"Oh, shit!" Corey said, rubbing his face. "My pager's in my room."

Chino pushed Corey to the side and walked into the house. He found Chris J sitting on the couch laughing, while Tish was still fumbling with her buttons.

"You two muthafuckas in here tricking, instead of getting

paper!" Chino yelled. "See, y'all full of bullshit. You ain't trying to make no money!"

"Hey, Chino!" Tish said, waving.

"Hey, bitch," Chino acknowledged. He had fucked Tish
back in high school, when she was really a star. She was nothing to him now.

"Fuck you," Tish told him.

"You wish you could," Chino replied with a smile.

"I already did." Tish stuck her tongue out.

"You two niggas need to get out there and get that paper!"
Chino told Chris and Corey. "It's the fucking first of the
month." Chino turned to leave the house.

"Where you heading, kinfolk?" Corey asked.

Chino turned around. "I gotta go and meet this nigga
Malik over in the Sticks."

"The Sticks?" Chris J asked, lifting an eyebrow. "You want
me to roll with you?"

Chino waved him off. "Naw, I'll handle it. Just answer
your pagers and get that paper. I gotta get them fools up in NY
they paper."

Corey and Chino exchanged their traditional one-armed
shoulder bump. "Be careful, kinfolk," Chino advised.

Chino headed for the door, then turned back and eyed
Tish. "No, you be careful. That bitch'll have your nose wide
open. She'll have your ass up in Columbus Mall shopping and
shit."

Chris J and Corey laughed. Tish shot Chino the finger.

"I'm out!" Chino told them.

Chapter 32

Tick Tock

Chino passed out thirty keys the first day and moved six more the second day. He had four more keys to get rid of and the others, he would just have to sit back and wait for his crew to pay him the dope he fronted them. If all went well, he would more than double his weekly intake. He was at the point where he couldn't even spend money fast enough. His two safes were quickly filling to capacity.

Young Mike had moved five of the ten that he had given him and was proving everybody wrong. *That kid is a natural born hustler,* Chino thought. He could get Santa Claus to buy toys from him. The kid was cold-blooded. Young Mike was definitely doing his part, and so was Infa. Now it was his turn to step it up another level.

Chino was parked in an uptown park, meeting a new client. The cat's name was Malik. He watched as Malik parked his Delta 88 and walked over to him.

"What's up, black?" Malik asked, exchanging handshakes with Chino.

"What up, black?" Chino said, returning his greeting. He knew where Malik was coming from.

Malik had his hair in long dreadlocks and was wearing a red, black, and green patch of the African continent around his neck. He wore an olive green shirt with X-Clan on the front of it. He wore red, black, and green knit wristbands and black Dickies. He also had a red, black, and green beanie over his dreadlocks.

Chino had been briefed on what type of brother Malik was. He wore his black power T-shirt for the occasion. It was a shirt with pictures of Malcom, Martin, and Mandela on the front of it, with the words "Strong Men Keep On Coming" above the pictures.

"Love the shirt, black!" Malik told him.

"Same here, bro," Chino replied. "I love X-Clan. I bump they shit all the time."

"Yo, them, Professor X, Poor Righteous Teachers, and Afrika Bambaataa is my dudes," Malik said. "That's all I pump out my system."

"Word, word," Chino said nodding. "Got that, black?"

"Got it," Malik said, handing Chino a black shoulder bag full of money.

Chino peered inside the bag, counted the stacks, and ran his finger through each stack, making sure that each bill was in fact a C-note. When satisfied, he pulled a gym bag from the floor of his Benz and handed it to Malik, who looked inside the gym bag and then shook Chino's hand again.

"Bet! Got to fund the movement, my dude!" Malik told him. Chino and Malik gave each other dap. "Got to free Mandela, support Jonas Savimbi, and our oppressed brothers and sisters the world over."

Yeah, five kilos at a time, Chino thought. He glanced around the park. He had been there way too long. He was in another crew's territory and dealing with a third crew's customer. Malik usually scored from the Young Brothers Incorporated, or YBI for short. He said YBI had told him that their connection was dry for right now, but to hold tight.

YBI was a combination crew. They had niggas from Columbus, Dayton, Cleveland, Cincinnati, and all over Ohio. They pushed yayo all over the state, and were known as a crew of ballers and killers who didn't take no shorts. They were serious about their money and serious about their clients. That's why Chino knew that it was going to be some shit as soon as he saw some of them pull into the park in a dark blue Chrysler New Yorker.

"Damn!" Chino said.

Malik peered over his shoulder and saw the New Yorker. He ran for his Delta 88. Chino could hear someone shouting Malik's name, just before the gunfire erupted.

Chino climbed out of his Benz and fired his Beretta. He couldn't just sit and watch Malik go down like that. Besides, once they gunned down Malik, he knew that he would be next. He had to give Malik a fighting chance to get to his wheels.

Malik dove to the ground and pulled out a Sig Sauer 9 mm. He fired back at the dark blue Chrysler, leaving a trail of bullet holes on the passenger side of the vehicle. Chino added his gunfire to the shootout, and Malik was able to rise and race to his vehicle. He fell and grabbed his leg just as he made it to the driver's side door.

Chino knew that Malik was a dead man. He poured gunfire into the New Yorker.

"Get up, kid!" he shouted, praying that Malik would pull himself up and climb inside his car. "Get up!"

Chino knew that he was running low on bullets and that if he stopped to reload, Malik was dead, and he was next. Suddenly, he heard gunfire to each side of him. There were park rangers in the park today and they were firing at the New Yorker, trying to protect a wounded Malik.

The New Yorker was riddled with bullets. Both tires on the passenger side of the vehicle were flat, and all the glass on that side had been shot out. But the big worry was the driver's side, the side facing Malik. The New Yorker had crept in between Chino and Malik and was now stalled out. The park rangers raced to the vehicle and surrounded it.

"Hands!" they shouted. "Let me see your hands!"

Chino tossed his gun inside his Benz and dropped inside.

"Freeze!"

Chino looked up. A third park ranger had his weapon trained on him.

"Shit!" Chino said, kicking the floorboards of his vehicle. He slowly raised his hands into the air.

"Don't move, muthafucka!" the park ranger threatened.

It was just his luck. He had gotten caught up in another crew's territory, gotten into a shootout, and now he was being arrested by some fake-ass wannabe cops. The good thing was that he had gotten rid of his yayo. The bad thing was that he had over a hundred thousand dollars on him and Malik had five keys of pure Puerto Rican flake on him. The cops were going to put two and two together and figure out what was going on. He had a pistol case at least and had lost a hundred grand that the police were definitely going to seize as drug money. Pushing the dope for Dragos had caused him to take an unnecessary risk and get caught slipping. Now he was headed to fucking county jail. More courts, more lawyers, more judges, more bullshit. He had been involved in a shoot-out, so he could pretty much forget about bond. The gun made him a danger to society, and the money that he was dealing with made him a flight risk. No judge in the world would give him a bond.

"Damn, Pooh," he said softly, shaking his head. Just when everything was going well. The shop, the money, the new apartment—within seconds, everything fell apart.

Chino was pulled out of his Benz, thrown to the ground, and handcuffed. He watched through tear-filled eyes as more police cars pulled into the park. He was on his way to prison, and nothing was going to stop that now.

Chapter 33

Doing Time

Pam walked into the visitation booth, took a seat at the thick glass window, and waited for Chino to appear on the other side. Never in a million years had she thought that she would be making this kind of trip. She had always thought those women who spent all their free time running down to the jail to visit their men were weak bitches. Her philosophy had been that if he loved you, he would have stayed out here with you. He would have thought about the consequences of his actions and wouldn't have done what he did to get locked up. But now she was one of those bitches.

Pam looked around the visitation room. There were twenty glass booths, with a telephone in each. Each booth had a mirrored booth opposite it, for the prisoner to sit in and talk to them through another telephone. There was a steel wall with a thick glass window that separated them. There were numerous pregnant women inside booths today, several with children, some older women whom she assumed were mothers, and very few men. Was that the reason why these men were in jail in the first place? she wondered. A lack of men in their lives? No fathers to kick their asses and keep them straight. Or did they have fathers who just cut them loose after they got locked up?

She assumed that it was the former instead of the latter. Chino grew up without his parents, and the streets had raised him. It was the streets that had made him who he was, it was the streets that made him hard. This was one of the reasons why Pam was determined to go to college and graduate. She had watched the news in Detroit and seen a constant parade of young black men being carted off to jail. They were losing an entire generation of young black men to prison, and she desperately wanted to do something about it. She went to college to change her destiny, but then she met Chino and got caught up. Her idealism seemed like it was years ago. And after a while, she had thought it to be so childish and naive. But now, now she remembered. She realized who she was, why she had gone to college, and what she wanted to do. Staring around that visitation room made her realize where she had gone wrong.

My God, Chino, she said to herself. *How did we get here?*

Chino walked into the visitation room and searched for the right booth. He found Pam seated in booth number fifteen, toward the end of the row. She looked miserable, as if she had actually been crying. Her appearance made him feel as if he were two feet tall.

He had never wanted this for his Pooh. He never in a million years imagined that he would put her through something like this. When you're young and balling, you feel untouchable, invincible even. Death and prison were something foreign, circumstances for other people, never for you or the people immediately around you. He never saw Pooh as being one of those women who trekked off to jail or to a prison yard every Saturday to visit their men. His Pooh was better than that; she deserved more than that. And so now he had a major decision to make. Should he tell Pooh to go on with her life, so that she could have a better life? Or should he try to hold on to her, fight for their relationship, and hope that it survived the rigors of time, distance, stress, and loneliness? Prison was a lonely experience. It was lonely for the prisoner, and just as lonely for the loved ones left behind. He would be in there; she would be out in the free world. Guys would get at her. What would she say? What would she do? Would loneliness get the best of her? Having someone to hold, to talk to, to laugh with, to share things with was a powerful narcotic. Letters and pictures from a prison yard couldn't compete with physically being there.

Chino seated himself in the booth opposite Pam. He brought the telephone receiver to his ear so that he could talk to her.

"Hey, Pooh."

"Hey, Chino," Pam said. She tried to smile, but it came out halfhearted. "Love the outfit. Is that Gucci?"

Chino laughed. He was happy that she was trying to make him laugh. That meant that there was still something there. And whatever was there was something that they could build on. Most of all, he was relieved. Their first words since his arrest had just been spoken, and they weren't full of anger, and she didn't say that she had told him so. She was trying to uplift his spirits. It made him feel good. He held back his tears and smiled at her.

"What, you don't like my outfit?" Chino asked. "This just so happens to be Versace orange, and I even have some Versace sandals to match."

Chino raised his foot to the window so that Pam could see the clunky plastic jail sandals that he was wearing. She laughed.

"So, what's been happening?" Chino asked.

"Nothing," Pam said, shaking her head. "Just missing you."

"I miss you too, Pooh," Chino said softly. "How are things at the crib?"

Pam nodded.

"Do you have enough bread?"

Again, she nodded.

"I'll let you know where the safe is so you can get some bread anytime you need it."

"The shop is supporting everything," Pam told him.

"It's making good money?"

Pam nodded. "It's doing real good."

"That's good news." Chino paused for a moment, then spoke seriously. "Hey, Pooh, I need for you to listen up real careful. These people might be coming at you with some bullshit, and I need for you to be ready for it."

"Bullshit like what, Chino?"

"Like a conspiracy charge or something," Chino explained. "They might try to put pressure on you in order to get to me."

"Put pressure on me how?"

"Because the cars and the apartment and everything was in your name. They might come at you with a money laundering charge or something."

Pam nodded.

Chino winked at her. "If they ask, just let them know that you got the paper from your parents, and if they trip, just make sure that you hip your parents to the game."

Pam laughed. "They are going to love that. That's going to be one helluva phone call."

Chino joined in the laughter. "I can imagine that one."

A guard pulled up behind Pam and placed a pink cupcake on the counter in the booth she was sitting in. The cupcake had a single candle in it. The guard pulled out his lighter, lit the candle, and then gave Chino a quick thumbs-up before disappearing.

"What's this?" Pam asked.

"You didn't think I'd forget, did you?"

"Forget what?"

"Your birthday," Chino told her.

"Oh my God!" Pam exclaimed. "My birthday is coming up. With all of this going on, and I've been so busy with the shop that I'd completely forgot."

"I didn't forget." Chino smiled. "Happy birthday to you, happy birthday to you, happy birthday, dear Pooh, happy birthday to you!"

Pam was in tears. "Thank you, baby."

"Don't tell me my singing made you cry."

Pam broke into laughter. "No, baby. Your heart makes me cry. You are so good to me."

Chino nodded toward the cupcake. "Make a wish, and blow out the candle."

Pam closed her eyes, leaned forward, and blew out the candle.

"I wished—"

"No!" Chino said, lifting his hands. "You can't tell me what you wished for. If you do, then it won't come true."

"Come home to me, Chino."

"I will." He nodded.

"Do you love me?"

"Of course."

"Then my biggest wish has already come true."

Chapter 34

A Down Chick

Pam's weekly trips to visit Chino left her more depressed than ever. She knew that she was supposed to put on a brave face so that he could keep his spirits up. And for the most part, she did. The only problem was the leaving. She had to leave him in that terrible place and come home alone. Sure, Young Mike was in and out, and she had the beauty shop to run, and Erik, her buddy from college, was always available to hang out with, but still, she missed Chino. There was nothing like eating dinner with your man, or snuggling up under the covers with him, or just having him around to talk to. She missed laughing all the time, she missed being called Pooh, and she missed seeing the smile on Chino's face. She could close her eyes and see his waves, his dimples, and his pearly whites.

Her sadness was growing exponentially by the day. Soon it would pass over that mystical demarcation line that separated sadness from depression, and she would fall into a despair that she wouldn't be able to shake. The house was growing quieter with each passing day. The walls were growing whiter, her food was tasting blander, and her days were beginning to run together. She had to get out of the house; she desperately needed a change of scenery. It was for these reasons that she had agreed to let her friend Erik get her out of the house and take her to see a movie. Some movie with Patrick Swayze was playing. It was an action movie, but it would take her mind off her troubled life. Seeing other people in a world of trouble made her troubles seem less abundant.

Erik always made Pam laugh. He got her through some of her toughest days, waiting for Chino to come home. She considered Erik a true friend. He was someone she could talk to, someone she could relate to, particularly as there existed a side to Erik that few others on campus knew about. Erik was also a baller.

Because Erik was in the game, she could confide things in him that she couldn't to anyone else that she knew. And with Chino being her man, Erik knew that he could talk to her about things that he couldn't talk to anyone else about. They understood each other. They understood the stresses and pressures of the game, and its toll on relationships. Erik reminded her so much of Chino.

Erik knew that Chino had gotten knocked, and he knew what Pam was going through. She was his friend, and he wanted to be there for her. So he stepped to her and arranged to get her out of the house to take her mind off things.

Pam and Erik walked across campus toward BW3's. She was frustrated about Chino's incarceration, about her mother, about life in general.

"Why you letting this bullshit stress you out, Pam?" Erik asked. "You too good to be going through this bullshit. Why you stressing and waiting on a nigga who ain't gonna be faithful to you in the end no way?"

"How do you figure that?"

"Because that nigga is a known player around town. He known for banging broads, and you not just some broad. You need to be my woman, Pam."

"Your woman? And how will things be different?"

"'Cause I'm a good man. I'm in school. I'm getting my paper so that when I graduate, I'm gonna open my own business. Together, we can write our own ticket. Two young black college graduates with paper. We can have it our way."

"This ain't Burger King!" Pam laughed.

"You know what I'm saying. Together, we are the perfect couple. You have your beauty shop, plus your education. I'ma have my businesses and my degree too. Pam, we can be living large together."

"You forgot one thing."

"What's that?"

"That I love Chino."

"Why? That nigga is in jail, and on his way to prison. Pam, face it, he got caught with all of that dough, and that nigga Malik got caught with all of that yayo. You don't think the cops put that shit together? Plus, that fool was in a shootout in the Sticks. Man, he's hit. He's going away for a while."

Pam started crying. "Don't say that. You supposed to be making me feel better."

"I don't just want to make you feel better; I want to make things better for real. Pam, he's gone. Just accept that. I can make you happy. I know that I can."

"I'm happy now . . . with Chino."

Erik pulled her close and wrapped his arms around her. "Look at us. See how we are together? We fit like hand and glove. No arguing; we both want the same things in life. Chino doesn't want anything in life but the street life. What are his prospects for the future, Pam? Is he just going to sell dope for the rest of his life? And by that, I mean once he finally gets out of jail."

"Erik, why are you saying these things?" Pam sniffled. "I thought that you were my friend. I thought that I could come to you. I thought that out of all people, you would understand!"

"You can come to me, and I do understand. I am your friend, and that's why I can't lie to you. If that's what you want, then you've come to the wrong place. I can't lie to you. I care about you too much. Fact of the matter is, Chino is going away; you're gonna be out here all alone." Pam wiped a tear away from her cheek. "I'll be here for you if you let me," Erik continued. "Do you want me to be here for you, Pam?"

She nodded. "Of course. You're my friend."

"Then I'll be here for you. You don't have to go through this alone. You don't owe Chino anything . . . absolutely nothing. He knew what the nature of the game was when he chose it. You can get locked up and killed anytime. He knew the risk, and that was his sacrifice, not yours. You don't have to sacrifice or be alone."

Erik was getting to her. Pam felt like she needed to get away from him.

"I want to be there to hold you at night," Erik continued. "I want to be there when you need someone to talk to. I want to laugh with you, whisper in your ear, and tell jokes to you.

We can grow old together, Pam. We can raise a family, and we can have everything that our hearts desire. We can have a vacation home in Sag Harbor and another home down south for the winter. We can have it all, baby. I can move you out of Chino's apartment and get you one of your own. Or you can move in with me."

Pam pulled away from Erik. "I love Chino. He's my man. What kind of woman would I be if I left him when he really needed me?"

"Sometimes you have to cut your losses."

"Sometimes you have to stand up and be strong for your man," Pam countered. "Would you really want a woman that cut and ran at the first sign of trouble? Or would you want a woman that you knew was down through thick and thin?"

Erik nodded and listened, but he couldn't care less about agreeing.

Erik was definitely a catch, but he was a catch for someone else. She loved her Chino and would do anything for him. If she had to ride with him for a million years, she would do it. Chino was hers forever. He was her life.

Pam and Erik made it to the movies and Erik opened the door for her. "After you."

"Thank you," Pam told him. She stopped him before they went inside. "Erik, I just want to clear something up."

"What's that?"

"I love Chino. I love him with all my heart, and I really like you as a friend. I don't want my friendship with you to become a problem. My heart belongs to Chino. Can you accept that and still be a true friend?"

Erik nodded. "Pam, I don't have no choice but to accept

it. I'll be there for you, but I want you to know that I'm feeling you. I want to give you a better life. I don't want you to suffer."

"I won't," Pam told him. "I'm tough."

"After this, let's hit a restaurant."

"A restaurant?"

Erik nodded. "Just to get your mind off of things."

"That'll be cool."

"Then it's a done deal. As a matter of fact, we can make Thursdays our official get-out-of-the-house night."

Pam smiled. "I can work with that."

"I'll even pay for everything."

"You better," Pam told him. "You're the big baller."

Erik put his finger to his lips, silencing her. "You trying to get me a case, girl?"

Pam laughed. She was going to have fun being friends with Erik, now that the ground rules had been established. She was Chino's woman, and Erik was just her friend. And that was that.

Chapter 35

Eyes Wide Shut

"Two tickets, please," Erik told the ticket girl. He pulled out a wad of cash and paid for the movie. "I heard that this movie was pretty good."

"I always like C. Thomas Howell, and Patrick Swayze," Pam admitted.

"Oh, you like them young white boys, huh?" Erik asked with a smile.

"I admit it. I like Anthony Michael Hall, Judd Nelson, River Phoenix, Molly Ringwald, Sean Penn, Emilio Estevez, and Demi Moore."

"The whole little Hollywood brat pack," Erik said, nodding. "I got it, you're really a white girl in black skin."

"Uh, just because I'm open to all kinds of movies and cultural experiences don't mean that I'm a white girl. You're closed-minded for someone in college. What are you in school for?"

"I'm just teasing you, girl."

"I like *Breakin'* and *Krush Groove* too." Pam smiled.

"I like *Beat Street* myself."

"Why, can you bust a move?" Pam asked.

"Girl, you didn't know?" Erik began waving his arms.

"Boy, you're silly!" Pam laughed. Erik was taking her mind off her troubles. She hadn't laughed since Chino had been locked up. It felt good to laugh and kid around again.

"Don't have me go and get the cardboard out of the trunk and bust out my funky fresh windmill, girl!"

"You do, you'll be here by your damn self!" Pam laughed. Her laughter reminded her of Chino, and so did Erik's silliness. Her thoughts of Chino suddenly made her go silent. Erik sensed the change.

"So, what's really going on, Pam?" Erik asked.

"What do you mean?"

"How are you holding up?"

Pam exhaled. "I'm doing as well as can be expected. My man is heading to prison for God knows how long. The beauty shop is a madhouse, and I just don't know what I'm going to do without Chino around to help me."

"Everything is going to be all right," Erik told her. "Plus, I'll do anything that I can to help you."

"I appreciate that, Erik, but the main thing that I need is for Chino to get out. I miss him so much."

"You just keep those prayers going up to the Man up above and everything will be all right."

"I hope so," Pam said. "I wish I had your confidence."

"You got my shoulder to lean on anytime," Erik told her. "Anytime you need to talk, anytime you need anything, you call me."

Pam nodded. "I appreciate that, Erik."

The two of them found the theater, walked inside, and found a pair of seats in the center. Pam was so focused on her thoughts that she hadn't noticed anyone else inside the theater.

Chris J held his hand up and silenced his date. "Hold on."

"What?" she asked.

Chris J squinted and focused his eyes to make sure that he was seeing what he was seeing. He was sure that it was Pam in the theater, and she was there with another cat.

"That's fucked up!" Chris J declared.

"What?" his date asked.

"My man just got locked up, and his girl is already stepping out on him. Man, that shit is fucked up. Scandalous-ass hoes, I tell you."

"Don't jump to conclusions, Chris."

"What do you mean, don't jump to conclusions? I got eyes, I know who she is. She's right there, in the middle of the damn theater, cheesing all up in another nigga's face while my homeboy is in jail for giving her the good life. Yo, it's fucked up for real!"

"I wouldn't do you like that," she declared, trying to win brownie points.

"Yo, what is your name again?" Chris J asked, annoyed.

"What? Nigga, don't play with me!"

Chris J waved his hand, dismissing her. He had more important things to think about. Like how he was going to break the news to his man that he had seen his broad dippin'. Damn, he hated to be the bearer of bad news, but his man had to know what he was dealing with. If he were in jail, and his main broad was dippin', he would damn sure want to know.

"Damn," Chris said, shaking his head. "I would have never thought she would break bad on my dude."

"It's always the ones you least expect," his date said, agreeing with him.

"Damn, I got to go see my man and give him the news," Chris J said sadly. "I know he got a lot on his plate already, but he gots to know. I don't want him coming home to no fake bitch or taking care of one while he's locked away. Sorry bitch!"

Chapter 36

Consequences

Pam walked into the visitation room to see Chino. This time he was already seated and waiting for her. Visitation had been crowded, and she had to wait in the lobby for a booth to become free. Chino had to wait in the rear lobby with the other prisoners for a booth to become free also. Both had had their patience tested today, and neither was in a very good mood.

"What's up, baby?" Pam said, exhaling, finally settling down to talk to him.

"You tell me," Chino said.

"Nothing, just missing you."

"Oh, you missing me?" Chino asked, raising his eyebrow.

"Yeah, of course."

"I can't tell," Chino told her.

"What do you mean?"

"You stepping out, going to the movies and shit!"

"Chino!"

"Chino my ass!" he said, pounding the counter in the booth. "What? Did you think that I wasn't gonna find out?"

"Find out what?"

"Find out that you creeping with some nigga!"

"Creeping?" Pam said exasperated. "I wasn't creeping with anybody!"

"I can tell! You bold with your shit. You all out in public at the movies with the nigga!"

"Chino! It wasn't even like that!"

"What's it like then, Pam? You fucking tell me!"

"I just went out with a friend."

"A friend, huh?"

"Yes, he's a friend, that's all!"

"What's this nigga's name?"

"Erik. His name is Erik."

"And where did you meet this nigga?"

"At school," Pam said softly.

"At school! So you *been* knowing this nigga! You probably been fucking with this nigga even before I got locked up! Man, this is some fucked-up bullshit!"

"Chino, I haven't been fucking with Erik, and I'm not fucking with him now! He's just a friend."

"A friend? How come I haven't heard of this friend before? How come this friend didn't pop up until I got up in here?"

"Because he wasn't important, Chino. He was just a guy at the same college, who I had some classes with. We became friends. That's it, nothing more!"

"So, you and this fool have classes together and shit. And now that I'm locked down, you two stepping out together and shit."

"Chino, we ain't stepping out. I just needed to get out of the house, and he was somebody to talk to."

"You can get out of the house with Tomiko! And what the fuck you mean, he was somebody to talk to? You know this nigga like that? You trust him? You confide in him? You two are that muthafucking close?"

Pam exhaled and lowered her head into her hand. She was growing more frustrated and flustered by the moment. "Chino, will you listen to me?"

"I'm listening! I'm listening to you tell me how you have a nigga at school that you can talk to and confide in and shit."

"Chino, all I talk about is you! How I miss you, how I want you to come home, how I love you. That's all I talk about!"

"You can tell that to me. How you gonna go out on a date with another nigga? Damn, Pooh, at least let my side of the bed get cold! That's fucked up!"

"I ain't fucking him!"

"That's what you telling me. Obviously, the nigga means something to you. Who is this mark-ass nigga?"

"I told you. His name is Erik."

"Who the fuck is Erik? Where this nigga from?"

"He's from New York."

"New York? You fucking with a New York nigga?"

"I ain't fucking with him."

"You know we got major beef with them niggas, and you fucking with one of them? Have you lost your muthafucking mind!"

"For the last time, I ain't fucking with him! He's just a friend. He understands what I'm going through."

"What the fuck you mean he understands what you're

going through? How the fuck he understand what you're going through?"

"'Cause he knows about this type of stuff."

"About what type of stuff?"

"About jail, and catching case, and stuff like that."

"What, is the nigga in law school or something?"

Pam shook her head. "No, he be hustling."

"He's a dope boy? A fucking New York dope boy! Bitch, you're fucking insane! You fucking a New York dope boy behind my back. You sleeping with the fucking enemy? I can't believe this shit!"

"I'm not sleeping with anybody, Chino!"

"I thought I could trust you, Pooh! I thought that you were different! But you turned out to be just like all the rest! You a skank just like all these other hoes running around here!"

"Chino, don't say that!" Pam said, crying.

"You a ho! A funky-ass slut!"

"Chino, you don't mean that!"

"The fuck I don't!"

"I haven't done anything. I would never cheat on you! I love you too much to do anything."

"And to think that I was going to marry you?" Chino said, shaking his head. "I would have been setting myself up. You probably would have helped them niggas jack me."

Pam was crying and shaking her head. "Chino, don't say that! I would never hurt you or allow anyone else to hurt you! I love you!"

"Get the fuck outta my face!"

"Chino!"

"I don't want to ever see you again, Pooh! I hate you!

You're a fucking slut, a ho, and a skank-ass bitch! Don't ever come in my face again!"

Pam rose from the seat inside the booth and ran out of the visitation room in tears. She was beyond hurt. She loved Chino with all her heart. All she had wanted to do was get out of the house for a little while, and now that decision would cost her the love of her life. It was too much for her to bear. If God took her Chino away, then he might as well have ended her life right then and there. She couldn't live without him.

Chapter 37

Betrayal

Pam burst into tears once again. She was in her and Chino's condo, sitting at the kitchen table. It was the dead of winter, and she had already been home from Christmas in Detroit for a couple of weeks now. Her family had begged her to move back home, but Pam refused.

She couldn't count the number of times that she had burst into tears, replaying her and Chino's last conversation. He hated her, all because of a stupid yet innocent little trip to the movies. And now here she was, desperately in need of someone to talk to, someone who would understand, and she couldn't talk to anyone. She damn sure couldn't talk to Erik. The last thing she needed was for someone to spot her talking to him again. Chino would probably break out of jail and kill her. So now she was stuck having to carry this burden alone. In fact, it was an even bigger burden now, because her man hated her. She was lost and felt like a rowboat adrift in an enormous sea.

"Pam, what exactly did he say to you?" Young Mike asked.

"I told you!" Pam snapped, through her sniffling. "He hates me now!"

Young Mike closed his GED book. "Look, you just have to look past all of that bullshit that my man was talking. You got to understand what he's going through. He's in there alone, missing you, without any of his family or partners; he's fighting a case and just trying to survive. You got to be strong, and you can't give up."

"He doesn't ever want to see me again!" Pam said.

"He didn't mean that." Pam looked at him with hope in her eyes. "Look, there's a lot of history between us and them New York cats. There's a long beef since back in the day. You gotta understand that. You not from here. You stepping out with a New York cat is like a Phillies cat wearing a Pirates jersey. Or a like the Celtics and the Lakers kicking it together. It's straight up bullshit. Granted, you didn't know that, but still."

"I wasn't stepping out," Pam said. "I just needed someone to talk to."

"Hey, no offense taken," Young Mike said sarcastically and shrugged his shoulders. "I do live here with you. I ain't been to college and I know I'm not the sharpest pencil in the box, but damn, ma!"

Pam laughed. "No, it's not that. You got to understand, you're never here. Especially when I need you. Erik is a friend from school. I ran into him at a vulnerable moment and broke down. It wasn't about me and Erik, it never was. It was always about my Chino, and me missing him."

"That may be so, but you got to look at it from my man's point of view. He's locked up, and all of a sudden this new cat appears out of nowhere. And you stepping out with the dude and telling my man that he's a friend from school, someone you never brought up before, and on top of that, you tell my man that he's in the game? Damn, that was twisted, ma!"

"I didn't mean it like that! Erik is just a friend!"

"That's how it always starts and that's what they all say. He's just a friend. And when you in jail, all you have is time to think and your mind be thinking some crazy shit. He's wondering every second what the fuck you doing and who you're doing it with."

"I'm not doing anything!"

"You know that, and I know that, but he doesn't know that!"

"He should! Chino should know by now that I would never cheat on him!"

"He knows, but prison is a fucked-up place. He's seeing these other niggas' women breaking left, and he's hearing these stories about how they are stepping out, and that's fucking with his head. His mind is playing tricks on him right now. The last thing he needs is to hear about another nigga."

Pam shook her head. She understood Young Mike's point. "I wasn't trying to hurt him."

"That's usually when it happens. The road to hell is paved with good intentions, ma."

Pam smiled. "You sure you're not the sharpest pencil in the box?"

Young Mike held up his GED book.

"That tells me that you're pretty damn smart," Pam told him.

"Why do you say that?"

"Because you're sitting here studying for your GED and trying to better yourself. A lot of guys your age wouldn't be thinking about getting their education. They'd be in the streets right now. I'm proud of you."

"Thanks, ma. And just so you know, I got your back. I'll let my man know what kind of woman he's got in his corner when he gets out."

"I wish you could let him know right now. I miss him so much."

"I'll write that fool a letter or something."

"Thank you!" Pam told him. She stood and hugged Young Mike tightly.

"Don't give up on him."

"I won't."

"Don't let that fool push you away. Right now he doesn't know whether to shit or go shopping. He's fighting his case, he's worried about you, and he's got a lot of other shit on his mind. By pushing you away, he's trying to get rid of one of his worries, but don't let him do it."

Pam stared off into space and nodded. "You're right. I'm going to fight for what we have."

"You two big heads belong together. Trust me. I knew my man since way before you came, and I see how my man is after you came. He's better because of you."

Pam kissed Young Mike on his cheek. "Thank you for saying that."

"Just telling the truth," Young Mike told her. He opened up his GED book again.

"What are you studying?" Pam asked.

"Just the basics. I got two more tests and I'm done."

"That's great! I am really proud of you. I can't believe that you actually did this."

"I had to do something. I didn't want to be in the streets my whole life. With my GED and the money I make hustling and boosting and fencing, I think that I might go to college."

"Are you serious?" Pam asked excitedly.

Young Mike nodded. "Maybe junior college at first, and then maybe transfer to a big college."

"That's great," Pam told him. "What do you want to major in?"

Young Mike leaned back and his eyes darted around the apartment.

"There's no one here but us," Pam said.

"I know. But promise me something."

"What?"

"Promise me that you won't tell anybody that I want to go to college. And promise me that you won't tell anybody what I want to major in."

Pam held up her right hand. "You have my word."

"I want to major in nursing."

"Nursing?"

"Kinda crazy for a dude to want to be a nurse, right?"

Pam shook her head. "No. But what made you decide on nursing?"

"My aunt is a nurse. She used to tell me how bad the hospitals need male nurses. And my counselor at GED class tells me that nurses are in demand and that they make a grip. He also said that I could go back to school and become a physician's assistant. He said that it was something like being a doctor."

"It is. Why not just go ahead and become a doctor?"

Young Mike nodded and winked at her. "One step at a time, right."

Pam smiled. She knew what he meant. He really wanted to be a doctor but was afraid to come out and say it. He told people something much lower than what he was shooting for, to keep people from laughing and telling him that he couldn't do it. His dreams would be their secret.

"One step at a time, Mike." Pam nodded. "But remember, you can do anything you put your mind to. And I just want to say this. You say that you're not the sharpest pencil in the box, but you're a pretty damn sharp one. I love you, baby boy."

Chapter 38

Keeping Secrets

Pam hesitated to see Chino. Walking away was definitely not an option. She had come to love her gangster husband. He was her Clyde, and she was his Bonnie. There was no more Chino without Pam, and no more Pam without Chino. She had to go to that place and make him see that. She had to make him understand. They could no more go their own separate ways than a right leg could walk away from the left one. They were one now. One body, one soul, one spirit. Their hearts shared the same rhythm. She could feel his pain, and she knew when he needed her. He needed her now. Especially now, more than ever. She would go to him.

"What are you doing here?" Chino snapped.

"I'm not going anywhere, Christonos," Pam replied. "You can say what you want to say, you can curse me out, but I'm not going anywhere. I love you, and I would never do anything to hurt you. And I'm going to fight to the death for what we have."

Chino exhaled and looked down.

"I know that you're going through hell in here," Pam continued. "I can't say that I know exactly what it's like, but I know that it's rough on you. I know that you have a lot on your plate, and this is where I come in. A real woman doesn't walk away and leave when the chips are down. A real woman stands by her man, and she fights with him. I don't know what kind of woman these other niggas in there have, but I'm not them. We're not them. Nobody knows what we've been through, and we can't put ourselves in somebody else's shoes, and nobody can walk in our shoes. This is our relationship, Chino. Only we can decide what's best for us. Only we know us. Nobody can tell me anything about my man, and nobody can tell you anything about your woman. You know me, and I know you. Let's fight through this thing."

Chino nodded. "Who is this nigga that you was with?"

"Chino, I told you. He's just a guy that I had classes with at school. I just wanted to get out of the house. I talk about you twenty-four seven, Chino. That's all anyone around me hears about. How much I love you."

"You got feelings for this nigga, Pooh?"

Pam shook her head. "No, not like that! Not at all. He's a guy from school, Chino, that's it. I love you. No one can take your place!"

"Tell me the truth, Pooh, have you did anything with this dude?"

Pam held up her right hand. "I swear to you, Chino. I have never done anything with Erik. I have never even thought of doing anything with Erik. You are my heart, Christonos. I could no more betray you than I could cut out my own heart."

Chino shook his head. "Man, are you still going to be going out with this nigga?"

Pam shook her head. "No. I realize now that it looked bad and I don't want to put you through anything more than what you're already dealing with."

"And you're going to see this cat on campus?"

"Chino, I'll switch my schedule around if that's what it takes. I'll drop the class that we have together. Whatever it takes to make you believe me. I'll do whatever it takes to make you happy, baby."

Chino nodded. "I didn't mean those things that I said to you, Pooh."

She raised her hand, silencing him. "I know, Chino. I don't want to talk about that. I know that you were just hurt and lashing out. Let's just move on from here, baby."

Chino nodded.

"Have you talked to the lawyer?" Pam asked.

Again he nodded. "I talked to that fool yesterday. I'm thinking about firing his ass. He only come down here when it's time to ask for some more money."

"You want me to look in the phone book for another lawyer?"

"Yeah. This big-time cat in here got this big-time Jew lawyer. He's supposed to be the best in Ohio. I got to get his name again. I'll call you when I get it, and I want you to call him and see what he'll charge to fight my case."

"I'll take care of that," Pam reassured him.

"This cat I got now is telling me that we are going to have a motion to suppress hearing. He says that's where the state has to present all of their evidence to the judge, who is going to rule on what evidence they can bring to trial. He says that we might be able to get the money suppressed, because the park rangers didn't have a search warrant and so they shouldn't have searched my car. He said that the state is going to say that they could, because of the shootout, and because they found the drugs on Malik. But that's bullshit, because old boy that searched my car wasn't nowhere near those other cats when they finally searched Malik. Those were two different searches and two different groups of police cats."

"So, you think you are going to beat it?"

"Well, not the pistol case. It was self-defense on the shooting, so they aren't charging me for assault with a deadly weapon. My lawyer was thinking that they were at first, just to try to throw a bunch of shit at me, so I can get scared and plead out. But right now he thinks that the only thing that they have is an unlawful carrying case."

"But the gun was legal, wasn't it?" Pam asked.

"The gun wasn't stolen or anything, so that part is straight. It's just that I didn't have a license to carry a weapon. And if I say that I was transporting it, then they are going to testify that I didn't go into my trunk to get anything out. You can transport a weapon, but the gun has to be inaccessible to the clip. One has to be in the glove box, and the other in the trunk, or something like that. They gon' say that there is no way I had time to pull a clip out of the glove compartment and then the gun out of the trunk, while being shot at."

"There's got to be something the lawyer can do."

"We're fighting it, Pooh. I'm in the law library every day, trying to fight this shit. I might have to plead out to the unlawful carrying and roll with that."

"What does that mean? You have to go to prison?"

"Just for a short time. Maybe go and get a number and do a

turnaround. That shit is like a five-year bid at the most, so I can't see me doing nothing but going through diagnostics and getting a number."

"No!" Pam said, shaking her head. "No, Chino! You can't go to prison! I can't do this without you. I need you out here with me. You find a way to beat it. You find something!"

"Baby, I'm looking! Trust me, I don't want to go. I'm just keeping it real with you. Would you rather me lie to you?"

Pam shook her head. "No."

"You just keep strong on your end, and keep it tight. You can wait for me, can't you?"

Pam nodded. "Yeah, of course."

"You promise? Promise me that you'll wait for me, and that there won't be no bullshit in the game."

"I promise you, Chino."

Chapter 39

Numbers

The state prison was an entirely different world. It was a place with its own codes, its own rules, its own laws and condition. It was a world unto itself. It was a place where the slightest sign of disrespect, whether real or imagined, could cost a person his life.

The rules were that you took nothing, and you expected nothing in return. It was a place where all a man had was his word, and he didn't break that word for shit. His word was his bond.

Another unwritten rule in prison was that you stuck with your own. Prison was divided not only along racial lines—blacks stuck with blacks, and whites with whites—but along geographical lines. Columbus stuck with Columbus, Cleveland with Cleveland, Dayton with Dayton, and Cincinnati with Cincinnati. You stuck with your city, and you represented your city. All the hoods and crews within the city came together and got down for one another. There were no hoods in the state joint, just cities and towns.

"What up, family?" Pee Wee said, greeting Chino and some other Columbus cats. "What it do?"

Chino and Pee Wee exchanged handshakes. "It do what it do, baby!"

"Little Chino, we balling tonight?" Pee Wee asked.

"Hell yeah!" Chino told him.

Pee Wee was a habitual. He had been in and out of the joint his entire life. He caught his first beef killing his stepfather in his sleep after he had beat his mother. The juvenile prosecutor had it in for Pee Wee and made sure that he did time for the murder. He'd never been out of prison for more than two years since that first conviction.

Pee Wee was prison built. He was six foot four, two hundred and eighty pounds of muscle. He looked as if he were a bodybuilder, straight off the cover of *MuscleMag*. His bald head and the hoop ring in his nose made him look like an evil bull. The jail guards avoided him and so did everyone else. He had killed more than three men with his bare hands. He was a trustee within the system, so he was allowed to reside in lower-security prisons.

Little Dice, another Columbus resident, put his arm around Chino. "Pee Wee ass can't ball! This nigga is just going to go up to the rec yard and jack rec. Old brick-shooting ass nigga!"

The Columbus boys broke into laughter.

"Who we playing tonight?" Chino asked.

"We got them Dayton boys tonight," Little Dice told him, "and if we win tonight, we play Cincinnati for the championship."

Chino high-fived Black, Pee Wee, and Little Dice.

Black was another prison-built cat that looked like he could be on the cover of *Muscle and Fitness*. He was doing a stretch for armed robbery. The fool had robbed a jewelry store and got caught when the automatic door closed and locked. The jewelry store workers locked themselves in the rear of the store and simply waited for the police to arrive. Black was showcased on the news as one of America's stupidest criminals. The fellas on the yard teased him about it all the time.

Little Dice was a street hustler that was down for yayo. He had gotten caught up with five keys and a trunk filled with weapons. The state gave him thirty and the feds gave him five on top of that. So when he left the state, he would have to go and see the feds. It was fucked up that they ran his time consecutive instead of concurrent. He swore that his lawyer sold him out and copped a deal with the feds so that one of his rich white clients could go free. It was the system, Little Dice often claimed. It was stacked against black folks and designed so that the white man would always win.

Chino and his Columbus partners made their way through the long, winding chow line toward the serving bar, where other prisoners would slop the day's meal onto their trays.

"I guess this shit is supposed to be spaghetti," Little Dice told them.

"Spaghetti surprise," Black added. "I know this ain't supposed to be hamburger meat."

"It looks like ground-up hot dogs," Chino said, staring at the slop.

"Y'all don't want it, pass it to old Pee Wee," he told them.

"Aw, nigga, your big hungry ass will eat anything!" Little Dice told him.

"You can have this shit," Black told Pee Wee. "You got some chips and a candy bar in your locker? Shit, a nigga gotta eat something."

"All right," Pee Wee said smiling. "I'll give you a candy bar, but you know what that means?"

"Aw, fuck you, nigga!" Black told him.

The rest of the fellas broke into laughter.

"Them candy bars is bait so I can trap my girls," Pee Wee told him, laughing while grabbing his dick.

"Fuck you, you Darth Vader head muthafucker!" Black shouted.

The crew was so busy laughing that none of them paid any attention to a Dayton cat creeping from around the serving bar. When Chino got to the corner of the bar and turned to get his drink, the Dayton cat stepped from around the metal serving station with a twelve-inch shank. Chino saw him just in time and jumped out of the way, while dashing his drink in the attacker's eyes. The blade caught Pee Wee in his side.

"YBI, muthafucka!" the attacker shouted. "Get yo hand outta our pocket, nigga!"

Pee Wee fell back, Black caught him and lowered him to the ground.

Chino swung his tray at the attacker, striking him in his nose. Blood splattered everywhere. The attacker charged at Chino full steam.

Chino swung his tray again, striking the attacking YBI member in his throat, but the attacker's forward motion sent the knife plunging into Chino's left forearm.

"Got dammit!" Chino screamed.

The attacker yanked his knife out and turned, grabbing

his throat. He was coughing severely. Chino grabbed his bloody forearm. Little Dice shoved Chino out of the way and kicked the attacker in his ass, sending him flying into another serving bar headfirst.

A crowd started to gather.

"Dayton!" somebody shouted. All of Dayton's prisoners raced to the front where the action was.

Columbus cats recognized Chino and Little Dice and muscled their way to the front. Dayton and Columbus stood opposite one another about to square off.

"What the fuck's happening here?" the Dayton shot-caller asked.

"This nigga shouted YBI and tried to stick my nigga!" Little Dice shouted.

"He stuck Pee Wee!" Black said to the Columbus boys.

The Columbus shot-caller looked at the Dayton shot caller. "Your boy representing YBI came at my dudes."

The Dayton shot-caller turned to his people. "Ain't no city thing." He nodded toward the attacker. "Mop his ass up for starting shit. I done told his ass. He either gonna roll with Dayton or not at all. Ain't no fucking cliques in here!"

A shot rang out.

"Everybody on the floor!" a guard holding a shotgun shouted. "Grab some dirt, cocksuckers!" He fired into the air again. Soon he was joined by other guards on the tier with M-16 rifles, while even more guards with long batons strolled into the cafeteria. The prisoners all hit the floor.

Lying on the floor, Chino shook his head. That shit was still following him. YBI must have put a hit out on him. Two of them cats in the New Yorker had gotten killed that day in the park, and they must be blaming it on him. But most of all, they were really mad about him doing business in their territory. Old boy shouted for him to get his hand out of their pocket, not that this was for his homeboys. This told him one really important thing—YBI was after his ass, and he would have to deal with them for the foreseeable future. Getting out of Columbus was now a priority. Getting out of prison and getting back to Pooh was a must. They would go after her too, just to get to him. They had no fucking morals or scruples. They were just cold-blooded dope boys and killers. And now they would have to send a message.

Chino glared across the room and watched as his attacker spit blood out of his mouth and continued coughing nonstop. Chino had hit him in the throat as hard as he could with the sharp edge of the tray. The guards were frantically working on him.

"Die, muthafucker, die!" Chino said under his breath. It would be one less muthafucka he would have to worry about.

Chapter 40

They Can't Hold Me

"Whose is it?" Chino asked, going pound for pound inside his Pooh. As much as he wanted to be gentle and make love, he couldn't help but explode and join the ranks of rumored minute men. Pam lay on her side thinking how fast he came, but she excused it because she was so happy to be back in the arms of the love of her life. Chino had come home after fifteen months under a first-time offender early release program.

Pam began to move from underneath the sheets when a hand grasped her firmly on her right ass cheek.

"Where you going?"

"I'm going to wash up," Pam explained.

"Nah, we not finished yet." Chino went at it again, and although he lasted several minutes longer, he still was only getting over the frustration of blue balls and Vaseline from his time in the joint. As Pam lay there, Chino ran inside the bathroom, relieved himself, and was back on top of her before Pam knew it. Pam could barely move. She too had been celibate for the last fifteen months, and with Chino ramming himself inside her like there was no tomorrow, her insides became dry and raw, but she couldn't quit now. Her only thoughts were of pleasing her man.

Pam pushed Chino back onto the bed and mounted him, pushing her legs alongside his body and pressing down, riding his member as deep as she could take it. Sweat began to roll down her back, as beads of sweat sat atop his top lip. Their rhythm, their lust, and the fifteen months apart got the best of both of them and they began to grope at each other.

"Uh . . . Uh . . ." Chino groaned.

"I love you, baby," Pam whispered.

"Whose is it?" Chino asked gripping her waist.

"Yours."

"Whose?"

"Yours!" Pam screeched repeatedly, bringing them both to a climax.

—

Chino pulled up to the hood park and climbed out of his new whip. As soon as he had touched ground in the free world, he had gone and copped himself a new Toyota Land Cruiser. This one was considered a big boy whip as well, but the color on this ride was ice blue with snow white leather interior, ice blue piping, and chrome AMG rims. He hadn't had a chance to take the SUV to the stereo shop and get a system put in it yet, but that was next on the agenda. He had other things to do first. He still needed to contact Dragos and pay him off, as well as pick up all the money that he had in the streets. Most of it from his crew.

"Chino! My nigga!" Rock shouted, rushing over to him.

"When did you get out, my dude?" Chris J asked.

"My nigga, my nigga!" Infa said.

"What up, kinfolk?" Corey shouted.

"Chino! Big baller!" Ant shouted.

They all embraced him one by one.

"Man, why didn't you let us know you was getting out?" Rock asked.

"I wanted to surprise everybody," Chino said. "Besides, I didn't want them YBI niggas to know that I was getting out. I need time to get my feet on the ground first."

"Man, fuck them hoes!" Chris J declared. "We got ya back, kinfolk. Them fools wanna trip, we can trip too!"

"I got me a brand-new AKM just for the occasion," Rock said.

"And I got me a tec-9 that I've been dying to try out," Infa told him.

"Yeah? Them niggas tried to get at me while I was in the joint," Chino told them.

"Bullshit!" Rock exclaimed. "Are you serious?"

"Serious as a heart attack. Them fools sent a nigga to dance," Chino said. "I busted his shit wide open. Fucked up his throat. They had to put a tracheotomy in that nigga's neck."

"Damn, kinfolk!" Corey said. "You put in work like that?"

"Hell yeah! I fucked that nigga up!" Chino bragged.

"Man, we gonna have to split them niggas' wigs and them GI Boys' wigs," Ant declared. The GI Boys were the Gary Indiana Boys. They were one of the out-of-town crews that had migrated into Columbus and set up shop. They were one of the most violent drug crews in Columbus—wild, take-no-shorts niggas. Their first and last reaction was to shoot and then ask questions later.

"What are we into it with them niggas for?" Chino asked.

"They tripped with Infa at the club," Ant told him. "And they jacked Joe Bub Baby last week. Caught him slipping at a 7-Eleven."

"Man, fuck Joe Baby!" Chino declared. "I ain't worried about his fat ass. They should have shot his bitch ass."

"That fool was asking about you the other day," Rock told him.

"Man, tell that nigga to keep my name outta his mouth!" Chino said. "So what them GI Boys tripping with you about?"

"Over a bald-headed bitch." Infa shrugged. "Man, fuck them niggas!"

"Man, how yo pockets doing?" Rock asked.

"I'm straight," Chino said. "I just need to get everybody's paper."

"You got that," Chris J replied.

"As soon as I get to the crib, you can get it," Rock told him.

"Same here, kinfolk," Corey said.

"I got you too, kinfolk," Ant declared.

"I got you." Infa nodded.

"Bet." Chino nodded.

"Man, you heard about Young Mike?" Rock asked.

Chino shook his head. "What's up?"

"Man, that youngster is doing bad."

"His mind is fucked up, kinfolk," Corey added.

"He flipped out," Chris J told him. "Got problems."

"Man, dude be walking around the hood talking to himself and shit," Infa said.

"What the fuck happened?" Chino asked, concerned. When he went down, Young Mike was still staying at the crib with Pam, and she had never said a word.

"Man, while you were gone, he caught a bid," Rock explained. "His girl broke bad on him, started fucking with this balling ass nigga from Cin town. Then cat daddy get out, he's broke, he started fucking with some down-south niggas and catch a fresh indictment."

"Man, kid running around the hood looking bad," Infa added.

Chino nodded. "I'll talk to him. As soon as one of y'all run into him, scoop him up and give me a call."

"So, is it on again?" Chris J asked, rubbing his palms together.

"Hell yeah," Chino told him. "I'ma get with Dragos in a few days and get us back on again."

"That's what I'm talking about!" Corey said happily.

"You been home, yet?" Chris J added.

Chino nodded.

Chris J, Infa, and Corey exchanged glances. Rock looked away, and Ant couldn't look at Chino.

"What?" Chino asked.

No one said anything.

"What the fuck's going on?" Chino asked.

"Man, this broad I'm fucking with be seeing your girl on campus with old boy," Ant told him.

"What? You talking about that nigga Erik?"

Infa nodded. "Old boy is papered up."

"So, that don't mean shit," Chino said. "He papered up. Y'all think Pooh is fucking with this nigga?"

Chris J shrugged. "That's for you to decide."

"Don't clam up now," Chino told them. "Tell me what you know."

I just heard that the nigga is papered up severely," Infa told him. "And that him and Pam be chilling and shit. Now, beyond that, I can't call it."

"What she tell you?" Rock asked.

It was the question that rocked his world. Chino thought about what Pam had told him. She had promised him that she wasn't going to go out with this nigga again. Apparently, they had just moved their relationship on campus, away from the eyes of the people she knew that he fucked with. She had lied to him, and what reason would she have to lie to him, other than the fact that she and this nigga must have something going on? His Pooh had been lying to him the whole time.

Chino felt like he had been kicked in his gut. He felt his eyes grow a tiny bit watery, but there was no way in hell he was going to appear weak in front of his boys.

"Man, fuck that bitch!" Chino said, dismissing the conversation. "Man, I'ma get outta here and go and make some collections."

Rock gave him dap. "All right then, kinfolk. I have that for you."

The rest of the crew gave him pounds and fist taps, and all promised to have his money ready for him. Chino climbed inside his Land Cruiser and pulled away. His thoughts turned to his Pooh. She had pretended the whole time that she had been down for him, and all the while she had been doing this nigga Erik. He was hurt, and also angry. He couldn't picture his Pooh lying under another man. He had been her first and he thought that he would be her only. The thought of her giving herself to another man was killing him. And he wasn't the type to take pain easily. It was eating him up inside.

Chapter 41

Don't Be Afraid

Driving back home, Chino thought about Young Mike. The boy had his hustle game tight. Pain wrenched deep inside of his gut. He just couldn't believe it.

He knew that Pam had grown close to his friend while he was away. She thought of him as a little brother. Why hadn't she said anything? Chino pushed open the door to the apartment and stepped inside.

"Hey, honey," Pam said. She stood over the stove cooking. "I'm making your favorite tonight. A big juicy steak, a cheesy baked potato, and some cream corn."

Chino walked up behind her and stood silent. Pam turned and faced him.

"What's the matter?"

Chino shook his head and looked down. His expression told her that something was wrong.

"It's Young Mike," Chino said, softly.

"What? Chino, what's wrong with him?"

"They found him."

"They found him? What do you mean, they found him?"

Chino exhaled. "He's dead, Pam."

Putting her hands up to her mouth, she exclaimed, "No! No, Chino!"

Chino pulled her close.

"*Nooooooooooo!*" she screamed. "*Nooooooo!*"

Chino wrapped his arms around her. Pam pulled away from him.

"Chino, what happened? Who did that to him?"

Chino shook his head. "No one. He killed himself."

"Why?" Pam cried out. "Michael, why?"

Again, Chino shook his head. "No one knows. No one but Young Mike." His story would be buried with him.

"*Nooooooo!*" Pam started falling to the ground. Chino held her up. "I can't believe this, Chino! I can't! Why, God? Why?"

Pam shoved Chino away and raced out of the apartment. She found herself racing down the street until she was out of breath. Breathing heavily, she looked around and found herself at a school. It was the weekend, and after hours, and so the school was empty. She leaned against the building and began crying like a baby.

"Why, God? Why?" she screamed. Why did He have to take Young Mike? Of all the people in this world He could have taken, why Young Mike? There were niggas out there not doing shit with their lives that He could have taken. There were people in this world hurting other people; why not take them instead? It was not fair. God was wrong for this one. Young Mike never hurt anybody. He never hurt a fly. He was just a youngster trying to get his life together. He was good.

Pam fell to the ground in tears. All Young Mike wanted to do was get his GED, go to college, get a good job, and take care of his grandmother and little sister. What was wrong with that? Why take somebody who wanted to do good? Why take somebody who wanted to be a doctor and help other people? Young Mike had a good heart. Whether or not he would have or could have become a doctor was beside the point. The point was, it was in his heart to help people. Despite all that he had gone through in life, despite the shitty hand that he had been dealt, he still wanted to do good!

Pam kicked the school building. "He never had a chance! You didn't give him a chance!" she shouted at the school.

That school, in her eyes, represented all that was wrong in life. It represented all the things that had conspired to destroy Young Mike. It was the place that had doomed him from the beginning.

"It's all your fault!" Pam shouted. She rose from the ground, searched the area, and found an empty soda can. She chucked the can at the building. "You did this! You failed him! You let him slip through the cracks, and you didn't give a shit! He was nothing but a statistic to you! Just another black face! You fucking asshole motherfuckers!"

Chino pulled into the parking lot and climbed out of his Land Cruiser. He walked to where Pam was chucking rocks and sticks and cans and bottles and whatever else she could find at the school. He grabbed her and pulled her close.

"They killed him, Chino!" she screamed. "They killed him!"

"No, Pooh! Nobody killed him! He killed himself! He killed himself!"

234

"Why, Chino? Why?"

"Things just got too tough for him, that's all. Life just got a little rough."

"He was going to make it! He was going to be a doctor and save people!"

Chino swallowed hard. "They say his girl left him, he was desperate for money, and he had just caught a new case."

Pam shook her head and pointed at the school. "They killed him."

"They didn't kill him, Pooh."

"He wasn't a street kid or a hustler or a booster or a fencer or a dope dealer! That was what everybody else expected him to be. He was sweet and innocent, and he had a heart of gold. He just wanted to help people. He wanted to help his grandmother and his sister, and save lives."

"I know, Pooh."

"It's not fair," Pam cried.

"I know, Pooh. I know." He held her tightly. "It's going to be okay, Pooh. Everything is going to be okay. He's in a better place now."

"He should have been in a better place down here, Chino. I failed him We all failed him."

"No, Pooh. He chose to take his own life. It's not your fault, my fault, or anyone else's fault."

"Chino, he sat at our table, studying for his GED. He told me that he wanted to go to college. I should have helped him study. I should have taken him down to the community college myself and registered him. I shouldn't have let him move out. I shouldn't have taken all that money that he owed you, Chino. When he gave it to me, I should have let him keep some. I should have made sure that he saved more of his own money and didn't blow it on bullshit."

Chino shook his head. "Pooh, he was grown. We loved Young Mike, but he wasn't our responsibility. We gave him a place to stay, we looked out for him, we did the best we could."

"We should have done better!" Pam snapped. "We should have done more, Chino. I just can't believe this! I can't believe that he's gone!"

"He's gone, and that leaves us, Pooh. That leaves us here to keep moving forward, to keep moving on. We have to keep on living now."

Pam wiped her tears. "I just don't understand how God could take someone like Young Mike."

"It's not for us to question. We just have to live our lives and do the best we can. You understand that, Pooh?"

Pam nodded.

"C'mon," Chino said, extending his hand to help her up. "Let's get out of here before somebody calls the police."

Pam rose, dusted herself off, and walked with Chino back to his SUV.

Chapter 42

Slow Down

"So, what's on the agenda for today, kinfolk?" Infa asked, while leaning in the window of Chino's Land Cruiser.

"Yo, you know what dude looks like fo sho?" Chino asked.

"What dude?"

"This Erik cat," Chino told him. "I know what he looks like, but not for sure. You know what I'm saying?"

"Yeah, yeah." Infa nodded. "I know what cat daddy looks like for sure."

"I need to roll up on dude and see what he's talking about," Chino said.

"Why you checking for dude?" Infa asked.

"I need some information."

"About Pam?" Infa asked, lifting an eyebrow.

Chino nodded. "I want to pull up on fool and see what he's talking about."

"Like what?" Infa asked. "What can dude tell you? He can be shitty and say he knocked boots, or he can be slick and claim that he didn't. Either way, you really won't know the truth."

"I need to see this cat," Chino told him. "I can tell what he's about once I look into his eyes. You rolling or what?"

Infa nodded, walked around the SUV, and climbed inside. "Man, I hope you know what you doing."

"What?" Chino grabbed his pistol. "You think that nigga wanna trip?"

"He might." Infa shrugged. "The nigga ain't no punk."

"Man, fuck that nigga!" Chino said.

"You right," Infa agreed. "But do you really want to go on campus and get into it with that fool? The campus police be tripping, and neither one of us belong on campus."

Chino turned onto the Ohio campus. "I'ma roll by the student center and see if I see that fool. Keep ya eyes out."

Infa nodded. "Damn, this shit must really be important."

Chino nodded. "It is. Nigga, you would do the same thing if it was your girl."

"If it was my main girl?" Infa shrugged. "Maybe. Maybe I'd just let her go, or get over it. I don't know if I would go and check the nigga. He can't do no more than she let him. Pimp rule 101. Don't check the nigga, check the muthafucking ho. Not that I'm calling your girl a ho, but you know the rules."

Chino nodded. Infa was right. Maybe he was out of order for checking to see if Pam had gotten out of line. Checking for this nigga was one thing, but checking this nigga was something completely different. He really didn't want to get arrested on campus, but he had to see this fool. He had to let this fool know that he was around and that he could find him and get at him. If he wanted to get at Pam, then he would play head games back with the nigga. I see you, nigga, is the message he wanted to convey. Plus he had to know if Pooh crept. He couldn't bring himself to admit it to Infa, but not knowing was killing him inside. He couldn't touch Pooh until he knew something.

"I got to find this nigga, Infa," Chino said softly. "I've got to find him."

"Let it go, bro," Infa told him. "You hold on to this, and it will eat you up inside."

Chino knew that Infa was on point. He turned the Land Cruiser around and headed off campus. He had to let it go.

Chino, Chris J, and Infa rolled to City Center Mall to pick up some suits for Young Mike's funeral. They were going to hit Foley's and Dillard's and do some more shopping. Chino was even going to buy a suit for Young Mike to be buried in and take it to the funeral home for his grandmother.

The first store the crew hit up was Dillard's. It was there where Chino ran into Tracey.

"Hi, how are you doing?" Tracey asked.

"I'm good, ma," Chino told her, returning her smile. *She cute*, Chino thought. She was a yellow bone, with long hair that she wore in a ponytail. She had full red lips and pretty light brown eyes. Her figure was on the slim side, but she had a nice curve on her backside and two nice little humps up top. The form-fitting knit overall suit that she was wearing accented her figure perfectly. It was black and white plaid, and she wore black shoes and sheer black stockings to complement her outfit. She also wore a white blouse and had a black tie holding her ponytail in place. She was dressed conservative and cute. More than likely, she was a college girl from the university.

"Is there anything I can help you with today?" Tracey asked.

Chris answered, "Yeah, how about your phone number?"

"Don't you go with my friend Debra?" Tracey asked.

"I was asking for it for my man here!" Chris J said, putting his hands on Chino's shoulders.

"Uh-huh." She nodded. "Sure you were."

Chino and Infa laughed. She was sexy and sophisticated. Unlike anything he had met before, Chino thought. Most girls he could easily charm, but this one was different. You could tell that she was smart and a spoiled little rich girl. She was working in the department store and she had a gold name tag on, which meant she was a department manager. She looked young, too young to be a department head. Unless she had just graduated from college, or she had worked for the store all four years that she had been in college and had worked her way up the ladder. Either way, she was smart, and ambitious, and classy. At least that's what her clothes and perfume said about her. Chino recognized the Chanel No. 5 she was wearing. It was his favorite.

"I'm looking for a suit," Chino told her.

Tracey turned and ran her hands across Chino's shoulders and chest. "I know just the right suit for your type of build. It's a Geoffrey Beene suit. It would fit you like a glove."

"I'm following you," Chino told her. He peered down at her firm, round behind. So did Infa and Chris. They gave each other dap.

"Like a muthafuckin onion!" Infa said. He, Chris J, and Chino laughed.

Tracey stopped, spun around, and faced them. "So, you like what you see, huh?" She spun back around and continued walking until she arrived at the men's suits section, where she led them to a mannequin dressed in a fine dark gray suit. "So, what do you think?"

Chino nodded. "I like it."

Tracey pulled a suit from a nearby rack. "This is your size."

"How do you know?" Chino asked. "Your boyfriend about the same size as me?"

"I don't have a boyfriend, and I'm a seamstress. I've been making my own clothes since I was fifteen. I can look at you and tell what size you wear." She handed Chino the suit. "I can ring you up over here."

Chino and the fellas followed Tracey to a nearby register, where she rang up his suit. Chino pulled out a wad of money and paid in cash.

"Are you getting married?" Tracey asked.

"Are you asking me?" Chino asked.

"Yeah," Tracey told him.

"Well, we just met," Chino smiled, "but I guess that I'll take a chance and marry you."

Tracey laughed. "Oh, a sense of humor! Silly! You wouldn't want to marry me."

"Why not?" Chino asked.

"Because I'm bossy. I don't think you could handle me."

"Wheeeew!" Infa ran his eyes up and down her body, and he and Chris J gave each other dap again.

Chino looked her up and down and nodded. "I can handle you."

"You think so?" Tracey smiled. "A few have tried, but none have managed to tame me yet."

"Hey, I'm an expert tamer," Chino said, biting his bottom lip.

"I'll bet you are," she told him. "What have you tamed so far?" She looked at Chino and her brown eyes sparkled, awaiting an answer from him.

Chino shrugged. "Whatever has come my way that needed taming."

"I have a really wild and mean cat named Pussy. You think you could tame my precious Pussy?"

"Hot damn!" Chris J shouted.

Infa bit his lip.

"I think that I could," Chino told her.

She wrote her telephone number down on the back of his receipt. "Here's my number. Call me and we'll see if you can tame that wild cat of mine."

Chino tucked her number away. "Bet."

Chino, Infa, and Chris J headed out of Dillard's through the mall toward Foley's. They were halfway through the mall when they ran across a group of GI Boys.

"There them niggas go right there!" Infa said.

They spotted one another at the same time. The GI Boys went for their guns, and so did Infa, Chino, and Chris. Chris fired first, putting a bullet through the chest of one of the Gary Indiana Boys.

Gunfire erupted like fireworks on the Fourth of July. Mall shoppers dove for cover and others began to flee. Screaming, shouting mall patrons ran from the scene, some getting caught in the crossfire. Infa tapped Chino on his shoulder and nodded toward Dillard's.

"Let's go back through the store and get the hell outta here!" Infa shouted.

Chino nodded. "Chris, we outta here!"

Chris took aim and popped another GI Boy in the back. "I'm Audi five thousand!"

The three of them fled through Dillard's, out the door, and into the parking lot. They passed the police on the way in but blended in with the other fleeing mallgoers.

"We served them hoes!" Infa shouted once they reached the Land Cruiser.

"Punk-ass hoes!" Chris J said, still hype. "They'll take their ass back to Gary now!"

"Showed 'em they fucking with the wrong niggas!" Infa added.

Chino climbed behind the wheel and thought about what had just taken place. The shootouts were coming too close now. He was supposed to have gotten out of the game and be long gone from Columbus by now, but all of a sudden, things in his life had taken a turn for the worse. Pam had went left with this nigga Erik. Young Mike killed himself. Things were way off from where he thought they would be. He had to get things right again. He had to. Maybe Tracey would bring him some good luck. Maybe that's what he needed, a complete change: a change of crew, a change of scenery, and a change in women. One thing was for certain, his life needed to change.

Chapter 43

If

"Hello?"

"Sissy, what's up?"

"Hey, Ty! What's my big bro up to?"

Ty Xavier was Pam's older brother. The two of them grew up real close and had remained so ever since. Ty resembled their mother on the outside but had his father's habits and mannerisms. He loved Pam and would forever think of her as his baby sister.

"I just got off the phone with Mom," Ty told her.

"Oh, Lord!" Pam said, rolling her eyes and sighing.

"You already know what it is," Ty told her.

"You know how dramatic Mom can be."

Ty laughed. "I know. That's your mother, Sissy!"

Pam joined in the laughter. "Uh-uh, don't put her on me. That's your mother too!"

"Sissy, what's this I hear about you getting married?"

Again, Pam exhaled. "I have a fiancé."

"What do you really know about this dude?"

"Chino?" Pam asked. "I know everything about him."

"You know he's in the game?" Ty asked.

Pam was stunned into momentary silence. "Where . . . where did you hear that?"

"Mom gave me his name and I did some checking. I called some partners of mine in Columbus. He just got out of prison?"

"It was a bad charge."

"You knew!" Ty exploded. "I can't believe this! You knew that he had been in prison before?"

"Ty, why are you tripping?"

"Tripping? You talking about marrying a nigga who just got out of the joint, and you say I'm tripping?"

"He's a good person."

"A good person? So you know that he's a drug dealer too, huh?"

Pam exhaled and allowed her silence to speak for her.

"I can't believe this," Ty told her. "You want to marry a dope dealer who's been to prison? What are you thinking, sis? What on earth has happened to you? You used to have more sense than this. I can't believe that this is the same Sissy that I grew up with."

"I'm the same person, Ty, and that's the point. I know what I'm doing. I'm not going to make any irrational decisions. Trust me and believe in me like you always have."

"You don't know this guy, Sissy. He's not like us, or like the people we grew up with. He's a real street cat."

"I do know him. He's really sweet, and vulnerable, and he has a heart of gold. He makes me laugh, Ty, and we have so much fun together. He reminds me so much of you."

Ty exhaled. "Be careful, Sissy. Please just promise me that you'll be careful."

"I will."

"I'm going to come into town and check on you."

"You don't have to do that," Pam told him.

"I'm going to come and check up on you. I'm also going to take you to a gun store and get you some protection."

"Protection?"

"You never know when this guy's activities can come back on you. You're far away from home, so I want to make sure that you're protected. Don't tell Mom, either."

"I won't," Pam said softly. "Thanks, Ty."

"For what?"

"For being a great lil brother."

"I love you, Sissy."

"I love you too, lil bro."

Chapter 44

Let's Ride

Chino had collected his paper from all those who owed him before he had gone in. He also made things right with Dragos, who gave him a massive ticket. He had more money than he knew what to do with. Everything in his life was going right, except for his shit at home. He was fucked up about Pam. She had him twisted. She had given herself to him first, and he was supposed to be her one and only. And now, that was gone. It was driving at him, that someone else might have tapped his Pooh. He needed a change, and so he decided to move. Moving to a new spot would give him a fresh start. Especially since that nigga might have been up in his crib while he was away. No nigga would be able to describe the inside of his crib to him. No, he was going to bust out a new spot. One he was certain that Pam hadn't screwed anyone else in.

The real estate agent walked him through the house, waving her hand around, showing off the place.

"This is the gourmet kitchen," she told him. "It has two sinks, including a vegetable prep sink. The missus will love that. It has two dishwashers, in case you do a lot of entertaining. It has granite countertops, Wolf stainless steel appliances, a forty-eight-inch stainless steel Sub-Zero refrigerator. Cherry cabinets with forty-two-inch uppers. A vaulted ceiling with these gorgeous pendant lights over the center island. It has a wine refrigerator and marble floors."

Chino nodded. He liked what he saw. Especially that big-ass refrigerator. He always liked those. He would see them in the giant mansions in the magazines he would flip through, and he would dream of the day when he could have one in his house. And now that day was upon him.

"This house has five bedrooms, five and a half baths, a formal living, a formal dining, an upstairs game room, an upstairs media room, a full basement. The master is on the first floor, along with one other bedroom. You can use the second first-floor bedroom as a nursery or a small child's bedroom, a guest suite, or a mother-in-law suite. The other three bedrooms are up. The master suite occupies its own wing of the house. It has two enormous walk-in closets, a luxurious master bath with a six-foot Jacuzzi tub, and a separate walk-in shower. It also has a small morning kitchen and a private entrance into the study."

Chino nodded and continued to follow her through the house, as she explained all the home's features and appointments.

"This home is convenient to the Corazon Club and Spa," she continued. "It is served by fantastic Dublin schools, and as you noticed when we came into the community, it is gated with a guard at the front. The streets are all tree-lined, the driveways are all brick, as are the sidewalks. All the homes are required to have manicured hedges out front to preserve that old small-town feel. The community does have a wonderful town center with gorgeous brownstone storefronts."

Chino walked through the house taking in the new home smell. He loved the smell of fresh carpeting and paint, and that wood smell that came with new construction. It was truly the house of his dreams. Perhaps it was in this new home that he would be able to get his new start. The stink of prison and another nigga around would be left in his old condo. He needed this house.

"Does this one have a pool?"

"Yes." She nodded. "A rather large one. Even larger than the house I showed you up I-Seventy-one. Do you have children?"

"Not yet," Chino told her.

"Oh, well. I was asking because I have another home, a French country design just like this one, and it's in the fantastic Olentangy school district. I also have an English Tudor design where your kids will attend Big Walnut schools."

Chino turned and headed up the dual staircase to the upstairs balcony, where he stared down into the family room. He loved this home. He could stand upstairs and look down into the family room, or turn around and look down into the foyer to see who was coming in through the front door. It was a crib for showing off. He was definitely going to change to marble tile in the foyer. He wanted to have a giant marble C added to the tile in the entrance. This was Chino's crib, and he wanted everyone to know it when they stepped through the front door. He could hear Rock, Infa, Corey, Ant, and Chris J right now. They would go crazy when they saw it.

Chino turned and walked into the media room. It was bare right now, but he could definitely visualize a ten-foot screen and a clean-ass projector dropping out of the ceiling. He turned and walked back into the game room, where he visualized a pool table on one side of the room and a card table on the other. There was already a wet bar in the corner. He would also buy some arcade games for the room. He thought that would be clever. Having Star Wars, Centipede, and Ms. Pac-Man video arcade games in his game room would be the shit. He would also need one of those jumbo gumball machines for his game room as well.

Chino walked to the game room window and looked out. He could see the pool and the adjoining spa. He looked forward to relaxing in a nice hot spa and sipping on some chilled Moët—or really, some Hen, or bourbon and Coke, or some gin and orange juice. He just wanted to be able to lay back in his hot tub and relax while sipping on a little something. And once he got rid of his cheating ass girl, he could have some hoes over and really have some pool parties. Some pool parties that would put Freaknik to shame.

Chino turned and headed down the rear staircase through the kitchen and into the dining room. The dining room was across the foyer from the living room. He turned and peered around both rooms. Both had wooden ceiling beams and chair rail paneling, as well as decorative crown molding. The home was built for a muthafucka with money. Everything inside and outside the house was straight on point. From the four-car garage, to the sprinkler system, to the intercom system, to the video alarm system, everything was on hit. The house even had a safe room in the basement. It seemed as though this house had been made just for him.

"So, what do you think?" the real estate agent asked.

Chino glanced around one more time, then nodded. "I like it."

"You want to see the house I have in the Olentangy school district?" she asked.

Chino shook his head. "No. No, this one is for me. I think I'll take it."

"You'll take it?" she asked, surprised.

Chino nodded. Now it was his turn to smile. The entire time this white bitch had been showing him houses, she had been smiling and smirking, like she was showing him the house because it was her job and she wanted to avoid a dis-crimination lawsuit. She didn't expect that he would actually buy a house from her. Not one of the gigantic homes that she had shown him. In fact, she had started off showing him homes in the two- and three-hundred-thousand-dollar range, until he damn near cursed her out. Now she was speechless.

"Yes," Chino told her. "I'll take it. Close your mouth be-fore something flies in it."

The real estate agent closed her mouth and frowned. "I imagine you already have your financing in order?"

"My finances are in order," Chino told her. "There ain't gonna be no financing shit. This is going to be a cash offer."

"Cash?"

"Cash."

"Anything over ten thousand dollars cash requires a lot of paperwork for the IRS." She smirked.

"I have a beauty shop that has done quite well. You may have seen it on the news. It's called L O Quent. Stop by and get your hair done. Tell 'em Chino sent you, and that I said it's on the house."

Her mouth fell open again.

Chapter 45

I Would Die for You

Chino felt that he needed a change, but still, he was willing to give Pooh a chance. They had been through too much together for him to not give her another chance. He felt weird around her now. He had made all kinds of excuses not to touch her after his boys dropped a dime on her, from being tired, to having a headache, to having a stomachache, to being busy. She was dirty to him now. She wasn't really his anymore, because she had been soiled by the touch of another man.

She had been dipping with that clown Erik, and ever since he had been home, she had been in his face like nothing ever happened. She was a snake in the third degree. The fact that she could grin up in his grille like she was all sweet and innocent, while the entire time he was down she had been dipping with dude, meant that she knew a level of deception that he hadn't known she was capable of. He hadn't mentioned it to her, because of the Young Mike situation. He wanted to get her through Young Mike's death before confronting her with what he knew. They had buried Young Mike two days ago, yet he still didn't know if he was going to mention anything to her. He was confused by the whole situation.

Chino felt like he didn't want Pam anymore, but he wasn't sure if he could let her go. After all, something had happened between them. Chino had shared everything with Pam—his deepest thoughts and secrets, the ins and outs of the drug trade. She knew who his boys were and what their roles were on the streets. If she ever used that knowledge against him, she could destroy him. He had nightmares about it.

The thought of her sleeping in the arms of another man each night killed him.

"We haven't been here since you proposed to me!" Pam told him. She was all smiles today. She and Chino were at her favorite restaurant, Red Lobster. It was like old times again.

"Was this the one I proposed to you at?" Chino asked, looking around.

"Yep!" Pam pointed. "Right over there!" Remembering the proposal, she smiled as she looked at the table they had sat in.

Chino nodded. "Yeah, I remember." *I remember that I was going to marry your funky two-timing ass*, he thought to himself. What he did know is that he would have killed her if he had put a ring on her finger and she had cheated on him. He would have cut her damn head smooth off and pleaded temporary insanity.

Pam held her left hand in the air and watched her engagement ring shine in the light. "We still haven't set a date yet, and you know we're not getting any younger!" Pam laughed to herself.

"No, we haven't."

"How may I help you?" the waiter asked.

"I'll have the shrimp platter, and my husband will have the steak and lobster." Pam peered at Chino and smiled. "Did I get that right, boo?"

Chino nodded.

"Baked potato, mashed, fries, broccoli?"

"Baked potato for both," Pam confirmed.

"Dressing for your salads?"

"Caesar." She looked at Chino. "Baby, you want some wine?"

"We're not celebrating anything," Chino said dryly. "We're just here for lunch."

Pam closed the drink menu and stuck it back in the corner of the table.

"Are you done with these?" the waiter asked, holding up the lunch menus.

Pam nodded. "Yeah, we're done."

The waiter nodded and disappeared.

"What's the matter, baby?" Pam asked. "You seem a little distracted."

Chino shook his head. "I'm focused like a laser beam."

"You're not in a real talkative mood."

"I'm just thinking."

"About what?"

"About a lot of things. About us, mainly."

"What about us?"

"About how three's a crowd."

"Chino, what are you talking about?"

"I'm talking about your little boyfriend, Erik."

"Not this again, Chino!" Pam said, sitting back in the booth. "Erik is not my boyfriend."

"I can't tell. You two muthafuckas look mighty cozy on campus together."

"On campus?"

"Yeah, Pooh! You lied to me! You told me that you cut this nigga loose! The only thing you did was start creeping with this fool on campus, thinking that the people I fuck with are too ghetto to be on campus and see you." Chino knew he was lying through his teeth, but his paranoia was in control.

"Chino, your fucking little spies don't know what they're talking about! I haven't been all cozy with Erik!"

"So, you was still grinning up in this nigga's face, while I was up in prison fighting for my life."

"No, I wasn't grinning up in anybody's face!"

"You sorry, Pooh!"

"No, you're sorry, Chino! You keep making me apologize and feel guilty over nothing! Nothing is going on between me and Erik!"

"What, is this nigga a punk or something? That's the only time a nigga is around a female and ain't trying to holla. Is that what you're telling me, Pooh? Are you saying he's a punk?"

"No, he's not gay. Yeah, he tried to holla at me. I put him in his place and told him that I had a man."

"So, he's just been laying in the cut, waiting for me to go to jail so that he could push up on you?"

"He ain't been laying in anything!"

"Now I know why you ain't need no money while I was gone! You had a dope-dealing nigga to pay for everything!"

"L O Quent paid all of my expenses!"

"Bullshit!" Chino shouted. "Damn, you're scandalous!

You can't even admit it. I've had all kinds of muthafuckas telling me that they seen you kicking it with this cat!"

"Chino, he's just my friend. So he might have walked with me to a class, or walked with me to the library, or been in a study group that the professor put together! Chino, that doesn't mean that I'm going to fuck him! How many times do we have to go through this?"

"We don't have to go through this at all," Chino told her. "We can end this bullshit right now."

"Chino, you are a trip, you know that? I've been nothing but loyal to you! It's been almost three goddamned years! I visited you every weekend, I took care of the beauty shop, I handled your business for you, I found you another lawyer, I did everything that you asked me to do."

"Except keep your legs closed!"

"I haven't slept with anybody! I never slept with Erik! Why can't you get that through your skull?"

The waiter brought their drinks to the table. He placed glasses of water in front of each of them. "Your food will be out in a moment."

"Thank you." Pam nodded.

"Man, I've lost my appetite," Chino said. "I wonder how many times the two of you came here."

"You seem like you just want me to make some shit up. When I tell you I haven't done anything, you don't believe me!"

Chino stood, grabbed his water off the table, and tossed it in her face. "You're all wet, bitch!" He tossed the empty glass in her lap and stormed out of the restaurant, leaving her sitting there in humiliation.

Chapter 46

Touch me. Tease me.

Chino tossed and turned and found himself breaking out into a cold sweat. He hadn't had this dream since he was locked up, and he had hoped that it wouldn't come back now that he was free.

He can see her clearly. She is wearing his crisp white button-down dress shirt. She also has his tie hanging loosely around her neck. Her thick, sexy, tight legs are smooth and creamy, as they have just been lotioned down. Her hair is long and wet, as she has just gotten out of the shower. She walks seductively to him. He lies on the bed naked, waiting for her. She climbs onto the bed, her legs glistening in the moonlight. She comes to him, slowly, carefully, deliberately. She is a woman on a mission. He is between a pair of crisp, white sheets. Pam pulls the top sheet down and licks her way up his leg to his dick. She doesn't engulf it at first. No, at first she teases it. She runs her tongue beneath his balls and then around his shaft, slowly making her way to the tip of it. Then she engulfs it.

In his dream Pam sucks ferociously, bobbing her head up and down on his manhood until he is ready to cum, and just before he does, her tongue glides up to his navel, and then to his nipple. He is rock hard. She takes his pole into her hand and places it inside her. He can feel it. He can feel every inch of her. She throws her head back and moans. Her moaning grows more and more passionate with each passing moment. She is bouncing up and down and practically screaming. She is a virgin again, and this is her first time making love. And then he is standing outside the window gazing inside. His woman, the love of his life, is getting the shit drilled out of her by Erik.

Chino finds himself banging on the window, but no one hears him. He finds himself screaming and shouting so hard that he is practically foaming at the mouth. Erik peers over at him and smiles. His Pooh is screaming and shouting and is in tears. She is getting stretched out like there is no tomorrow.

"Stop it!" Chino moaned. "Stop!"

Chino awoke from his nightmare covered in sweat. His dick was hard as a rock. He sat up and looked around the room. He was safe inside his new house, lying on the couch.

Chino rubbed his eyes, climbed off the couch, walked to his bedroom, and peered inside. Pam was lying in bed, sleeping soundly.

"Cheating bitch," he mumbled. He walked back into the living room and sat back down. He still had a hard piece, and he was now fully awake. He pulled on his Timbs and pulled out his cell phone.

"Hello?"

"Is this sexy Tracey?" he asked.

"It sure is."

"You hungry?"

"Maybe."

"Feel like meeting me at the Waffle House?"

"That could be arranged."

"See you in twenty?"

"See you in thirty."

"Bet," Chino said, disconnecting the call. He pulled his jersey over his head, threw some spearmint gum in his mouth, and he was out of there.

Thirty minutes later, Tracey and Chino met at the Waffle House.

"Hey, sexy!" Tracey told him, and gave him a friendly hug.

"Hey, beautiful!" Chino said, hugging her back. He inhaled the Chanel No. 5 that she wore.

"What, you couldn't sleep or something?" she asked.

"Sleep? It's only eleven-thirty. Who sleeps at eleven-thirty?"

"People who have to work in the morning."

"You don't have to work in the morning," Chino told her. "You don't have to be in until ten."

"Oh, you know my schedule now? You up on me like that?"

"Of course. You ain't know?"

Tracey held out her hand. "Give me some money, Chino."

"For what?"

"So that I can get my hair done after work tomorrow."

"What happened to you being an independent woman?"

"I am, but still. You have to pay to play in this kitty."

Chino threw his head back in laughter. "Damn, you're direct."

"Well, let's just be honest. You want to grip this onion and bust this cat wide open, right?"

Chino nodded. His dick started getting hard. "I wouldn't mind."

"You'll get it, I just have to get to know you first. I ain't about playing no games."

"I like that. I like it when a person is just straight up with me."

"I'll always be straight up with you, Chino, and I want you to always be straight up with me."

"I will." Chino nodded. "I'm liking this already."

"Do you have a woman?"

"Not really."

"What does 'not really' mean?"

"It means that I have a sorry-ass woman who cheated on me." Chino shook his head and stared off into the distance. His semihard dick went soft.

"Damn, boo. Sounds like you need to talk."

"Are you going to be my therapist too?" Chino asked with a smile. "What's that going to cost me, an outfit?"

Tracey laughed. "No, you're going to buy me outfits because you want to. The therapy is free; it comes with being your new flame. Besides, I can make my own clothes."

"Oh, that's right. You have to forgive me. I've never had a woman who could actually do something for themselves, or who had any kind of talent."

"Oh, baby, that's nothing." Tracey smiled. "I'm great at making clothes, but my real talent lies elsewhere."

Chino felt his hard-on coming back. Seeing Tracey in a long pantsuit made her look even finer. The girl was slim with an ass like a porn star.

"You're pretty, you know that?"

Tracey ran her hand through her long hair, pulling it back behind her ear. "Thank you."

"I want to make love to you so bad right now," Chino whispered.

Tracey held out her hand.

"Damn, baby. There's a word for women who demand money up front."

"Smart?" Tracey asked.

"That's the word I was looking for." Chino laughed.

"I'll bet. I'll tell you what. We can go back to my place, and if you packing at least ten inches, you can bust this pussy open. If you not, you got to go."

Chino laughed. "Shit, deal!"

Tracey stood and nodded toward the door. "Well then, let's get out of here."

Chapter 47

Dangerously in Love

Chino grabbed his Jordans and laced them up. He stood and headed for the door. He had gone out every night for the last two weeks. Not only was Tracey a tasty treat, but he had a few others now as well. Pam raced to block his exit.

"Out? You just got home!"

Chino pushed Pam to the side. "I don't like being here!"

"Why not?"

"Because every time I look at you, I think of you and Erik. Of all these niggas in the city, why did you need him for a friend when I was doing my bid?"

"What are you talking about, Chino? I didn't have any other friends to talk to, because you wouldn't allow me to have any. So Erik was around, and he was just somebody to talk to."

Chino gripped Pam's arm. "Fuck that! Did you think I wasn't getting out? You was supposed to stick to the program and wait! Did you think that I wouldn't find out that you was fucking that nigga? You just like the rest of these gold-digging ass bitches! Pooh, you ain't getting another dime from me.

You've booked yourself, baby! I do more for you than you can do for yourself. I taught you everything! I gave you everything! I clothed you, I fed you, I took care of you, I practically made you! Look at those rings on your fingers! I put them bitches there! Look at this muthafucking house! I paid for it! You can't pay the fucking phone bill without me."

Pam broke down into tears. Chino's words cut like a knife. She had been a virgin when they met, and he knew that she hadn't been with anyone else. He was talking about all of the stuff that he did, but what about what she did? They built that shit together. She was the one who held down the beauty shop. She was the one who had gotten his lawyer for him. She was the one picking up money for him, and dropping off money and product.

"What the fuck you mean?" Pam exploded. "How the fuck can you say some simple shit like that? You know that I've never been with anyone else but you! Can you say the same? Chino, you went to prison and I was left out here all alone. None of your crew would help me. And to top it off, you came home from the penitentiary with everything that you left with. Not one lock changed, not one phone number changed, your clothes hanging where you left them. I put your cars in storage, and I visited you twice a week. You came home to all of your loot. I sent clothing packages, food packages, and money to you and every nigga you told me to send them to, too. I accepted the collect calls and made three-way calls for you and all them sorry-ass niggas you met up in there!"

Chino tried to brush past Pam, but she cut him off.

"Chino, why are you doing this to us? You have to help me

be strong for us! Erik was just my friend from school!" She was at her wits' end as tears streamed down her face.

"You saved all my bread 'cause you didn't need it!" Chino shouted. "That nigga Erik is out in the street getting money just like me. You can save those tears, Pooh. Save that bull-shit ass drama for your mama. Them tears is because your ass is cut off!"

Chino tried to push past Pam again, and she braced herself against the wall, stopping him. The two of them stood face to face, like a drill sergeant had just yelled "Attention." It was then when she noticed the hickeys on Chino's neck and chest.

Blood rushed to Pam's head, and she felt flushed. She wanted to rip Chino's clothes off and examine his entire body, particularly his dick, but that would have only told her what she already knew: Chino was fucking somebody else.

"I'm in love with somebody else," Chino said softly.

"What? What was that you said?" Pam asked, leaning in closer. "You're in love with somebody else?" Pam lifted her hand and smacked the shit out of Chino.

The look on Chino's face filled Pam with fear. She turned and raced out of his reach just in the nick of time. She raced to the indoor pool and ran around toward a poolside chair, where she had hidden a .38 semi-automatic pistol the night before.

"You stupid, bitch!" Chino shouted. "You just made my day. Oh, now you wanna be a man? You wanna fight?"

Pam ran around a chair near their pool table with the thought of grabbing a pool cue, but changed her mind. A cue would have been too easy for him to take away and use on her. Chino continued to rant and rave while Pam danced back and forth around the pool table to avoid him. Her bare feet made her slide back and forth on top of the smooth ceramic tile.

Tired of chasing Pam, Chino pulled off his shirt to cool down. She could now see the handle of his 9 mm pistol tucked inside his waistband. She became terrified.

Pam had heard rumors of Chino's exploits in the streets. The beauty shop talked, the college-going, wannabe street cats talked, the girls in the mall talked. She knew that Chino was in the streets wilding out, and she didn't want his activities to come back on her. So she'd had her brother buy her a small handgun for protection. He had bought her a chrome Lorcin .38, and loaded it with hollow points. He believed that with such a small caliber, she would need hollow-tip bullets to take out her attacker. She had to take the guy out, he said, or he would beat the shit out of her for shooting him.

"Okay, Chino, stop!" Pam pleaded, breathing heavily. "Stop playing!"

Chino was growing angrier with each passing moment.

"Stop playing?" Chino shouted. "Naw, bitch, we gon' play! I should have whooped your ass a long time ago. When you was kicking it with that nigga Erik you wasn't worried, you didn't have no fear in your heart. Now you're going to see the real Chino. You're going to see what all them other niggas saw when I told them that I'll be to see them!"

"Chino, no!"

"You want to violate and curse like a man and swing at me like a man, now I'ma treat you like one!"

Pam tried to dart past Chino, but he snatched her by her hair and straight brought her to her knees.

"Chino, baby, please stop!" Pam pleaded. "I quit, I'm sorry. Let's stop playing!"

Chino pulled tighter. Pam could feel her face tightening and her eyes widening, as her skin was pulled back.

"Chino, please!" Pam cried on her knees.

"No! Say something!" Chino told her. "Talk shit! You always thought that you were better than me, you always thought that you were smarter than me, and that I was just a dumb-ass nigga! You thought that since you was from LeDroit Park that you was better than everybody else! Well, fuck you and your fake-ass family!"

Pam grabbed Chino's wrist, in an attempt to loosen his grip on her hair. She could feel clumps of her hair being pulled out, and a penetrating migraine formed in her forehead.

"Christonos, please, baby, don't do this, let me go!" Pam pleaded. She could feel her legs going numb because of her awkward position on the floor.

"How dare you call me that name!" Chino shouted. He was practically foaming at the mouth because of his anger. "You ain't got it like that no more!"

Fight or flee? Pam knew that she had to decide quickly. Chino's tightening grip on her hair told her that she had to fight. Not with her fist, but with a woman's mind.

"Chino, baby, please don't hurt me," Pam whimpered. "All I ever wanted, all I ever needed to know was that you loved me. I miss you, Chino. I miss how you used to make love to me."

Pam began to caress Chino's legs. Slowly, his grip on her hair loosened. Pam rose on her knees and brought her face close to his groin. "Chino, just hold me again. Make love to me like you used to."

Chino swallowed hard. He could feel the blood starting to flow to his dick. "Pooh, why you trip like that?"

Pam unzipped Chino's pants and moved her lips to his privates. Chino loosened his belt buckle and tossed his 9 mm from his waistband onto the same seat cushion that was hiding her .38. Once she felt him release her hair completely, she made her move. Pam balled up her fist and punched Chino as hard as she could in his genitals. He fell to the floor in mind-numbing pain, clutching his balls. Pam leaped to her feet and grabbed his gun off the chair. She quickly pulled back the slide, chambering a round.

"Now, muthafucka, who's the bitch?" Pam screamed. "Looks like you're the bitch now, Chino. If only you knew how to control your dick, we wouldn't be in this predicament in the first place. I wouldn't have bitches calling the shop, and you wouldn't be creeping out in the middle of the night, and we would be happy!"

Pam placed the gun to the back of Chino's head. "Now muthafucka, what?"

The air grew silent, and Pam glared down at Chino. Fear was not etched into his face, but an intense pain was. It brought back memories. Memories of when Chino had been abducted by a rival crew. He almost had tears in his eyes.

"Chino, I am so sorry!" Pam said, dropping the gun. She fell to her knees and wrapped her arms around him. "I am so sorry, baby! I remember that night. I wasn't going to hurt you, I promise."

Pam wiped away her tears and Chino's as well. She hugged him but he didn't hug her back. He gave no response.

"Chino, baby, I am here," Pam cried out. "Please, what is wrong with us?"

Chino abruptly pushed Pam off him and backhanded her, splitting her lip. He picked up his gun and stood. "How could you put me in that position after what I told you happened to me? I killed those niggas that did that shit to me, and now it's your turn to get what they got. So now you a trick bitch, huh?"

Pam placed one hand on her head and cried. Chino paced back and forth, ranting and raving. He was too busy to notice her sliding her other hand beneath the seat cushion. Pam found her Lorcin .38.

"You're the weak link, Pooh!" Chino shouted. "The only person that knows about them niggas is you. I buried the gun, and only you knew where it was. But I went back and got it and moved it, after I found out about you still creeping with Erik. I can't trust you no more, Pooh. And because I can't trust you, your ass has to go. Have you said your prayers, love?"

Pam panicked. She aimed the gun beneath the pillow at Chino and squeezed the trigger. A loud pop rang out. All Chino saw was feathers flying from the ripped pillow.

"Pooh, where did you get a gun from?" Chino asked, clutching his stomach. He dropped his gun. "Pooh, don't shoot me, just drop the gun."

Pam threw her gun down. "Oh my God, I'm going to call nine-one-one!"

Chino clasped her arm. "No, calm down and call my boy Darren."

Pam called Darren, and he was on his way. "Chino, Darren said to hold tight, and that he'll be here in five minutes! Are you okay? Do you want to lie down?"

"Just calm down, Pooh," Chino told her. "It'll be okay."

Darren's Jag screeched to a stop in front of the house, and he and Pam helped Chino out to the car.

"I'll drive!" Pam said.

"No, you're too hysterical to drive," Chino told her. "Besides, they'll arrest you for the shooting. I'm just going to go in and say that I had a little accident."

Darren and Pam rushed Chino to Mount Carmel East Hospital, while Chino lay in the back applying pressure to his gunshot wound. When they got to the hospital, Darren and Pam carried Chino inside.

"Pooh, go home," Chino said weakly. "Darren, take her home."

Darren pushed Pam out the door and made her get into his Jag. The two of them left as the police cars were arriving. Darren reached over and patted Pam on her leg.

"You know, Chino let you go free," he told her. "That's love, baby girl. That's love."

Chapter 48

I Belong to You

As he lay in his hospital bed unconscious, Chino's mind took him back to a place he didn't want to go. It took him back to that night; it was the worst night of his life.

Chino walked out of the store with a grocery bag in his hand. He was thinking of the brand-new Lorinser rims that he was going to cop for his Benz. They would be chrome, with a white center and a chrome center cap. It would give his Benz that powdered-out look. White on white, with a white AMG kit. His Benz would be the cleanest whip in Columbus.

Chino set his grocery bag down on the concrete next to his car so that he could fish his key out of his pocket. He was struck so hard over the head with a metal object that he instantly fell unconscious.

Chino woke and peered around the room. The room was full of junk. Chipping paint, spiderwebs, and holes were all over the walls. The scenery told him that he was in an abandoned building. Rats and roaches scampered across the floor, and the floor itself was missing some boards. The blood running down his neck told him that he had been struck over the head, and his change of scenery told him that he had been driven to a different location. He had been abducted.

"Wake up, sleepyhead," one of his abductors chimed.

Chino shook his head, trying to focus. His head was aching, and his vision was still a little blurry. He could make out that there were at least three of them.

"Wake up, punk-ass nigga!" another one said, slapping him.

Chino came to fully. He recognized them as members of YBI, Young Brothers Incorporated. It was Red, Dirty, and Slick, and they all had pistols in their hands.

Red was a Columbus nigga that he had actually grown up with back in the day. He was a red nigga, with reddish sandy brown hair and a raspy voice. He had dropped out in middle school, and Chino hadn't really seen him since. Dirty was a nigga from the NYC. And he actually resembled Ol' Dirty Bastard. He had gold teeth, a wild afro, and a crazy eye. Slick, on the other hand, was a dirty, funky nigga from California. He had moved to Columbus with his family when he was twelve. Somehow, their three paths had all led them into YBI.

"Stand up!" Red ordered. Chino stood, and Red yanked Chino's clothing off him. "You won't be needing these, pretty boy!"

Dirty punched a naked Chino in his stomach, causing him to fall back down to his knees. "What's up, pretty boy? You up in the club high-capping. Why you ain't celebrating right now?"

"What are you talking about?" Chino asked.

Slick struck him with his pistol. "I'm talking about you high-capping, big baller!"

Chino cried out in pain.

Dirty struck Chino with his pistol, sending blood flying everywhere.

Chino cried out again. "If it's money you want, you can have it. Just let me go."

"Let you go?" Red asked. "Nigga, they're going to find yo body on the evening news." He struck Chino again.

"Please, don't kill me," Chino pleaded. "You can have my car."

"We got your car," Slick told him. "We know exactly where to go and get it from."

"From the bullshit grocery store where we got your ass!" Red said, striking Chino again.

Chino cried out again. He knew that he was going to die. He wanted desperately to make it. He wanted to get back to his Pooh. He would do anything to get back to his love. To lie in her arms again, to have her caress his head. He needed his Pooh now more than ever.

Dirty kicked Chino in his face, and then in his stomach with his enormous hiking boot. Chino spit up blood.

"Don't kill me," he pleaded weakly.

"Look at this ho ass nigga!" Slick shouted. "He ain't such a big man now!"

Red struck Chino again with his pistol. "Bitch ass nigga!"

"Get on your knees!" Dirty shouted.

Filled with aching pain, Chino rose to his knees. Blood was pouring down his body. Red pulled out his penis and urinated on Chino.

"That's how we feel," Red told him. "We feel pissed on by niggas like you. Up in the club popping bottles and pulling all the bitches."

"Man, I ain't pulling no bitches," Chino told him. "I got one woman."

"Take us to your crib so we can hit your safe," Slick said.

"And then we can fuck your bitch!" Dirty added.

"And if she gives good head, we might let her live," Red said.

"Please, don't kill me!" Chino pleaded. He lowered his head to the ground crying.

"Man, this nigga's a real bitch made nigga!" Red said, laughing.

"If I weren't a straight up G, I would make him suck my dick!" Dirty added.

"This crying-ass nigga would probably do it!" Slick said. He kicked Chino in his side, causing him to roll over on his stomach. The three abductors broke into laughter. Slick moved in too close to Chino, while laughing hysterically. Chino made his move.

Chino grabbed the gun from Slick's hand, while kicking him in the side of his knee. Slick's knee snapped like a dry pretzel and he buckled instantly. Chino aimed the gun and shot Slick in his gut, then turned and popped Red in his chest, dropping him. He quickly shifted his weapon and fired several shots toward Dirty, who caught a round in the head. Chino quickly rose and backed up against a corner wall. He fired his gun at Red once again, striking him in the head.

"Piss on that, bitch!" Chino told him.

Suddenly he heard what sounded like someone running up some steps. He didn't know how many of them there were. He searched the room for an exit. Bullets ripped through the room. Chino ran for a window across the room and dove through it. To his unfortunate surprise, it was a third-floor window. Chino landed on the roof of the front porch, then rolled off into the yard. His back was hurting, and his leg felt like it was sprung, but he got up and ran anyway. He ran as hard and as heavy as he could. He was so busy trying to escape that he had forgotten that he didn't have any clothes on. He was running butt-ass naked with a bloody gun.

Chino huffed and puffed and raced down the street, making it to a main road. He raced into the road and stopped an oncoming car. It was an older white man inside.

"Help me!" Chino told him.

"Oh, my God!" the man exclaimed. "Get in!"

Chino made his way to the passenger side and climbed into the car. The old man raced off.

"Is anyone chasing you?" the old man asked.

"Probably," Chino said, breathing heavily.

"We need to get you to the hospital."

Chino shook his head. "I need to go home. I need a hot bath, and I need some clothes."

The old man looked at Chino's bloody and naked body. "You're bleeding bad, young fella. You need a doctor."

Chino shook his head. "Please, they'll ask questions, and then call the police. I'll be okay. I just need to get cleaned up."

"What happened to you?" the old man asked.

"I was kidnapped. But other than that, you shouldn't ask too many questions."

The old man nodded. He knew when to shut up.

———

The nurse ran into Chino's room and pressed the emergency alarm. Soon she was joined by several other doctors and nurses.

"What happened?" one of the doctors asked.

"I just came in here because his heart monitor was going off, and I found him like this."

Chino was covered in sweat and convulsing violently. His nightmare had caused his heart to palpitate excessively.

"We need a sedative!" the doctor shouted. "We need to make sure that he doesn't go into cardiac arrest."

Chino's dream found him in his bedroom kneeling, and Pam rushing to him. She found him naked, bloody, and weeping. But in his dream, his Pooh was with him now, and so his heart calmed down to near normal beats. He had his Pooh with him in his dreams. He was better now.

Chapter 49

The Future

The nurse walked into Chino's room and checked his monitors. She wrapped a blood pressure cuff around his arm and placed the end of a stethoscope against his arm, just beneath the cuff. She pumped up the cuff and listened and timed his heartbeats as it deflated. His blood pressure was still a little on the low side.

Nurse Jen then checked his IV fluids and placed a thermometer in his armpit to measure his temperature. It was also a little low. Chino was not doing well.

Nurse Jen shook her head. Chino was on his way to being another statistic. She had seen way too many of those in her ten years as a triage nurse. Gunshot wound victim after gunshot wound victim poured into the Columbus hospital night after night with alarming regularity. Almost always it was an African-American male who had been shot by another African-American male. Black-on-black crime was the reason she had gone into the medical profession in the first place. It was black-on-black crime that had taken her younger brother from her.

Nurse Jen's younger brother Jarod had gone to a party one night, and for no apparent reason, while he and his friends were leaving the party, a crew from the Southside rode by and unleashed on them. Northside against Southside, Eastside against Westside, it was always the same shit. Blacks killing other blacks for bullshit reasons. And now she had another one. This one was, more likely than not, a victim of crack violence, she surmised. One way or the other, crack was going to destroy all in its path. Whether you used it or sold it, it was going to catch up to you in the end. It caught up to the users by making them addicts. It caught up to the dealers by sending them to prison or, even worse, to the morgue. This one was headed to the latter, if he stayed in the condition that he was in. That thing about the first thirty-six hours being critical was true. But what they don't tell you is that if you haven't gotten better in the first thirty-six, then you were in more and more trouble with each passing day. Open wounds, infections, low blood pressure, low body temperature, and so many other things all conspired against you. Time was not on your side.

Nurse Jen rubbed Chino's arm.

"Fight, baby boy," she said in her thick West Indian accent. "Fight. I need you to fight for your life."

Chino moaned and turned his head to the side.

—

"Pooh, those muthafuckas tried to play me," Chino said.

"It's okay, you're home now," Pam reassured him. "What happened?"

Chino shook his head. "Pooh, this is murder one, baby. Ain't

*no turning back if I tell you. From this point on, you my accom-
plice. Either you down, or you can turn and leave now."*

"Chino, you know I got you, boo. Now, what's up? Whatever
happened, I'm sure that they got what their hand called for."

Chino held up a gun. It was a gun that Pam didn't recognize as
one of his.

"Pooh, baby, this is murder," Chino repeated. "Without this
weapon, they got nothing, though."

"Chino, let's do what we gotta do," Pam told him. The two of
them stared into each other's eyes and embraced. She could smell
the blood on him.

Chino kissed Pam gently on her forehead. "You all I got,
Pooh."

———

"Christonos!" Nurse Jen called out to him.

Chino was turning his head rapidly from side to side and
moaning. She was scared that he was going to become unset-
tled or even violent and pull out his tubes. They should have
strapped him down after his first episode.

"Help!" Nurse Jen shouted into the hall. "Help me!"

———

*The park was near their new home up I-270, off Route 161, near
Dublin. Chino and Pam walked through the darkness toward the
boat docks.*

"Keep an eye out, Pooh," Chino told her. "We don't want nobody to see us. If somebody sees us and wonders what we're doing,
they may call the police or come and see for themselves."

The two of them made their way to the docks, and then down
an embankment to a shed beneath the docks where ropes for the
boats were stored. Chino pulled on the shed door, but it was locked.

He pulled out the tire iron that he had hidden beneath his jacket and tried to pry open the door. The bolt was too strong.

"Damn!" Chino cried out.

"What's the matter, boo?" Pam asked nervously.

"It's locked, and I can't get it open!" Chino told her. He peered around the area. There was a green steel bench about twenty feet away. He walked to the bench, dropped to his knees, and peered underneath it. The structure of the bench was such that nothing could be hidden underneath it.

"Someone would find it there," Pam told him.

"I know," Chino nodded. Again, he searched the area. A water fountain sat next to the park bench, and next to the fountain was a drain for the overflow from the fountain. Chino rose, walked to the drain, and examined it. He pulled out the tire iron, stuck it in one of the openings, and pried open the grate. He then lifted the grate and sat it down next to the hole. It was heavy.

Chino dropped to his knees, stuck his hand inside, and found the perfect spot. There was a shelf just below the surface of the drain that couldn't be seen. A person would have to stick his hand deep inside to find it. And as slimy as it was, no one would go there and purposely stick their hand inside. It was perfect!

"Hand me the piece, baby," Chino whispered.

Pam handed Chino the wrapped-up gun, and he placed it inside the hole on the shelf. He rose and replaced the heavy grate, then examined the hole. Nothing could be seen from the surface. Pam grabbed Chino's hands and dropped to her knees.

"Dear God, please protect us, and forgive us for everything that has happened. Please keep us together, and let nothing but death separate us. We humbly ask that this secret goes with both of us to our graves. Amen."

Chino stared at Pam. *"Pooh, this is the spot, and you hold the secret to my freedom. You're not my wife, legally, but in my heart I trust you with my life."*

Nurses flooded into the room and grabbed Chino's arms. Nurse Jen bent over and whispered into Chino's ear as she caressed his head.

"It's all right, baby," she said softly. "Everything is going to be all right. I'm here with you. Nurse J has your back. You hear me, Christonos?"

There were two people in this world who called him Christonos. His mother, who was dead, and his Pooh. He could hear his name being called. It was soothing. Calming. He stopped twisting and turning, and found himself relaxing. Slowly, and just barely, Chino cracked open his eyes.

Chapter 50

Giving My All

The wedding was taking place outdoors in the park. A trellis with flowers around it had been set up near the altar, while another was set up near the front so that the bride would walk through it before her journey down the aisle. All their friends and family were in attendance, as the bride's family had made sure of it. They had spared no expense, including flying in relatives from all over.

A pianist banged out the bridal march, and the wedding began.

Chino stood at the altar waiting for his soul mate. Rock stood next to him as his best man, while Chris J, Infa, Ant, and Corey stood to one side as his groomsmen. They were all decked out in white Armani tuxedos, while Chino had on a black one.

Chairs had been arranged on either side of the aisle; floral arrangements made a pathway for the bride to walk down. White doves sat in cages throughout the area, and a white panther with a diamond necklace snarled from a cage toward the rear of the area.

The bride cut the corner in her dress, and Chino gasped. She was more beautiful than anything in the world to him. Her white silk wedding dress was designed by Carolina Herrera, and it had over ten thousand Swarovski crystals sewn into it. Her silk shoes had the same crystals sewn into the same pattern in them, and they matched the dress exactly. She was a vision of loveliness floating down the aisle on her father's arm.

"Congratulations," Rock leaned over and whispered.

"She's beautiful, man," Infa told him.

Chino smiled and nodded. He knew that he had found the perfect woman for him. She was smart, funny, and she had proven that she had his back. She was the woman that he was going to spend the rest of his life with.

The beautiful bride stopped at the altar, and her father placed her hand into Chino's and then took his place of honor.

"Who here gives this woman away in holy matrimony?" the minister asked.

"I do."

The minister turned to Chino. "Do you, Christonos, take this woman to be your lawfully wedded wife in holy matrimony? Do you promise to love her, honor her, and cherish her, in sickness and in health, till death do you part?"

Chino turned toward his bride and smiled. "I do."

The minister turned toward the bride. "Do you, Tracey, take this man to be your lawfully wedded husband in holy matrimony? Do you promise to love, honor, and obey him, till death do you part?"

Tracey faced Chino and smiled. "I do."

"Do you have the rings?" the minister asked.

Rock pulled out the rings and handed them to Chino, who handed his to Tracey.

"Repeat after me," the minister told them. "With this ring, I thee wed."

"With this ring, I thee wed," Tracey said, placing the ring on Chino's finger.

"With this ring, I thee wed," Chino repeated, placing his ring on Tracey's finger.

"I now pronounce you man and wife," the minister declared. "You may kiss the bride."

Pam cried out in pain and arched her back. The techs rushed her into the delivery room and helped her onto the delivery table.

"*Aaaaaah!*" Pam screamed, and then started breathing out heavily.

"Breathe, baby, breathe!" Mrs. Xavier told her.

The doctor on call breezed into the room. "What have we here?"

"First-timer," the tech told him. "Her water broke in the ambulance on the way here, and she's already dilated to six."

"She's at six?" the doctor asked, not believing what he was hearing.

"Yes, sir," the paramedic told him. "She's already at six."

The doctor walked to the glove dispenser, pulled out a pair of gloves, and put them on. "Let me take a look at you."

Pam screamed as another contraction hit her.

A nurse in the room reclined the bed Pam was lying in and held her hand. Another nurse placed Pam's legs in a pair of stirrups. The doctor pulled up a stool and stuck his fingers inside Pam to see how many centimeters she had dilated.

"She's at seven now," the doctor proclaimed. "She'll be at nine in no time. I'm going to go and get scrubbed up. Get everything ready for me. Looks like we're about to have a baby."

Two delivery nurses brought in some carts with several prepackaged tools for delivery and pieces of equipment. They began opening packages and arranging all the necessary delivery equipment on the stainless steel delivery carts. They were already scrubbed up and had their sterile gowns and masks on.

Another contraction hit Pam. "Chino!" she screamed.

"Chino's not here, baby," her mother told her. "But I'm here. Don't worry, we're going to get through this together, baby. Mama's here."

"Chino!" Pam cried out again. This time, she broke down and began crying. "Where are you?"

"Mama's here, sweetheart."

"You said that you would be here!" Pam cried.

"Forget about him, Pam!" her mother snapped. "We have a baby to bring into this world, and a baby to raise. Forget about him."

"Why am I alone?" Pam cried out. "Why?"

"I'm here, Pammy," her mother told her. "You're not alone."

"You promised," Pam cried.

———

Chino lifted Tracey's veil and leaned forward and kissed her. *Damn, Pooh. I can't believe this,* he thought. *I can't believe this isn't you. How could you have shot me, Pooh? How could you have tried to kill me?*

A tear fell from Chino's eyes. Everyone thought that he was overcome with emotion because of the wedding. In reality, he was saying good-bye to his past and stepping into his future. He was saying good-bye forever to his Pooh.

The cries of a newborn radiated throughout the room.

"It's a boy!" the doctor declared.

The delivery nurses suctioned the baby's nose and mouth with a tiny aspirator and wiped him down.

The doctor pressed against Pam's stomach. "I need for you to push for me again. We're going to get the afterbirth out of you. The tough part is over with; we just have to finish the job, though."

Pam pushed, and the doctor pulled out clumps of afterbirth and placed it in a metal tray.

"What are you going to name him?" a nurse asked. She wrapped the baby in a warm cloth and handed him to Pam.

"Christon—" Pam stopped herself. "No. No, his name is Antonio."

She too was making a break from her past. She was not going to burden her newborn child with her past luggage; she was going to give him his own name and his own future—a future that they were going to march into together.

"Good-bye, Chino," Pam whispered.

Tracey wiped the tear from Chino's eye. *Good-bye, Pooh,* he thought, staring into the eyes of his new wife. He was staring into the eyes of his new future. His break from the past was complete.

Chapter 51

The End

Pam found herself sitting in her apartment in the dark, thinking about her life. Everything had come crashing down on her, and she didn't know how or why. Chino was gone; he was out of her life for good. He couldn't get over her relationship with Erik. She had shot the love of her life, and then borne a child by him. Chino's son, Antonio, was seven months old now. He was safe and sound in his crib, not understanding the mounting bills, stresses, and pressures that his mommy faced.

She had gone from being a young, sweet, innocent college girl to this: a college dropout, a single unwed mother of an infant son, a person dodging phone calls from bill collectors. She had gone from not worrying about money, and sitting on top of the world, to worrying about catching her own case. She had gone from virgin to call girl. From brand-new to tired and used up.

Her life had left her behind, and somehow, in some way, fortune had given her a life that belonged to someone else.

She had gone from Pammy to Pam to Pooh to Carmen. She had gone from a dorm room to a luxury condo to damn near a mansion, and now she was back in an apartment. Life had spit in her face, and now she found herself having to get up, wipe it off, and keep on moving.

"Keep on moving, Pooh," is what Chino had told her after Young Mike's death. "We have to live our lives and keep on moving."

And so she had, and so she would.

If she was anything, it was a survivor. Like millions of sistas who had walked this world before her, she did whatever she had to do to make a life for herself and her child. Whether it was sleeping with the enemy or working for them as a domestic. She did what she had to do. At least that's what she had told herself the first time she slept with a man for money. But then again, it really wasn't her first time.

Chino had promised her that she wouldn't miss her job, and she didn't. He gave her everything she ever wanted, in exchange for her being his girlfriend. And what was a girlfriend but an exclusive piece of pussy on lockdown? So no, she had turned tricks before. She had been Chino's private trick. But then she stepped out from beneath that umbrella and became a public trick. And now she had moved beyond that. She was now arranging for others to turn tricks. She had learned the game, and she had started her own escort service. It was time for her to stand on her own two feet and get her own paper. No more turning tricks for private boyfriends or public johns; either way, you had to please another motherfucker to get paid.

Now it was about pleasing herself. Now it was about depending on herself to pay her bills and get paid. Now it was time for her to reach for the stars.

Ring, ring.

Pam answered the telephone. "Hello! May I help you?"

"You got any girls that speak Greek?" the caller asked.

"No!" Pam said, slamming the phone down.

Acknowledgments

My Reasons Why

I exist is because of God's grace.

I have a writing is because of my readers.

I strive is for my sons: Valen-Mychal, Victor-Amon.

I take walks is because of my dogs.

I never cry alone is because of my family.

I never doubt my talent is because of my twin: Linda Stringer.

I was a part of a legendary crew is because of Joe (Bub) Johnson, Triple Crown Posse founder/leader.

I stay on the path is because of my godmother Elder Vera Jackson.

I believe in friendship and forgiveness is because of Christ.

I love myself is because of my journey.

I never quit is because they can't hold a good woman down.